[See page 8

IT WAS OBVIOUSLY IMPOSSIBLE TO TELL HER OF HIS LOVE

Lovers' Knots

*The whimsical twists
and tangles of a dozen
youthful love affairs.*

BY

ELIZABETH JORDAN

AUTHOR OF

"MAY IVERSON" "MANY KINGDOMS"
"THE LADY FROM OKLAHOMA" ETC.

WILDSIDE PRESS

Books by

ELIZABETH JORDAN

LOVERS' KNOTS
MAY IVERSON—HER BOOK
MAY IVERSON TACKLES LIFE
MAY IVERSON'S CAREER
THE LADY FROM OKLAHOMA
MANY KINGDOMS
TALES OF DESTINY

———

HARPER & BROTHERS, NEW YORK

CONTENTS

LOVERS' KNOTS

LOVERS' KNOTS

MAN PROPOSES

BY the count of the hostess, there were twelve at dinner. By that of her youngest man guest, Teddy Hapgood, there was exactly One. Far removed from him, but, fortunately, on the other side of the table, where his adoring eyes could reach and linger on her, Dorothy Winter sat. Though she was so pervadingly present, she seemed in another way incredibly remote. He could hardly realize that she was the girl he had met dozens of times during the past summer, and with whom at first he had chatted and danced and, yes, flirted, too, with heart-free abandon. Now it was all different. He tried to remember just when it had begun to seem different, but he couldn't; and what did it matter, anyway? He was in love with her—fathoms deep in love—and as yet she didn't know it. But she was going to. It was this certainty which had strengthened the lines of young Hapgood's mouth. He was a bit afraid of her, but in their first moment alone together he would tell her all that was in his heart.

LOVERS' KNOTS

Between them, besides an endless expanse of embroidered linen, were flowers and candles and bobbing human heads that sadly interfered with the most wonderful view in the world. This was well, for the existence of these barriers steadied the nerves of the impetuous young man, enabling him from time to time to drop a casual word into the ears of vague shadows on his right and left, who also imagined themselves women. As he listened to them and pretended to eat, his mind worked busily. This was Saturday night, and the hour was nine. Within a few minutes the women would leave the table. After a decent interval with the men—the smoking, say, of half a cigarette—he would follow Dorothy to the drawing-room, and, being the only man there, he would quite naturally take her out on the veranda for a glimpse of the moon or the stars. Given five minutes, uninterrupted, he could pour into her ear the story of his love, tell her of his new prospects and his impending journey west, and ask her to be his, thus putting an end for all time to the suspense that had tortured him for weeks.

If she loved him—oh, *if* she loved him (his heart melted within him at the thought)—they would have a glorious Sunday together in this hospitable home where they were fellow-guests for the week-end. If she didn't—for a second his heart stood still, then dropped into some bottomless void—well, if she didn't, he would simply go off and die in the shrubbery. Or, if that seemed inconsiderate toward his

2

hostess, he would take an early train Sunday morning and get back to town, where he would live through the day in some fashion. In any event he had to leave for Kansas City, the field of his new duties, on Monday morning. There, a young captain of industry, with brooding eyes and stern, set lips, he would make Work his goddess, and possibly find in the piling up of millions a dreary compensation for his loveless life. As his reflections reached this mournful stage he became conscious that the girl at his right was talking.

"—tell me what you think of it," was all he caught, but it was addressed to him, and Miss Bigelow's blue eyes, wide with interest, were fastened on his face. He made a desperate clutch at the trailing end of what, he vaguely surmised, had been a detailed account of one of her experiences. Betty was always having things happen to her, and making interesting stories of them.

"I think it was *great*," he said. "Awf'ly nice for you, too," he added, conscious that he was on thin ice, but heedless of his peril.

"Why, Mr. Hapgood! How perfectly *dreadful!*" Betty Bigelow's voice was pitched on a high note of horror.

"Just think!"—she was addressing the general assemblage now—"I told Mr. Hapgood there were nine cases of typhoid in our settlement district this month, and three deaths, and he thinks it's great! And so nice for me!"

Under the surprised stare in the many eyes now turned upon him, the unfortunate young man's pink face deepened into crimson.

"I—I—was saying," he explained, wildly, "that I think it's a great opportunity to learn things about typhoid and—and—stamp it out, you know. That's what I meant."

His voice failed him. *She* was looking at him across the table, and in the quizzical gleam of her brown eyes he saw something that made his nerves sing.

"She understands," he told himself. "At least she knows I haven't heard a word Miss Bigelow's been saying, and she jolly well guesses why!"

Comforted by this thought, he beamed back at her until she looked away. Then, turning, and impressed by the continued silence, he realized that his immediate neighbor at the table was still awaiting the expression of his views on the opportunities attending typhoid.

"They're learning a lot about how to cure it now, you know," he told Betty, his eyes again drawn irresistibly to their magnet. "But ten years ago" (why the deuce was she listening with such interest to that ass, Howe, on her left? Howe had never uttered an original remark in his life)—"why, ten years ago," he added, "they let a fellow I knew die of typhoid."

What further idiocy he might have uttered he and his hearer never knew. Mercifully, his hostess gave the signal for departure to her women guests, who in another minute had made their rustling exit; and Mr. Hapgood, having crawled under the table for two fans and one pair of gloves, was resting after his exertions and moodily chewing the end of a cigarette.

To propose, yes—but how? In what well-chosen words? They must be few, of course, but exactly right—the kind of thing that thrilled a girl with the knowledge of a man's tremendous earnestness.

"*Dorothy, I can't live without you! Will you trust yourself to me?*"

No, he didn't like that. It sounded like the stuff men said in books.

"We were going fifty miles an hour," the man next to him was saying, "and we turned out to let another car pass. The next thing I remember was feeling the earth drop away from me, and seeing Kennedy sail through the air, head first, toward the nearest tree, his legs working exactly as if he were swimming—"

Hapgood wondered if she liked automobiling. If she did, of course they would have a car. His salary, added to his private income, would stand it. But unless she was really keen on motors, they might do well to wait a year or two. However, anything—everything she wanted! Think of buying her things—of having the right to do it! And one thing was certain. He'd give her a big allowance, so she wouldn't have to come and ask for money. He knew what that meant to a proud woman. He had read about it in magazines. His happy thoughts ran on.

"We hadn't been out of the room more than a minute before my wife smelled smoke, so we went back."

Perkins, the host, was leaning back in his chair, telling his best story.

"Tongues of flame were shooting out from the electric fixture and the surrounding woodwork, and the next minute the whole place was blazing. We were on the tenth floor, with no fire-escapes, and my wife was ill—"

They would have to select a house together, Hapgood reflected, buoyantly, and furnish it. *That* would be interesting. That would be something *like*. But what infernal twaddle were these fools talking now? It interfered with serious thought. He rose to his feet.

"If you don't mind, old man, I'll join the ladies," he remarked, as he started for the door. His host, who at that instant in his narrative was clinging to a window-sill of the tenth floor with his left hand, and supporting his wife in his strong right arm, regarded him with natural irritation. This was not only his best story, but it was also true. Teddy Hapgood, in blithe ignorance of his disapproval, was already on his way to the drawing-room. Pausing on its threshold, he studied the scene before him with an anxious eye. *She* was off in a corner with Miss Bigelow, and their faces wore the look of patient waiting which dims the features of most women guests during their lonely after-dinner vigil. But

6

even as he started rapturously toward her the picture changed.

"And I lost ten pounds," Betty Bigelow remarked, casually. As the words left her lips, four women who had been sitting together at one end of the room rose to their feet. Simultaneously they swept toward Miss Bigelow. Simultaneously one word burst from their lips:

"*How?*"

By the time Hapgood had reached her, Betty Bigelow was launched upon a recital of such absorbing interest that at first even the Only One was oblivious to his approach. When she finally saw him, he could not escape the knowledge that her recognition was wholly devoid of personal emotion.

"But *I* never got the slightest results from buttermilk," he heard her say, pathetically, while her gaze drifted across him as impersonally as a rose petal drifts across a garden path. Young as he was, Teddy Hapgood knew the world. Moreover, he had sisters. He strolled away from the absorbed group and stood gazing moodily out of the window, his hands in his pockets, his ears strained to catch the first word of a new topic in which he could take an intelligent part.

But flesh-reduction held the women enthralled for ten minutes, and then the men came in. Three tables of bridge were promptly arranged, and Mr. Hapgood, who had hoped that a malignant fate had exhausted itself in the outrage of the reduction episode, discovered that he was still its helpless victim; for he was not even at her table, and there was to be no pivoting. Until almost midnight he played bridge solemnly with three stern and exacting players, whose resentment of any absent-mindedness on his part was strong and freely expressed.

When the party broke up for the night, he went with Dorothy to the foot of the stairs, gazing at her with such touching appeal that she wavered uncertainly for a moment on the lowest step. But it was obviously impossible to tell her of his love with his late partner at his elbow urgently pointing out some fault in his last game. He could only look deep into her eyes and spend the remainder of the night in alternate hope and belief and doubt and fear over what he read there.

His wakefulness led to his sleeping until after nine o'clock the next morning, and when he came down to breakfast at ten it was to find her gone to church with her hostess. This blow was severe, for he had planned a walk and talk with her along quiet country roads, with the glory of the autumn foliage as an excuse. He had but little time to mourn, however, for he was promptly selected for a foursome by his host, whose interest in golf was second only to his absorption in money-making. Hapgood accompanied his friends to the links willingly enough. He had to do something to kill time, and golf would answer his purpose as well as the next thing. His plan was to go over the four-mile

8

course once during the morning, and then return to the house for luncheon and a long afternoon with Her.

But this was not to be. The morning match was intensely interesting. Knowing that she was, for the time at least, beyond his reach, he put his mind on what he was doing and played brilliantly—so brilliantly that he and his host finished all square with two opponents who were really much their superiors. Perkins was shamelessly jubilant. He immediately issued a challenge for an afternoon match, and ordered luncheon at the club-house. From this program there proved to be no possible escape. Hapgood developed a frightful headache, but it did not save him. During the early afternoon he was the victim of several alarming accidents. He injured a kneecap, he sprained a thumb, he almost broke an ankle. In fact, he was sure he had broken it until Perkins insisted on examining its fair, unblemished surface, afterward turning his eyes from it to Hapgood's face with black suspicion in their depths. When each of his injuries in turn had been thoughtfully scrutinized by a fellow-guest in the foursome, who was also a physician, the game went on, and for very shame Teddy had to cease his frantic efforts to break it up. His play, however, was abominable. Whereas in the morning he had earned the golden opinions of his fellow-players, this afternoon he pulled, he sliced, he topped, and he drove out of bounds. The language he evoked from Per-

9

kins was enough to cause a sulphurous haze to rise over the links. But it was five o'clock before he got back to the house, disgusted and, incidentally, badly defeated, and saw Her for a moment, pouring tea for an animated group of guests who had come in automobiles to swell the house-party. He was desperate by this time, but, short of actual physical force, there seemed no way of getting her to himself for a moment before dinner.

As he dressed for that function he experienced almost a sense of panic. To-night was his last chance. To-night the word must be spoken—and would be, he decided, casting aside the third tie he had ruined—if he perished in the effort. He remembered that his hostess was a good sort, and he decided to ask her to help him out, at least to the extent of putting him beside the Only One at dinner. He met Mrs. Perkins in the hall as he was going down-stairs, and breathlessly made his plea. She listened, with sympathy and understanding in her rather prominent gray eyes.

"I'm sorry, Teddy," she said, "but I just can't do it to-night. I've already promised both Mr. Howe and Arthur Bryce a place beside her."

Then, seeing his despair, her heart yearned over him.

"But I'll help you to get her away after dinner," she added, "and I'll put you next her at breakfast."

Teddy thanked her gloomily. He hadn't much faith in the after-dinner promise, or, for that matter, in the breakfast plan. Half the guests were leaving on early morning trains, and the women would have their hats on and would all talk at once about en-gagements for dress-fittings in town. There was sure to be an indescribable atmosphere of confusion and haste around the table—not at all the right scene for an avowal to the One Woman. However, if breakfast was all he could get, he would take it. Besides, there was still to-night. But what did Howe want to say to her? Had Howe asked her, and had she, perhaps, consented to let him sit beside her? And how did it happen that Bryce was also in the running—Bryce, who had been devoted to Betty Bigelow all summer? Was it possible that Miss Winter liked Bryce? He told himself gloomily that no one could possibly like Bryce, ignoring the fact that he himself had liked him very much until this minute.

If stern disapproval in the gaze of one human being could blight another, both Mr. Howe and Mr. Bryce would have shriveled up as they sat beside Her half an hour later. They remained, however, in excellent health and spirits, and it was evident even to the prejudiced eyes of Mr. Hapgood that they were entertaining. She seemed absorbed in them, and not once during the endless, maddening meal, with its foolish laughter and its silly talk, did her gaze stray toward Teddy.

After dinner, in the drawing-room, that young man approached her with a look of stern decision on his handsome face. Bryce and another man were in the group around her, and he added himself to the circle with something of the effect of a corner-stone settling into place. Before he had a chance to speak, however, a sweet, old, quavering voice addressed her, and Mrs. Tremaine, eighty and still a spoiled belle, was drawing the girl's arm through her own.

"You've promised to play for me, my dear," she said, gently, "and I'm not going to let you off. I've been looking forward to your music all through dinner—and at my age, you know, we don't postpone our pleasures longer than we can help."

Hapgood followed them to the music-room, with several of his fellow-guests, and for an hour listened dreamily and almost happily to Chopin, Richard Strauss, and Grieg. It was not what he wanted, but it was better than seeing her talk to other men; and he could dream that she was playing for him alone, far away, in their own home. While he was mentally shaping the opening words of his proposal his host entered suddenly.

"Will you come and make up a table, Ted?" he asked, catching the young man's eye. "I know you don't care for bridge," he added, apologetically, "but we're just one player short."

Hapgood planted himself, as it were, and pulled back with all the strength that was in him.

"Old man," he said, solemnly, "I've got such a splitting headache that I couldn't tell the difference between an ace and a ten-spot. Awfully sorry, but my playing would simply spoil the game for every one else."

"Oh, all right. Sorry. Why don't you ask Thompson to fix up something for your head?"

Perkins spoke absently, his gaze roaming round the room; and now it fell upon its victim. He was a man of one idea. He descended joyfully upon the Only One, who was at that moment rising from the piano.

"All through, Miss Winter? Good!" he exclaimed, tactfully. "Come and make a fourth at bridge. We're one short."

He offered her his arm, and Dorothy Winter, with a surprised and somewhat dazed expression in her eyes, was firmly led past Hapgood and away to the card-table. Ted looked after them, struggling with a conviction that darkness had settled permanently over the universe. Suffering, rebellious, he finally followed her, stopping long enough to swallow a nauseating mixture which Perkins, now in high good humor, had thoughtfully ordered for his headache.

It was all over. Fate was against him. That was evident. He would have to go away without telling her, and then he would have to write, and the whole business would probably take another week, and he would be kept in this unspeakable misery just that much longer. Of course, he *could* telegraph, but who wants to do the thing as crudely as that?

Love you. Will you marry me? Got new job K. C. five thousand a year. Answer collect.

13

The message flashed across Ted's mental vision as vividly as if some one had written it out. He uttered a groan of self-disgust, turned on his heel and, dazed by his misfortune, half sick over his disappointment and the nervous strain of the whole experience, went sulkily up-stairs and to bed.

That night he slept, to his own great surprise as he subsequently realized the fact, but the next morning he was the first person in the dining-room. He had already investigated the contents of the hot dishes on the sideboard, and was beginning his breakfast when his hostess appeared. Behind her trotted her three-year-old daughter, Marjorie, a small, fat infant with upstanding curls, whose maiden heart had long since been openly and shamelessly bestowed upon Hapgood.

"Goin' to sit by Teddy," she now announced promptly, forestalling objection by climbing into the chair at his left.

"Darling, mother doesn't know whether she'll have room." Mrs. Perkins, however, was as clay in the hands of the small potter. "Wouldn't you like your own little table better?" she added, weakly, "with Nellie to wait on you all the time?"

Miss Perkins would not, and said so. She was already mentioning her preference in the matter of food, and Hapgood waited on her tenderly, effecting a judicious compromise between what she wanted and what she was allowed to have, but incidentally keeping an anxious eye on the empty chair at his right. If any one tried to take that chair—

MAN PROPOSES

Fate and his hostess were with him. Half a dozen guests entered almost together, Miss Winter among them. Mrs. Perkins caught her glance.

"Will you sit next to Mr. Hapgood, Dorothy?" she asked, "and help him to keep Marjorie in order? She *would* sit beside him, and I'm afraid that five minutes from now he'll be simply *kalsomined* with her breakfast food!"

Other duties called her, but if death itself had claimed her now, the radiant young man next to Miss Winter would have remained unmoved. To him, Mrs. Perkins had fulfilled her mission on this earth. Beamingly he rose and went to the sideboard for Dorothy's breakfast. She wanted poached eggs and bacon and a muffin, she said, and the largest cup of coffee Mrs. Perkins knew how to pour. When Hapgood returned to her side with the well-filled plate, it nearly fell from his nerveless hand. Howe was sitting placidly in the chair he had vacated, while the protestations of Miss Marjorie Perkins rent the atmosphere.

"Why, Mr. *Howe*, that's *Teddy's* place! That's my Teddy's place. He's sittin' 'tween me an' Miss Winter," she was ejaculating, in despairing accents.

"Marjorie!"

The look in Mrs. Perkins's eye was not to be mistaken. Marjorie studied it an instant, and her voice sank to a whimper, then was lost in the mug of milk in which she sought to drown her grief. Howe, calmly ignoring the little episode, devoted

15

himself to Dorothy, while Hapgood, choking over his bacon in the place he had taken at the end of the table, looked at his watch and told himself that now, beyond any question, all was indeed lost. His train left in forty minutes, and it would take half an hour to drive to the station. His bag, hat, and coat were in the hall. As others were to take the same train, breakfast was a hurried meal. Very soon every one was out of the dining-room and the bustle of their impending departure filled the house.

Marjorie and Dorothy came into the hall hand in hand, the child's chin still quivering over the disappointment of a few minutes before. Even the blue bow on her short curls seemed to droop. Her Teddy was going away on the cars, and he had already told her that she might be a big girl before he saw her again. With a gulp she dropped Miss Winter's hand and ran to him, and he knelt down and took her in his arms, laying his face against her yellow head. He felt as if his chin and lips were quivering, too. Then an inspiration came to him.

"Marjorie," he whispered, "will you do a favor for me—a great big favor?"

"Yes."

The answer was gratifyingly prompt. Marjorie's quivering chin steadied. The tears which had begun to flow were checked.

"Then listen."

Hapgood whispered earnestly in her ear. It

seemed to be a very important message, for he repeated it several times.   Then, to be quite sure she
understood it, he made her whisper it to him.   After
this rehearsal Marjorie walked slowly over to Miss
Winter, an expression of vast earnestness on her small
face, her manner that of one carrying a full pitcher
whose contents she might spill.

"I got to whis'er to you," she exclaimed, impressively.   "It's a secrek!"

If it was a secret, it promptly ceased to be one.
Miss Winter knelt, and Marjorie's small mouth approached her ear.   In the next second the half-
dozen men and women who were drawing on coats
and gloves in the hall had the pleasure of listening
to Ted's message, uttered as distinctly as the tradi-
tional stage aside.   Delivered in an auditorium, it
should have reached the last row.   Clear, sharp,
penetrating, it filled every nook and corner of the
wide hall.

"Teddy says he loves you awf'ly, Miss Winter.
An' will you *p'ease* mahwy him!"

Miss Winter stood up hastily, her fair face scarlet.
There was a second's hush around her, then a general
rush toward the front door.   Teddy Hapgood had a
passing vision of fleeing figures, of waving scarfs and
veils, of coat-tails erect in the haste of departure.
The next moment the place was deserted save by
three persons.   *She* was in his arms, and no one was
left to view the picture save Marjorie, who shamelessly drew nearer, wide-eyed and wondering, to

give her whole attention to the appealing spectacle of Miss Winter crying on her Teddy's breast.

"Oh, Ted, I've been so perfectly *wretched*," sighed the Only One, when her lips were free for speech. "I was dreadfully afraid you'd have to go away without saying it!"

THE YOUNG MAN IN PEACOCK ALLEY

M R. ALLEN RENFEW sat in a gaudily up-
holstered chair in the corridor of a great
New York hotel at seven o'clock one spring evening
and scowled at the care-free throng that indifferently
surged past him. He was an exceedingly lonely
young man, and his resentment over this unusual
and mournful condition was not lightened by the
knowledge that he had no one to blame for it but
himself.

He had come to New York without deigning to
write or to telegraph his intention to his few intimate
friends in the city, as he should have done; and
to-day, on his arrival, he had found two of them out
of town, a third strenuously engaged for the evening,
and a fourth apparently out of all touch with human-
kind, judging by his lack of response to notes, door-
bells, and telephone-calls. Young Renfew knew
that any one of the four, if properly warned of his
arrival, would have been delighted to see him, and
might even have broken an ordinary engagement for
the pleasure of his company; but the reflection did
not soothe him. If anything, it added to his gloom.
Here he was, a truly companionable human being,

loving his kind and loved by them, yet going to waste, as it were, for an entire evening, simply because he didn't happen to know any of the hundreds of equally companionable human beings around him.

"They call this Peacock Alley," he mused, looking down the long corridor with its kaleidoscopic effects. "Good name for it, too. Place for women to show off their plumage, and for men to strut around and exhibit themselves. Nothing attractive about this!"

He had spent more than half an hour in the occupation of dressing, deliberately drawing it out as long as he could. Now he could kill an hour or two over his dinner.

He rose and strolled along Peacock Alley toward the dining-room, telling himself glumly that to eat from seven to nine, and then sleep from nine to seven, seemed the sole solution of his simple problem. He was smiling sardonically over the contrast between this program and the jolly evening he had expected to have with his friends, when he saw a very charming woman, who was passing with an equally charming girl, glance at him indifferently, then look again more sharply, and suddenly stop. Possibly she had been misled by his smile, for their eyes had met before it ended. At any rate, she was approaching him now with a very beautiful smile of her own and a hand outstretched in cordial greeting.

"Why, how do you do?" she exclaimed, with evident pleasure in the unexpected meeting. "How do you happen to be here?"

Mr. Renfew took her hand and beamed upon her with the sudden warmth he felt. For a moment he honestly believed she was some one he knew and had forgotten—though that he could have forgotten her was even then incredible. Whoever she was, it was simply great to meet her again here and now. Wildly searching his memory for some clue to her, he filled the interval with a simple statement of fact.

"I'm only here for the night," he said. "I'm sailing for Europe in the morning."

She drew back and looked at him in obvious and extreme surprise.

"For Europe?" she repeated. "But how can you get away? Jack wrote that you were absolutely indispensable."

This was flattering, but puzzling. Who the deuce was Jack? Allen racked his brain in vain. He knew many Jacks, but none, alas! by whom he could possibly be regarded as indispensable. He held to a straight course in what he was beginning to realize was difficult sailing.

"Joseph Pulitzer said," he reminded her, cheerfully, "that the indispensable man is not yet born."

She looked at him, still puzzled. "But I can't see how Jack let you go," she murmured, "with the strike on."

Then, suddenly remembering the quiet girl who was standing at her side, she said: "But I must present you to my niece. Mildred, this is Mr. Hutchins, Jack's new manager of the Rightaway Mine."

So that was it. The whole thing had been a blunder. Allen Renfew's disgust and disappointment seemed a physical weight settling down upon him. This woman was simply delightful—the kind his sister Maud would be twenty years hence—and the girl with her was the loveliest, most exquisite being he had ever seen. For a moment they had stretched forth their friendly hands as if to pull him out of his abyss of loneliness. But it had all been a mistake, and the only possible thing for him to do was to say so and withdraw forever from their presence. There wasn't the slightest excuse for prolonging the conversation a second beyond the time of the necessary brief explanation.

To do him justice his lips were parted for the fatal words even as he bent his handsome head in response to the introduction. But as he raised it to speak he looked straight into the girl's eyes, and something there, deep down but looking shyly out at him—something fresh, virginal, trustful, and indescribably appealing—checked him. "Isn't this nice?" the glance seemed to say. "But don't imagine it is the first time we've met. Why, I've known you all my life. *Don't* you remember me?"

Suddenly it seemed to him that he did remember. Of course he knew her. They had met, where, when, he did *not* remember, in this world or some other— it didn't matter where. Why, he had even dreamed of her. And was he to lose her now, for a silly convention, because he didn't know her aunt?

Never! His young jaw set. Without an instant's hesitation he decided to stand pat, as it were, in the odd situation, and to play the cards chance had put into his hands. To the voices of tradition and breeding he resolutely refused to listen. Here was something bigger than convention, more vital than tradition. Wherever it led he would follow.

"I'm in their class, anyway," he told himself. "There's no reason why I shouldn't know her aunt. We must have lots of friends in common. I'll just see this thing through."

The older woman was speaking again, in her wholesome, cordial manner. There was something of the spirit of the West in her, together with the poised assurance of the experienced and cultured woman who has known many men and women and traveled much.

"This is so interesting and unexpected," she said. "Shall we sit down and chat a few moments? It's just a year, isn't it, since you went West?" She led the way to a little group of empty chairs clustered under an ostentatious palm. "We've ordered our table for seven," she explained as they sat down, "and it's not quite that yet. But Mildred insisted on seeing Peacock Alley in its fullest flower."

Allen looked at the young girl. He was very anxious to meet those wonderful eyes again, but now she seemed too much absorbed in her surroundings to do more than glance at him. Her eyes traveled rapidly here, there, and everywhere, lingering on

3   23

some groups, quitting others at once, but full of an almost childish pleasure and excitement, and invariably returning to his for an instant's sympathy and understanding. She was not a child. She must be all of twenty, Allen reflected. In dress and carriage she was as much a woman of the world as her aunt. In manner she combined dignity and poise with an adorable reserve. Her eyes alone spoke eloquently.

"You like this sort of thing, don't you?" he asked her. It seemed a wonderful thing to be speaking to her—at last. He even remembered the little dimple at the left corner of her mouth. Where, where, *where* had he watched it before?

"I love it!" she said. Both her hands were clutching the arms of her big chair as if she feared to be torn away from it by some strange force in this new world she had entered. "I love every minute of it, and everything in it," she added, almost under her breath; and now she looked at him again. "I really grudge the moments we're in our rooms. It seems a crime to miss all this—there's so much life in it. Think of what these people represent—the homes, the types, the lives. I like to look at them and try to guess what is in their hearts."

"It is great," he conceded, and surveyed the pageant with an expression of proud proprietorship. He forgot that only a short hour ago it had bored him beyond endurance. Now it had suddenly become brilliant, fascinating, alluring to the highest degree — something that he himself had arranged for Mildred. "But I don't think I want you to know what's in their hearts," he concluded, cautiously. "Except in mine, of course. Read that, please."

Her soul looked out at him for an instant. Then, without answering, she turned her eyes away.

The music was superb now, crashing and triumphant—in keeping with one's mood. It had seemed almost diabolically mournful an hour ago, but Mr. Renfew, who was not analytical, abandoned himself to the phenomenon of the sudden change with entire content.

Mildred's aunt spoke to him again, and they talked for ten minutes, the young man showing much skill in controlling the subjects discussed. He was exceedingly anxious to keep away from the subject of Jack, whoever Jack was, and he succeeded so well that when Jack's sister and her niece rose to go to the dining-room that able Western capitalist had not received so much as the tribute of a word from the little circle to whom his interests should have been so vital.

Mildred said very little, and said that little to "Aunt Helen," as she called her chaperon: but it was plain that she listened and was interested. And with each moment that passed the conviction that somewhere he had seen her, known her, strengthened in Allen's mind.

The breaking up of the party was a tragic awakening from this fair dream. For ten glorious minutes he had been the happiest of men. He had, somehow, taken it for granted that those minutes would extend indefinitely into the future. And here they were, those women, hurling him back into the outer darkness from which they had only now rescued him. His expression, as he rose to his feet, was so openly and utterly despairing that it moved the older woman to sudden sympathy.

"What are you doing this evening, Mr. Hutchins?" she asked, kindly. "If you have no—"

But "Mr. Hutchins" was already assuring her of his complete freedom for the evening, with such passionate earnestness that both she and her niece smiled irrepressibly.

"Then if you care to dine with us—"

"Mr. Hutchins" cared. He cared more ardently than he had ever cared for anything before in his life. He was quite shameless about it; so much so, in fact, that Mildred turned a pair of wonderfully sympathetic brown eyes upon him.

"How dreadfully lonely you must have been," she murmured. "You must never be so lonely again," her eyes seemed to add.

Mr. Renfew gazed into them, lost to his surroundings, until they turned away. Then, seeing his opportunity, he drew such an affecting picture of his experience alone in New York for five hours that Mildred laughed for the first time. She was a rather serious young person, on the whole, but her rare laugh was a wonderful thing—almost as wonderful, Allen decided, as were her eyes.

The dinner was very pleasant—even gay. Though the young man had cast most of his scruples behind him, he was still keenly conscious of his obligations as the guest of a hostess who had not the privilege of his acquaintance. He exerted himself to be agreeable and entertaining, and succeeded. Moreover, he began to feel a certain exhilaration in the danger of the situation. He was like a sailor handling a boat in a storm in unknown waters. There were rocks and reefs to be avoided. There was sail to be taken in—very suddenly at times. The rock which rose most often above the waves was "Jack"—that mysterious and rugged personality, whose very surname he did not know, yet with whom he was supposed to have the closest, most confidential business relations.

With an intelligence and skill preternaturally sharpened by consciousness of all these dangers Mr. Renfew navigated his social craft. Several times he narrowly escaped shipwreck; and, notwithstanding his quickness and cleverness, it began to dawn on the mind of his hostess, before the dinner ended, that something was wrong between Jack and his brilliant young manager. She wondered what it was, and finally dismissed the subject mentally, with the hope that it was merely a misunderstanding which time might straighten out. She liked the young man, and it was increasingly evident that

Mildred liked him too. Also that he liked Mildred. True woman that she was, she let her thoughts dwell on the possibilities of this mutual liking, while the young people, left to themselves, talked together in tones that grew more intimate and confidential with each moment that passed. As he talked to Mildred, Allen's guard unconsciously dropped. Indeed, consciousness of the need of a guard deserted him. Concealment, subterfuge, such things could not survive in the light of the wonderful eyes that seemed to search his soul. It was his realization of this, and the tribute of responsive sincerity he offered her, that carried him to his destruction. She mentioned that just a year ago she had been in Spain. Allen leaned toward her breathlessly, his blue eyes ablaze with excitement.

"Then *that* was where I saw you!" he almost shouted. "In Algeciras! My sister Maud and I were there last May. Oh, don't you remember that night at the Reina Christina, when we gathered on our balconies to hear the nightingales sing in the moonlight? And you were in the balcony next to mine. There was a moon in the heavens too big to be true, and the lights of Gibraltar in the distance, and the Mediterranean sighing at the foot of our garden wall, and the nightingales singing their hearts out among the pomegranate blossoms. You were there. You had a veil over your head, but I saw your mouth and your eyes, and ever since—" He stopped. "I've seen them ever since," he added, more quietly. Then he realized that his hostess was looking at him; and under the expression in her eyes a sudden chill swept over him.

"Why, Mr. Hutchins," she asked, slowly, "how *could* you have been in Spain last May? It was the first of May that Jack brought you to see me, and the next week you and he left for Montana to begin work on the Rightaway."

It was all over with Mr. Allen Renfew, and he knew it. Her manner was perfect. It assumed that an explanation would be forthcoming; it withheld judgment until that explanation was offered. But it tolerated no more evasions, no more half-truths; for during his rhapsody over his recognition of Mildred the older lady had had time to think. Flushed, wretched, Mr. Renfew writhed under the steady eyes fastened upon him. Desperately he turned and looked at Mildred. Her eyes were fixed on the table-cloth and she did not raise them. To experience such abject humiliation as he felt in that moment seemed almost as bad as anything could be. To experience it in her presence, to have her observe his further ignominy, was not to be borne. He turned an imploring look on his hostess.

"It's—it's a rather long story," he said. "I want to tell it to you—but not here."

"Very well," she said, quietly.

They had finished their coffee. She summoned the waiter, signed her check, and in silence led the way out of the brilliant room to the corridor.

As they followed her Allen had time for one quick question: "It *was* you, in Algeciras, wasn't it?"

"Yes," she said, "I was there." And she added, "I saw you, too."

Her aunt stopped before one of the elevator doors, and when the car appeared gave Mildred a key and motioned her into it.

"Go to our rooms, dear," she said. "I will be with you in a few moments."

Her niece obeyed dumbly, with a last glance at the despairing youth, which he returned with a look that spoke regret, remorse, and something more.

When the girl had been borne aloft he followed his hostess to their former places, the chairs under the spreading palms. There she sat down, and motioned him to follow her example. He did so, but the absence of Mildred was a mitigating feature of the miserable situation, and it was with something like self-control that he next met the steady look of his hostess's suddenly keen and worldly eyes.

"So you are not Mr. Hutchins, after all?" she asked, dryly.

"No, I am Allen Renfew, of San Francisco."

He had hoped that the name of Renfew, well known and honored in the West through the business activities of his distinguished father, might impress her, but it seemed to have no such happy effect.

"You look and speak like a gentleman," she said, slowly. "I suppose there is some explanation of why you have not acted like one?"

"Yes, if you will listen."

Allen felt that she was very hard on him.

"At first, for a moment, I thought I knew you," he began, lamely. "Then, when I realized I didn't, I was so abominably lonesome I couldn't resist—"

But the lady had risen, and was drawing her lace scarf around her shoulders.

"I am sorry," she said. "I hoped you would have some excuse to offer. Good night."

Allen pursued her breathlessly along Peacock Alley.

"But, Mrs.— Great Scott! I don't even know your name!" he cried. "But listen to me, for Heaven's sake! Though I don't know you, it's only chance that I don't. We must have many friends in common. Surely you know my father, Henry Renfew, of California?"

They had reached the elevator doors again, but the car had just started slowly upward. Inwardly, but fervently, Allen blessed it. His hostess was speaking.

"I do know Henry Renfew," she said, coldly. "But I do not know that you are his son; and, if you will pardon me, I have no reason to take your word for it."

He took that without offense, knowing it was no more than he deserved.

"I'll prove it!" he cried, eagerly. "I'll prove it right now! The night clerk knows me. I was here last spring."

She smiled ironically. "I'm afraid that would not convince me," she said, coldly. "But, after all, we are perhaps magnifying a trifle. You are sailing in the morning. Our acquaintance ends naturally. Good night."

The car was descending again. Allen waited for it as the victim of an execution might wait for the knife to drop.

"But—but—I can't let it end that way!" he cried. "Listen just a minute, Mrs.— Oh "—he paused impotently—"*Aunt Helen!*" he brought out in a despairing wail.

The austere face of the lady relaxed. She struggled with and barely conquered a telltale twitch of the lips. But Mr. Renfew saw it, and, with reviving courage and great presence of mind, followed her into the elevator.

"I'll have father telegraph you," he went on, breathlessly. "I'll get the Reverend John Menick, of the Fourth Presbyterian Church, to come and see you to-morrow. You know him. He's my godfather. He'll tell you all about me. My sister Maud's going to be married in London this month, to Captain Winchley of the Scot Guards. She and mother are over there now. I'm going over to give her away. Father has the gout and can't travel. I'm all right—honestly I am," he finished, hopefully.

They had reached her floor now and were hurrying along the corridor.

"It will be all right in the morning," he repeated,

"after you see dad's telegram, you know. But I'll be gone then. So, Aunt Helen"—she had reached the door of her sitting-room, but he checked her further progress by pinning her resolutely against the wall—"Aunt Helen, you'll let me see Mildred again, won't you? Just to say good-by?"

"Aunt Helen" succumbed to helpless laughter. "My young friend," she said, when she was able to speak, "I don't know whether you are what you say you are, or the rank impostor I have every reason to believe you. But at least you have greater audacity than any other human being I have ever met. Once more, good night."

"But wait," begged the young man. "Here, see this!" He pulled out his card-case. "Here's my card. Here's my steamer ticket—and, by Jove! here's my letter of credit! Look at it. That ought to clear me! Now won't you let me see Mildred for just a moment?"

He forced the collection into her hands. She examined them slowly. She was beginning to believe that this extraordinary youth was telling the truth. She had read in the newspapers of the coming marriage of Henry Renfew's only daughter to an English officer. From the same source of information she had learned that Henry Renfew himself was the victim of an attack of gout and could not attend his daughter's wedding. She returned the ticket and letter of credit to their owner. Her manner was milder, but still firm.

33

"You cannot possibly see Mildred to-night," she said, quietly. "But while you are abroad I will look up your—your references. When you come back—"

"But I can't go off with nothing more definite than that!" he wailed. "I'll be gone almost three weeks!"

As if in answer to his mournful cry the door opened tentatively, and Mildred, still inside the room, looked out at them. Then, in answer to his imperative gesture, she stepped across the threshold and stood beside him. The long hall was deserted. Mr. Renfew assured himself of this by one swift glance down its length, and seized both the young girl's hands.

"It's all right," he said, swiftly. "She knows who I am. She's going to let me come and see you as soon as I get back. I'll sail for home the minute Maud's married. And when I do get back I've got something to say to you—Mildred, oh, Mildred—"

He had one wonderful look from her—shy, adoring, hinting divinely at the things she could not say. Then she was taken from him by a stern and capable pair of hands and pushed gently back into the sitting-room, the door of which was closed upon her.

Still holding the knob, the lady who had executed this manœuver faced the importunate lover. "Now, Mr. Renfew," she said, "I am sure you will obey me when I ask you to say good night to me and go away at once."

But the radiant young man she addressed was

34

quite a different person from the crushed worm of half an hour ago. Had he not seen that never-to-be-forgotten light in Mildred's eyes? Had he not felt the soft response of her hands in his?

"All right!" he said, with an exultant swing of the shoulders. "But you understand, of course, that I'm going to marry Mildred!"

She shook her head at him. "You're wholly incorrigible," she said; and then, to stem the Niagara of words that so obviously beat against his lips, she added, "If that subject is ever discussed it will be *after* you return from Europe."

"Very well," he said. "We'll let it go at that. Maud's to be married on the tenth. I'll be back on the sixteenth. If there's no boat I'll swim."

She gave him her hand and he pressed it rapturously.

"Good-by," she said, and went in resolutely and closed the door. Five seconds later there was an excited knocking on its solid panels. Reluctantly she opened it, and at her expression the young man in the corridor lost no time in stating the urgency of his business.

"I'm going," he said, anxiously, "but you forgot to give me your address. And say, Aunt Helen"—his voice sank to a whisper and ended on a note of touching pathos—"what's the rest of Mildred's name?"

A GAME OF TAG

THEY had parted forever. That fact, the one certainty in a most uncertain world, filled "Billy" Bailey's consciousness.

To him, at twenty-three, both life and love had lost their glamour—that is, if she had *really* thrown him over. All that lay before him now was work, and work, someway, had never especially appealed to him, probably because he had never given it a fair chance. Even at this moment, when it offered its bony breast as a refuge from his misery, he regarded it without enthusiasm. There was no hurry about going to work. First, he would see Edith again, make one last appeal, grovel if she wished— and perhaps she would give him another chance.

His black depression lifted a little as he made the decision, and he crossed the room to his desk with a swing and vigor in his movements which they had wholly lacked during the past week. He even whistled softly as he selected a pen and began his note, begging for an interview.

It was short, but every word was a tribute to the glory of Edith, and an admission of the utter insignificance of everything in himself save his great

36

love for her. He sealed the letter, called a messenger-boy, and sent it to her at once. Then, with Hope once more at his elbow, he went down to the hotel dining-room and ate a highly satisfactory luncheon.

His sense of well-being, however, was rudely jarred by the phenomenally prompt return of the messenger, who, having been earnestly charged to hurry and to bring back the answer, had done his best according to his opportunities. He was back, but he was still conspicuously grasping Billy's note, which bore evidences of having passed through several hands.

"Nothin' doin'," he announced, defensively.

Stunned, young Bailey regarded the letter, then addressed him as man to man.

"She didn't send it *back?*" he stammered.

"Naw. She wasn't there. She's gone to Europe."

"Gone to Europe!"

For an instant Billy could not take it in. He had imagined everything but this.

"How do you know?" he added, quickly. "Who told you so?"

"House all boarded up. Saw the caretaker. And, say, you said you'd gimme a dollar if I hustled."

Billy gave him the dollar, got rid of him, and thought hard.

He and Edith had hosts of friends in common. Undoubtedly they had been restrained from telling him of her departure by what they considered the most delicate tact. Quietly but fervently he confided his opinion of them and their tact to the unresponsive walls of his room. Then hurrying to the telephone, he called up one of them, and, fortunately, found her at home. Breathlessly he poured forth his story, and, as she listened, the heart of Mrs. Mayhew softened.

"I'm so sorry, Billy," she said. "I supposed, of course, you knew. Edith and her mother sailed for Triest yesterday. No, I don't know how long they'll be gone. They didn't say. It was all arranged so hastily that I fancy they didn't make any definite plans beyond just going over. But they're going straight from Triest to Vienna, and I heard Edith say something about Hungary and Roumania and Greece."

Billy listened in sick dismay. This was worse than he had expected, for in the days before the engagement Edith and her mother had thought nothing of remaining in Europe a year at a time.

"Does any one else know any more about it than you do?" he bluntly asked Mrs. Mayhew.

She was sure no one else did.

"Why don't you foolish children kiss and make up?" she asked, kindly. "I thought Edith looked wretchedly unhappy the other night."

"Oh, *did* she?" Billy grinned widely over these sad tidings. Edith jubilantly sailing toward the Adriatic was a picture he could not have contemplated. But Edith hastening to the world's end to deaden the dull ache of a broken heart was a wholly reassuring vision. At the same time he did not intend to let her suffer a moment longer than was necessary.

He was a singularly energetic young person, and, once resolved to "get Edith back," as he expressed it to himself, he lost no time in pursuing that laudable purpose. He counted his ready money, cashed a check for more, and sailed for Europe the next morning. It seemed safe to assume that, taking the leisurely voyage of the southern route, they would be in Vienna in two weeks.

"I'll take the northern route and beat them to it," Billy told himself, elegantly.

But he had failed to take into consideration the fickle nature of women. On the second day of his voyage he received a wireless message from Mrs. Mayhew.

Just learned they decided to leave ship at Gibraltar and travel in Spain. First hotel Reina Christina, Algeciras.

Mr. Bailey read the message and then hastened to a lonely spot on the upper deck, where, untrammeled by convention, he could express his feelings to the unsympathetic sea. The expedient of making the captain change the ship's course at once occurred to him, but was dismissed as he remembered that other desperate men had attempted this in vain. A wild desire to try to swim back he wrestled with and conquered. But these and similar mental struggles so preyed upon his mind that before he reached Cherbourg the entire ship's company were discussing the metamorphosis of a sunny-natured young man into an embittered being whom none cared to approach more than once.

Taking into consideration the admitted uncertainties of travel by airships and automobiles, young Bailey decided that the safest and quickest method was to travel by rail. As long as his journeying was confined to France, this theory was quite correct, but when he reached Spanish soil the difficulty of getting anywhere by any means seemed at times so insuperable that even the intrepid lover almost gave up hope. All trains, leaving for any point, seemed to start at some gray, mysterious hour toward dawn. Like sluggish serpents the engines crawled over the Spanish landscape, pausing whenever they reached a particularly bleak and desolate "junction" to let their passengers linger a few hours on the sunbaked platform of some primitive station. By night a wonderful moon swam in the heavens, and the love-songs of nightingales came pregnantly from olive-trees, for it was still spring, though it began to seem to the unhappy young man that he had been traveling for months. But at last he reached Gibraltar, and with leaping heart embarked in the little packet-boat that plies between "the Rock" and Algeciras.

The dignified young Englishwoman in the office

of the Reina Christina was pained by the abruptness of his manner.

"Here," cried the young man, irritably. "Their names wouldn't be registered last month. Look at this week's entries. They must have arrived two or three days ago."

Thus guided, the slow fingers of the clerk moved toward the more recent registrations. "It.mightn't be Mrs. Henry White, of Albany?" she suggested. *She* had been there four days ago. No?

"Might this be the lady?" she then asked, timidly. It might be, and indeed it was. With difficulty the young person recalled her. According to the records (and this required another search), Mrs. White and Miss White had remained only until morning. The clerk's manner was becoming weary. She had not the remotest idea where they had gone next; and now there was a distinct edge to her voice.

The porter who attended to the luggage of his friends might remember to what destination he had booked it. She summoned that excellent and intelligent employee, explained the gentleman's wishes, and the whole situation cleared almost miraculously. The porter's memory, stimulated into hectic activity by the gift of five pesos, recalled facts in almost embarrassing detail. He had attended to everything for the ladies, and had booked their luggage through to Seville. It was only nine hours to Seville; one ought to reach there inside of two days. They were probably just arriving. Following them, the gentle-

man could leave on the earliest boat in the morning—
there was, alas! no other boat to-night. And, yes,
sir; thank you again, sir, Billy should be awakened
at dawn and presumably—so great was the porter's
zeal—carried on board.

Mr. Bailey retired gloomily to his room. It
opened on the famous garden, and there was a
balcony outside of one window, on which, until midnight, he lounged and smoked. To be here with
Edith would have been a joy he hardly dared to
picture to himself. To be here without her was
an irony which turned the incredible beauty of
the night and the place into mockery. Yet it
bore its reassuring message, and insensibly he felt
calmed and soothed by it. Surely, somehow, in
a world as wonderful as this, things *must* come out
right.

He reached Seville two days later, and went at
once to the principal hotel, at which he expected to
find Mrs. White and Edith. They were not there;
but awaiting him, having traveled with something
approaching speed *via* Spain's "fast mail," was a
letter forwarded by the attentive porter at Algeciras.
It was from his sister, and had been at the Reina
Christina when he arrived, but the exacting duties he
had put upon the young lady at the desk, he gathered, had driven it from her mind. Without much
eagerness Billy opened the envelope, then, a sentence claiming his attention, reread it with shining
eyes.

A GAME OF TAG

The day after you sailed a letter came to your hotel addressed in Edith's handwriting. The clerk remailed it to father, as you had left no other instructions. I'm not at all sure where you're going to be, so I'm sending this note on a chance. But I don't want to risk remailing Edith's letter until I hear from you. It may be important. So I'll hold it here.

A letter from Edith—that *was* news. Should he cable his sister to read it and cable the contents? No. It might be merely another "farewell forever," and Mollie, he remembered, had a confoundedly keen sense of humor. Besides, he'd see Edith herself in a day or two more, and she would tell him what was in the letter.

But two days passed and he found no trace of the Whites in Seville. It seemed obvious that they had changed their plans and not come there at all. In his inquiries he was greatly handicapped by his ignorance of Spanish and by the national Spanish ignorance of any other tongue. They might yet come, so he dared not leave. They might have gone straight on to Madrid, so he was afraid to remain. He waited, however, but on the edge of his nerves, whiling away his time by cabling inquiries to Mrs. Mayhew. At the end of his fifth day in Seville he received a cable from her. It read:

Hear they abandoned Spanish tour, and sailed from Gibraltar to Naples on seventeenth.

Billy ground his teeth. The seventeenth! That was the day he had started from Algeciras for Seville. And even as he started Mrs. White and Edith had

43

been just twenty minutes away from him, comfortably taking ship at Gibraltar. He went to Gibraltar in a desperate frame of mind. He would take the next boat that sailed from there. If its destination happened to be Naples, all right. He would go to Naples. If, on the other hand, it was sailing for New York, he would take it and go home. He was sick of this wild-goose chase.

By a stroke of luck—the first he had experienced since he left America, he told himself, bitterly— a steamer stopped at Gibraltar the day he arrived there. Within two hours he was sailing toward Naples. He knew Edith's favorite haunts in Italy. She would stay in Naples a few days, he thought, at Bertolini's. Then she would surely go to Amalfi, stopping for a day or two, perhaps, at Sorrento. It seemed certain that in or near Naples he would catch up with her at last—and where could there be a more perfect spot to meet Edith again than on the Capuchin terrace at Amalfi?

At Bertolini's Billy was greeted with seeming rapture by the head clerk, who remembered his visit there the year before. But the face of this gentleman clouded with a deep sorrow when he had heard the young man's eager questions. Was Mrs. James Frederick White in the hotel now, or had she been here? Alas! no.

Slowly, heavily, Billy turned away. Then he went down to the steamship office and took passage on the first ship home.

"Ought to have had sense enough to do that from Gibraltar," he told himself. "There's Edith's letter; everything is in it, the whole thing settled one way or the other. And here I've been gadding about like a maniac."

He did not linger at all in New York, but hurried on to Boston, going straight from his steamer to the train, delighting his sister as well as impressing his father by this unusual expedition. He arrived in the early evening and found them both at home. Almost before their greetings were said, he drew Mollie to one side and demanded this letter. His sister stared at him.

"Didn't you get it at your hotel?" she asked. "I sent it there—mailed it last night." Then, at the expression of his face, she put her arms around him. "Oh, Billy!" she cried. "You poor boy! And I thought I was so clever to have it waiting in New York, so you'd get it without an hour's delay. I never dreamed you'd rush home without going there."

Billy bowed his head. The whole world seemed topsy-turvy. Everything, he felt, and every one, had conspired against him.

"Well, never mind," he said, ungraciously. "Let me have what mail there is. I suppose there's some."

"Oh yes, a heap."

Mollie went for it and brought the pile to his room, lingering lovingly with him while he opened the letters. He had glanced at all the addresses and postmarks before he opened any, but Mollie saw by his expression that he had not found what he wanted. He tore open the envelopes listlessly, dropping bills on the floor, half-reading and tossing aside personal letters and invitations. Then he rose.

"You'll look after these, won't you?" he asked. "Just say 'No' to everything."

"But, Billy, where are you going?"

"New York," he announced, briefly, and started down-stairs. Mollie followed him, and while he was picking up his hat and hand-bag, hurriedly explained the situation to his father. That gentleman appeared in the hall just as his erratic son was opening the door leading to the street.

"Hold on, Billy," he called. "What nonsense is this? Can't you bear with us one night at least?"

"Sorry," said poor Billy, stopping reluctantly; and he added, vaguely, something that sounded like "'portant 'sness."

The elder Mr. Bailey uttered a sound expressing contempt. "Business!" he repeated, ironically. "Billy, you're acting like a fool."

"I know it," admitted Billy, ignobly, and closed the door.

When he reached his hotel in New York he checked the buoyant greeting of the night clerk by demanding his mail.

"Everything's gone on to Boston, Mr. Bailey," said that unfortunate, blithely. "We've forwarded all your mail since you went away."

His victim glared at him. "But the letter—the things that came yesterday from Boston," he stammered, "to catch me here. How about them?"

"Sorry," said the clerk. "But, you see, we didn't know. No instructions, and we don't stop to examine postmarks. So if anything came from Boston it went right back to Boston." He smiled happily upon Bailey, and received one of the surprises of his life.

"Damn you!" said that young man, intensely, and retired to his own rooms.

Rising in the morning, and glancing out of the windows as he moodily dressed, he was almost surprised to find that the portion of the outer world around his hotel seemed much as he had left it, little more than a month ago. It had been May then. It was now June, but there was the same deceptive tang in the air, the same mocking sunshine, and, yes, somewhere near by, an organ-man was making a street organ senilely betray its age.

After breakfast he strolled out on the Avenue, with some vague notion of looking up some one who knew something. His mind, dazed by recurrent disappointments, was apparently failing him, too. And then, as if Fate had wearied of him as its toy, it tossed a favor his way. Before he had gone three blocks from his hotel he met Mr. Horace White, unimportant in himself, but great in the eyes of Billy Bailey as the uncle of Edith. The fervor of the greeting Mr. White received was so great that

the phlegmatic gentleman was unable to conceal
his surprise. He was hurrying to his office, and had
stopped reluctantly, obviously unable to see why he
should waste precious business time in conversation
with Billy Bailey. But after a sharp glance at the
young man's face his expression changed.

"What's the matter with you, Billy?" he asked,
kindly. "You're looking seedy."

Billy had entered upon the jocund day enveloped
in a wretchedness so complete that it scorned concealment. It was from the depths of this that he
answered.

"I guess you know what's the matter," he muttered.

The other looked at him again, thoughtfully.
Then he yielded to a rare impulse of friendly sympathy.

"Edith, I suppose?" he asked.

"Of course."

Edith's uncle glanced at his watch, then snapped
it shut with a movement of decision. He could give
this young man another minute.

"Sorry," he said. "But, since you feel that way,
why don't you fix things up?"

Billy uttered a laugh he intended should sound
sardonic, but which merely sounded pitiful.

"Takes two," he explained. Then, with a wild
impulse of hope, "Would Edith—"

Horace White was a busy man, with no time for
beating about the bush.

A GAME OF TAG

"Would she?" he echoed. "You bet she would. Been eating her heart out ever since the quarrel. Fix it up. Good-by."

He was off, but Billy pursued him.

"Here, wait a minute," he begged. "Where can I write her?"

The other paused. "Write the devil," he exclaimed. "Go and see her. That's the best way."

"But where, *where?*" cried poor Billy, grasping his elbow. "I've been chasing her and her mother all over Europe. Where is she now?"

Horace White turned and stared at him. Then he seemed to understand.

"Why, you young idiot," he said, almost affectionately, "it's my daughter that's in Europe with Mrs. White. At the last minute Edith wouldn't go. She's been right around the corner for a month, ostensibly keeping house for me, but really waiting for you to call!"

MR. BRINKLEY TO THE RESCUE

"YOU will admire greatly the *pension* of Madame Bouvier," said Madame Olivier, "and you will like also that excellent woman herself. In appearance she is of a size remarkable; but her heart is no less large than her body."

Mrs. Reynolds Hartley, of New York, listened to this tribute with an absent smile, while she fitted her plump figure into a desirable corner seat of the compartment *pour dames seules*, to which the porter had just escorted her and her daughter. Her own French was uncertain, but "Maudie," she reflected, comfortably, would talk to Madame Olivier. Maudie did everything. Maudie was an extremely pretty girl, slender and dark, with an efficient air that perched rather ostentatiously on the arrogant shoulder of her twenty-two years. In fluent and courageous French she now rose to the demand of the moment.

"You've been so good to us, Madame," she said, cordially. "I don't know what we'd have done without you during our two weeks in Paris. If Madame Bouvier makes us half as comfortable, we shall be fortunate."

Madame Olivier sighed and made a gesture consigning herself to an abyss of despair. She was genuinely sorry to see these Americans depart, and her regret was not wholly based on the loss of the temporary income they had given her. She expressed her appreciation volubly.

"And now it is to say good-by," she added. "You are comfortable, yes? And you have forgotten nothing? No, here are the packages, the journals, the fruit. *Au revoir*, then, *chère madame et mademoiselle*. It is but a ride of a few hours. At two o'clock you will be in Tours, in the home of the excellent Madame Bouvier. Had you changed your plans less suddenly I would have written her. But you are sure of a welcome."

She shook hands with them again and departed, and an instant later the shrill whistle of the French engine sounded its final warning as the train began to move. The mother and daughter exchanged a look of quiet satisfaction.

"Well, we're off," remarked the older lady, comfortably. "Nothing to do for a few hours but to sit still and watch France pass by. I must say I'm glad of it. Another week of gadding about would have finished me. I hope, Maudie," she added, earnestly, "that you'll settle down quietly in Tours for a little while and study your French, and let the châteaux wait till we're rested. They'll be here next month, which is more than I shall be if you drag me to see them to-morrow."

Maud Hartley laughed. "Don't worry; I won't," she said, affectionately. "Snub every château in Touraine if you want to."

Her voice held the cajoling accents with which one addresses an infant of four. In the year of leisurely travel that had followed her graduation from a New York school she had directed her mother's destiny according to the highest traditions of the executive American daughter. "She even thinks for me," Mrs. Hartley boasted, shamelessly.

"Now read," Maud directed, gravely, and handed her mother a magazine. And that lady, her mind at ease about the châteaux, dutifully read.

They reached Tours, as the time-table and Madame Olivier had predicted, about two o'clock. Once out of the train, Miss Hartley, as usual, took full command of their affairs. She directed her laden porters to a *fiacre*, which she selected from the congested mass of vehicles at the station. She saw to it that the cab was fairly clean and that the horse was in as good a physical condition as one could expect that hard-worked animal to be in France. To the driver she paid absolutely no attention. When she had helped her mother into the cab, and had seen that the hand-luggage was packed around her and the cabman, she stood with one stout little boot on the foot-rest of the *fiacre* while, in her best French, she gave the driver Madame Bouvier's address. He had lifted the reins above the back of his lean horse. At her words he dropped them, while the look of one hopelessly bereaved fell upon his expressive features.

"But, Mademoiselle," he explained in mournful accents, "there is no longer in existence the Pension Bouvier!"

Miss Hartley regarded him, an annoyed crease disturbing the smooth outline of her brow.

"No Pension Bouvier?" she repeated. "But we have the address."

"The address, yes," explained the *cocher*, "but Madame Bouvier, alas, is no longer there. I trust," he added, piously, "she is in heaven. She died last month."

Miss Hartley reflected rapidly, her manner implying that the act had been inconsiderate of Madame Bouvier, to say the least—not at all what she had been led to expect of her.

"But her *pension?*" she asked, with a sudden gleam of hope. "Isn't some one else conducting that?"

"No, Mademoiselle; it is closed, locked, empty. It is of indescribable desolation." He waved his arms to indicate the width and depth of the desolation, and his steed, misinterpreting the motion, took two reluctant steps forward. Miss Hartley accompanied him, on one foot, preserving her balance by clutching wildly at the swinging cab-door as she hopped. The incident did not improve her temper, though it was warmly appreciated by a group of French urchins, who stood round and grinned delightedly, while a few men and women hurriedly added themselves to the select circle.

"I suppose there are some good hotels," murmured Miss Hartley, crossly, when the driver had checked his horse with a flow of language whose full eloquence was happily lost to her. She did not care to go to a hotel. It was, instead, her strong desire to be in a *pension*, where she could try her imperfect French on her helpless fellow-boarders, instead of finding her opportunities limited to the usual hotel staff, who always leaped half-way to meet her meaning.

Of a certainty there were hotels. Her *cocher* rattled off an impressive list. But even while he was doing so a motherly Frenchwoman stepped out from the surrounding group, her broad face alight with good feeling, her hand on the head of a toddling baby whose fat arms fervently clasped her knee. She addressed Miss Hartley diffidently, but with a charming smile.

"If Mademoiselle and Madame desire a *pension*," she suggested, including the older lady in her deprecating bow, "possibly they will permit me to give them the address of a most excellent one." And as Miss Hartley hesitated an instant, she went on: "Does Mademoiselle desire that I tell her *cocher* to go there, that she may at least look at the place?" '

Mademoiselle promptly decided that she did. To go and look at a *pension* could do no possible harm, and to go somewhere at once was highly desirable, as public interest in her affairs was already blocking traffic.

"If you please, Madame," she said. "And thank you very much."

The good samaritan confided the address to the cabman, who received it with beaming approval. Maud entered the cab. The farewells, of somewhat extended beauty and ceremony, were finally over, and the depressed cab-horse started off, his mien suggesting that his darkest forebodings were realized. In something less than half an hour he stopped before a large, square, white house surrounded by a high wall, and set, as his passengers afterward discovered, in a garden which they entered by means of a wooden door. Mrs. Hartley remained in the cab while her daughter briefly investigated the attractions of the *pension*. These, she soon realized, were numerous. The garden was a delight, and the living-rooms of the house she entered were large and bright and furnished in admirable French taste. On the walks that ran around the garden two happy American children rolled French hoops. Within, several pleasant-looking Americans and a middle-aged English couple who, as Maud put it to her mother, "fairly oozed the domestic virtues," lounged comfortably in the long *salon*.

The appearance of the mistress of the house was equally reassuring. She was a dark-eyed, agreeable Frenchwoman, with the suave manner of her class. She confirmed with grief the announcement of the

5   55

death of Madame Bouvier, her very dear friend; she sympathized with the Hartleys in the inconvenience it had caused them; she intimated that it would distinctly dim the celestial content of Madame Bouvier herself could she realize the annoying position in which she had placed these American ladies. For the rest, by a happy chance, she herself had now vacant two most desirable bedrooms and a sitting-room on the second floor, the whole being a suite sure to suit the exact needs of Mademoiselle and her mother. Mademoiselle permitted herself to be escorted to them, surveyed them, and promptly engaged them—paying for them a week in advance. This duty accomplished, she descended to the cab again, escorted by her new landlady and half the household staff, and within the next five minutes the Hartleys and their luggage were established in their new quarters, and their cabman, paid and extravagantly tipped, had gone his care-free way.

The travelers had lunched on the train. The *pension* dinner, they learned, would not be served until seven. To fill this dragging interval Mrs. Hartley promptly went to bed, murmuring something about a slight headache.

For an hour Maud busied herself, with the assistance of one of the maids, in unpacking bags, laying out the gowns she and her mother would wear at dinner, and moving the furniture about the rooms to give them the occupied effect they lacked. When she had done all this she went to a window and looked out. Below was the garden with the hoops and the children. Around it was the high, protecting wall. But off to the right were wonderful stretches of green and pink, French fields with almond-trees in full bloom; and farther away still was a curving silver line she knew must be the Loire. In the light spring breeze the branches of the almond-trees waved a salute to her, and she seemed to hear the voice of the river calling her out into the open. Glancing into her mother's room, she saw that she was fast asleep. Without awakening her, she put on her hat, jacket, and gloves, and strolled out into the streets.

She would not, she decided, go into the country this afternoon, though that was where she longed to go. There would hardly be time. It was now about four o'clock. She would see something of Tours itself—getting her first impressions quite alone, as she preferred to do.

Comfortably and happily she strolled along, leaving the wide thoroughfares for quaint side-streets, which always most attracted her in foreign cities. She had her Baedeker in her hand, its tell-tale red back concealed by a special cover of dark, rich leather which she had bought in Italy. She did not open it, however; she merely wanted to absorb the atmosphere of Tours, to look at its people, to hear the click of their *sabots*, to admire the little red soldiers, to return the town's smile, indeed, until she was ready to go home.

Until she was ready to go home! A sudden reflection caught her by the throat. Under its force she stood still in the street, momentarily aghast. When she was ready to go home, *where would she go?* She realized now, for the first time, that she had not the remotest idea. The kindly Frenchwoman who stepped out of the group at the station had given her new address, not to her, but to her driver, and he had driven her to the house. Incredible as it now seemed, when she reached there she had taken everything for granted. It had not occurred to her to ask the proprietress her name or the address. So, when she had left it, she—Maud Hartley, the capable, the executive, the experienced traveler— had ventured out into a strange world as irresponsibly as a baby, and with as little knowledge of how to return to that starting-point. For a moment the humiliation of the experience occupied her mind more fully than its practical aspects. Then, resolutely, she forced herself to think of these.

The house, she recalled, had been a large, white house, behind a high wall. Large, white houses behind high walls were to be found upon every hand in Tours. Half a dozen of them faced her even now, as she stared around her, trying to control the unpleasant little tremor that was shaking her nerves. This wasn't at all serious, she told herself. It was merely funny—a huge joke on her, which she would tell with gusto when she returned to America. But in the mean time there was that mysterious house to return to here in Tours, in which her mother was waiting.

She looked at her watch. Five o'clock! She had been walking more than an hour. She might be three or four miles away from that white house, wherever it was. She was obviously in quite a different part of the city. The white houses around her now looked old and grim and forbidding. They seemed to stare back at her with a strange aloofness, as if coldly repudiating any association with an American girl who was foolish enough to start out from a strange *pension* without making a note of its location. What should she do? What *should* she do?

She had been standing still for several minutes, in the middle of the sidewalk, unconscious of the curious glances of those who passed her. Now, realizing that she must not attract another crowd, as at the station, she uncertainly moved away. She had gone only a few steps when she caught the eager but respectful gaze of a young man who had been leaning against an old wall and quietly watching. When their eyes met he at once came toward her, his tweed cap in his hand, his tanned, boyish face slightly flushed with embarrassment.

"I beg your pardon," he said, "but can I help you? Have you lost anything?"

She looked uncertainly into his handsome, eager face, met the clear regard of his gray eyes, observed the diffidence of his American manner, and straightway felt at ease with him. As promptly, she dropped her burden of anxiety on his welcome masculine shoulders.

"Yes," she admitted, ruefully, "I've lost myself."

He smiled. "That's very easy in Tours," he told her, "especially for strangers. But I know the place pretty well. If you'll tell me your address I'll see that you reach it."

His tone and manner were exactly what they should have been—comforting, reassuring, matter-of-fact.

"But that's just what I can't do," she told him. "You see, I don't know my address."

"You mean," he asked, uncertainly, "that you've forgotten it?"

"No," she said; "I mean that I've never had it."

At the expression of his face she laughed outright. Then, as briefly as she could, she explained the situation. At first he laughed with her; then his eyes grew grave.

"But that's rather serious," he admitted, soberly.

"Would you think that any human being could be so silly?" she asked. "I'm afraid mother will never trust me again. Poor mother! She must be worrying about me dreadfully this minute. What shall I do? The worst of it is that I walked out of the house without my purse. I haven't a cent."

He gave his mind to it, his boyish face very serious. At first sight she had thought him about her own age. Now she decided that he was several

years older, and found the reflection oddly interesting.

"The cabman might remember the address," he
mused, "if we could find him." He faced her with
sudden decision. "Will you let me take charge of
the search?" he asked. "Let me see if I can find
the place for you?"

"Oh, if you only will!" she murmured, gratefully.
She felt like a lost and frightened child to whom a
friendly hand had been outstretched. If he turned
and left her, she told herself, she believed she would
run after him, crying.

"I oughtn't to trouble you," she added, dutifully.
"It may be ages before we find the house."

"Then we'll wander hand in hand for years," he
laughed, "keeping up our mysterious quest while
our hair turns white and our steps grow feeble. And
if my end comes before we find it," he added, "I'll
expect you to mourn for me and put a monument on
the spot where I dropped."

She shivered. "Don't," she begged. "I can see
myself now, a helpless, heartbroken old woman,
weeping at the grave of my one friend."

"Would you be heartbroken?" he asked.

"Utterly," she smiled.

Their eyes met. The smile in both pairs faded.
In his a sudden flash took its place. Why, in
Heaven's name, he asked himself, did he feel at the
end of half a dozen sentences as if he had known this
girl all his life? He had never felt that way before

about any girl, least of all one he had known only five minutes. With an effort he recalled himself to duty.

"Then it's all understood," he said, briskly. "For the time you're under my orders. We'll see how obedient you are."

He dropped into the big outside pocket of his Norfolk jacket the sketch-book he had been holding, and signaled to a cabman who was driving slowly past them, his eyes alert for passengers. When the man stopped he helped her into the cab and took his place beside her.

"Drive to the station," he directed the *cocher*.

"Oughtn't we to walk while we're young and strong?" she asked, "and save the cab-fare for later years?"

Already the affair had begun to seem to her like a joke.

"I've figured that out," he answered, gravely. "We can spend freely now, while I'm strong enough to earn more."

"But with most of your life given to the search," she insisted, "how can you find time to earn more?"

He met her eyes again; then, dropping his own, caught the adorable effect of the lift of her upper lip over her teeth as she smiled. As if drawn by a force beyond his control, he leaned toward her.

"I'll have plenty of time," he said, quietly. "You see, the thing most men spend their lives looking for, I think I've found already."

She raised her eyebrows. "Fame?" she asked.

He shook his head. "No, nor money," he told her.

Miss Hartley mentally retreated. Whatever it was, it was no affair of hers. She sat up suddenly, as one who has been dreaming and is rudely awakened.

"How far is it to the station?" she asked.

Under the rebuke he bit his lip. She should not have to pull him up again, he resolved. The unusually intimate note with which their talk had started at the first instant must be his excuse.

"Only a few blocks," he said. Then, in the same breath, he produced his credentials and his plans. "My name is Brinkley," he said. "Edward Brinkley. I'm an American, from New York, studying architecture in Paris. I've been in Touraine for a month, making notes and sketches." This introduction over, he passed on resolutely to the task before them.

"Would you remember your cabman, if you saw him again?" he asked. "The one you picked up at the station?"

She nodded. "I think so," she said, doubtfully.

"If you can, it may be very simple," he told her. "Perhaps we'll find him at the station, if that's his stand; and if we do, the chances are that he'll remember the address."

His companion leaned back in the cab in restored peace of mind. Of course the cabman would remember it. That was beautifully simple. She would have thought of it herself, given a little more time. Meantime, from the corner of her eye she studied her companion, and he, as if conscious that such observation might still further reassure her, sat quietly by her side, looking straight before him. It was not going to be easy to find that *pension*, he reflected, if her cabman could not be discovered. To ask police help was unthinkable. The thing would be all over town the next day and the girl would be the talk of Tours. It might be necessary to get a list of *pensions* and visit them all. It would take some time—half the night at least. She wouldn't like that! Unconscious of his forebodings, his charge continued to study him, mentally tabulating her impressions.

He was tall, she observed—possibly almost six feet tall—erect and athletic. His gray-green jacket and knickerbockers were of heavy tweed, and his dark-green stockings matched his tie. He looked extremely comfortable, but had evidently dressed with an eye to detail. The soft tweed cap he had replaced on his brown, curly hair was gray-green, like his clothes. His face was smooth, his eyes gray, his young jaw very firm, his smile quick and boyish. Altogether, he was distinctly reassuring. She was sorry she had snubbed him, but he had brought it upon himself. However, he was evidently forgiving. He flashed his brilliant smile upon her now, as if he had understood her close scrutiny.

"Will I do?" he asked, teasingly. "Or would you prefer a *gendarme?*"

She shuddered. "You'll do," she said, emphatically, and looked it.

"Keep an eye out," he advised her, restraining the response on the end of his tongue. "If your man isn't at the station, he's driving somewhere in these streets, and you may catch a glimpse of him at any minute. Was there anything noticeable about him? Anything distinctive, I mean?"

She thought there wasn't, but she described him as well as she could. The description fitted perfectly the man who was driving them at the moment, as well as a dozen other cabmen they passed. She was equally vague in her memories of the house. It was white, and behind a wall. As she brought out these banalities she was conscious of a tingling sense of humiliation. What an idiot she must seem to him! Even to her it seemed incredible that she or any other girl could have been at once so absent-minded and so blind. But he appeared to think it all the most natural episode in the world, and, comforted, she began to accept his view. Certainly, it seemed oddly natural to be riding about with him now.

At the station they both looked around eagerly. There were several cabmen lounging on the boxes of their *fiacres;* none of them stirred the chords of memory. Nevertheless, Miss Hartley's escort alighted and made numerous inquiries. The minds of the cabmen, stimulated by the swift passage of coin from hand to hand, grappled eagerly with the problem presented to them. But after a great deal of talk nothing had been discovered beyond the fact that none of these was the right man, and that none knew who the right man was. Their combined mental effort finally evolved the theory that the lady's cabman might be Marcel Frechette, a new-comer among them, who had gone home sick an hour ago. He had mentioned having had a good day, and had boasted that he could afford rest when he required it. He lived, they said, in the suburbs of Tours, five miles from the station, and they gave minute directions for reaching the spot.

"We'll go and look him up," said Mr. Brinkley, blithely. "Meantime we can watch the streets and the other cabmen, and see if you recognize yours. Go slowly through the town," he added to the driver.

Hope again whispered her welcome message in Maud's ear. Frechette must be the man. The generous payment he had exacted for handling eight pieces of luggage, combined with the usual fares and her handsome tip, had made him feel like a capitalist, and he had gone home to the delights of well-earned repose. Brinkley, to whom she con-fided this theory, was as confident as she was. It was hard to be pessimistic, or even practical, when her mere presence beside him was making his heart sing in his breast. She was here. He had found her, and almost at the first glance he had known her for his own. What did anything else matter? He remembered how often he had scoffed at the notion of love at first sight. Well, he knew better now. For twenty-five years he had been wholly indifferent to girls; now, in an instant, his whole life seemed hanging on this girl whose very name he did not know.

He wondered what she was thinking of. Was she worrying, or was she trusting him? Was there any echo of his feeling in her heart, or was she wholly indifferent? He stole a glance at her. She was sitting with absent yet happy eyes fixed on the far horizon line, relaxed, content. He knew how quickly an unwise word of his would change that attitude of perfect trustfulness—for she did trust him, he realized that now. And, though she was not yet conscious of it, there must be some response in her to the depths she had stirred in him. Silently he studied the lines of her face, the arch of her black eyebrows, the soft curve of her lips. He knew how cold a look those brown eyes could hold; he had seen it only half an hour before. He wished never to see it again. Was it possible that he had known her only half an hour? He felt as if he had known her for centuries. It was hard not to be able to tell her so. But he must be careful—very careful. Only—how could a fellow be careful when the Only One had come at last, and when he was wholly alone with her in a world of almond-blossoms, and when she smiled like that?

She had, he decided, the most charming smile he

had ever seen. It came often—whenever he spoke to her. To keep it in play, he chatted of his work, his life in Paris. He told her about his family. It would save time later, he reflected, wisely, to tell her such things now. Also, he drew her out about herself. She talked of America, and of her travels. They discovered that they liked the same countries, the same pictures. At the end of an hour they both felt an extraordinary sense of long acquaintanceship, even of intimacy. The pleased cabman, grasping his opportunity, also, drove them on and on, reaching his destination by long détours, each détour representing at least fifty centimes added to his account. Occasionally, as in duty bound, Brinkley directed Miss Hartley's attention to some object of interest while they were passing.

"That is the church of St. Martin," he remarked, when that venerable shrine of pilgrims loomed before them. She cast a half-hearted glance at the sacred spot. There were moments, she had just decided, when his eyes looked almost brown, instead of either blue or gray. She liked his nose, too, and his way of throwing back his head when he laughed, and his little trick of compressing his lips occasionally, as if he had started to say something and had suddenly checked himself. She did not know what eager words were trying to make their way past that firm barrier.

The cabman's expedition had frankly resolved itself into a drive about Tours, and Brinkley, sud-

denly realizing this, quieted his conscience by re-
flecting that his charge might recognize her street or
her own cabman at any moment. He added to his
companion's knowledge by discoursing learnedly on
the Maison de Tristan l'Hermite, pointing out its
picturesque façade, and by showing her the remnants of Plessis-les-Tours, at which she hardly looked,
and the cathedral, and the birthplace of Balzac, all of
which left her cold. Historic ruins, she felt, paled
before the charm of the new world in which she was
driving with this stranger who fitted so wonderfully
into it. It was a very beautiful world, a world
wholly without care or convention. It seemed to be
a world without memories, too, or she might have
recalled some reason why she should not be wander-
ing through it in this detached and happy way.

Neither of the two realized how late it had grown;
but darkness was falling when they reached the rural
home of Marcel Frechette and summoned that unattractive person to its forbidding exterior. He had
been asleep and apparently intoxicated, but his
manners were better than his appearance.

Alas, no. He had not had the pleasure of driving
mademoiselle from the station. Indeed, he had
never had the extreme felicity of seeing mademoiselle
before. He could not have forgotten her if he had.
If he might be permitted to say so, the face of
mademoiselle was one that must be engraved forever
on the memory of one fortunate enough to behold
it—

Brinkley checked his flow of Gallic eloquence, gave him a franc, and ordered his driver to depart. As he lashed his weary horse into a jog, both his passengers were startled by a sudden realization of the swift coming of the night and the nearness of an approaching storm. The fields around them lay dim and silent; lights winked meaningly at them from the windows of scattered cottages, the wind began to sweep the dust in a small whirlwind before it, and the sky, which had seemed so near and friendly an hour ago, was obscured by ominous clouds. Even as they stared up at it the first heavy drops of rain began to fall.

"By Jove!" said Brinkley, with deep contrition, "I'm making an awful mess of this. I ought to have had you home long ago. Did you realize it was so late?"

"No," she said, gently, "I didn't."

He stopped the cab and asked the driver a question or two, and that personage responded with a flow of rapid and urgent French, of which she caught only occasional words. Brinkley turned to her with a worried look.

"The *cocher* says," he explained, "that he thinks it's only a passing storm, over, probably, in an hour. There's a good inn half a mile farther on. He suggests that we go there and wait till the worst of the storm is past. Incidentally, we can get something to eat."

With a sigh Maud Hartley awoke from her dream.

They *had* made a mess of things—there seemed no doubt about that. They should never have come out into the country on this wild-goose chase. But they were here, and the storm was here also, and two hungry men and a starved and weary horse were dependent upon her common sense. Very well, she decided. They should rest and eat—for an hour. If at the end of that time the storm was not over, they would start for Tours if the old horse had to swim. Once in Tours—but now her imagination refused to pass the point of their arrival in Tours. She communicated her decision to Brinkley, and he, seeing her pallor, and appreciating both her panic and her courage, gave his orders to the *cocher* between set teeth, and swore to himself that in some way, *any* way, he would have her with her mother before ten o'clock.

It was raining hard when they reached the inn, and the wind was shrieking around the corners of the old stone building. But the dining-room to which the landlord led them had a fire on the hearth, and the glow of candles on table and mantel was reflected in the polished wood of the paneled walls. The meal he brought them was of the perfect kind found in France alone, but neither did it justice. They ate absently and almost in silence, listening to the gusts of wind that seemed to shake the building, and to the rain that dashed itself against the window-panes. Both had the odd sense that sometimes comes in life of having been in the same situation

6   7I

before, and together. There was no self-consciousness in their long silences. They had reached the point where words were not necessary.

When they went out into the dripping court of the inn the storm was at its worst. But their cabman was awaiting them, enveloped in a huge waterproof cape, and the old horse, cheered by his rest and meal, and protected by a heavy blanket, seemed ready for the road. The driver helped them into the rickety cab, and fastened its curtains securely around them. Sitting close together, on the back seat, they were protected from the storm, enveloped in the darkness of the night, and drawn together by an extraordinary sense of interdependence and intimacy. Yet, secure in this safe retreat, started toward Tours, and with arrival there in an hour fairly certain, Maud suddenly buried her face in her hands and burst into tears. A full realization of her situation had rolled over her, as clearly as it had done in the first moments on the street of Tours. And now, as then, she found herself in the clutches of an incipient panic.

When they reached Tours, where should she go? She was as far from knowing as she had been five hours ago—and during those impossible, incredible five hours she had been blithely, happily, driving around the countryside with a strange young man. What must he think of her? What could she think of herself? What must her mother be thinking now? —her distracted mother, whom she had almost forgotten. A childish gulp broke from her, and at

the sound the wretched young man beside her grew
desperate. Seizing his handkerchief, he drew her
hands from her face and wiped her eyes. Then,
resolutely, he held the hands that tried to draw
away, and bent toward her, his eyes shining into
hers in the dark. Frightened, she shrank from him.

"Don't!" she cried.

He held her hands tightly in his. "Why not?"
he asked, gently.

She wrenched her hands away, and faced him with
sudden decision.

"I don't know what I've been thinking of," she
cried. "It's night, and I'm lost, and I'd forgotten
all about it, and I'm miles from home—wherever
home is. Oh, how could I have acted this way! And
you didn't care. It was all a lark to you!"

"You know better than that," he said, quietly.
"You know perfectly well that the reason we both
forgot your little predicament was because we were
facing something bigger—the biggest thing in life.
You know that, don't you?"

She shook her head.

"You do," he insisted. "Do you think anything
else would have made you forget? Do you think
I don't understand that? I loved you the minute
I saw you, and something in you answered. I knew
it when we got into the cab and drove away. Home
is any place where we two are together. That's why
you weren't afraid. You know it. Say you know
it! Say you love me!"

The old horse stumbled, and was jerked up by the impatient cabman, with winged words of protest. The storm was growing wilder, but neither of them noticed it.

"Say it," he whispered.

She drew her hands away, but very gently.

"Wait," she murmured.

"But there's so much I want to tell you," he urged. "We've got our whole future to plan!"

She smiled in the darkness. "Wait," she said again. Her voice held both a promise and a command. He exulted in the one and obeyed the other.

For a long time they sat in silence, while the horse made its weary way toward Tours. Impassive against the stormy sky, the huge back of the cabman rose above them. He did not know where they wanted to go next, and he thought it did not matter. The rain beat upon him, but he did not feel it. His reins slack on the back of his aged animal, his chin on his breast, he almost dozed. Behind him, Brinkley looked at the white oval of her face in the darkness, and told himself that he and she had been together, just like that, for a thousand years, and would be together, just like that, for a thousand years to come. He could not picture life without her, here or hereafter. With an exultant thrill he told himself he need not try.

"We're very near town," he said, suddenly. "Can you remember anything else about the house— anything you haven't told me?"

"There was a garden," she murmured, dreamily, "with a straight path from the gate to the house, fringed with almond-trees. There was a little fountain at the left, but it wasn't working; the basin was held up by cherubs. I think the iron lamp over the wooden gate was held by cherubs, too. And—"

The old *fiacre* creaked under his sudden start. He gave the driver a quick order. "Why didn't you remember that before?" he asked, smiling at her.

"I don't know," she said. "I suppose it was because at first I was so nervous and frightened. I couldn't think of anything except that I didn't know the address or the woman's name."

"And then," he explained, "when you stopped being afraid it began to come back. Your memory developed the photograph it had unconsciously taken. Doesn't that sound impressive?"

The cab stopped before a large, white house set in a walled garden. Brinkley paid the driver and followed her through a wooden gate, under an iron lamp supported by cherubs.

"This must be it!" she cried. "And here's a number on the gate-post—thirty-seven. I remember now," she said, proudly, "that there was a number —thirty-seven, I think."

"Of course it's thirty-seven," agreed Brinkley, placidly, and accompanied her into the house.

"But how did *you* know?" she demanded. "And how did you happen to recognize the fountain when I described it?"

"By the luckiest of chances," he laughed. "You see, I happen to be boarding here myself!"

"Hello, Mr. Brinkley!" shrieked a shrill-voiced American boy from an upper window. "You're dreadfully late for dinner. And everybody's worried about Miss Hartley!"

Brinkley waved his hand to him and pursued Maud along the hall to the foot of the wide stairs.

"Mayn't I come up for a moment and meet your mother?" he begged. "I don't want to wait till morning."

Mrs. Hartley, wide-eyed and excited, heard her daughter's voice and opened an upper door as he spoke. Her torrent of questions was checked by the wanderer, who accounted for her adventure in one pregnant sentence, and introduced Mr. Brinkley, of New York.

"But what I can't understand," said Mrs. Hartley, after she had shaken hands and thanked him, "is why it should have taken you so long to find the place."

"There's a reason," admitted Mr. Brinkley, gaily. "Our minds weren't on it!" Then, as she stared at him uncomprehendingly, his manner changed. "We were a little slow in that," he explained, gently, "but we made record time in another matter. It took us five hours to get here—but it didn't take us half as long to find each other!" And to Maud he added, urgently, "Now that you're safely home, *admit* it!"

She admitted it.

THE FAR-AWAY ROAD

"SO you see, Joe," Evelyn said, "it's the end of the story. We've got to say good-by and part forever, the way they do in books. And I hope," she added, trying to speak lightly, "we can do it without working up a dramatic climax that will wear us both out."

Rand, huddled together in a chair behind her, took this in black silence, his head bent forward, his eyes fixed on the floor. Only a sudden contraction of the muscles of the jaw as he set his teeth showed that he had heard her, but she did not see it. She could say the words which would separate them— she had whipped herself up to that—but she could not and would not look at him while she uttered them. She realized too well how horribly she was hurting him, and she wondered if he would ever realize how horribly, at the same time, she was hurting herself. She was doing it all for his sake; some time, if not now, he would understand that, as he went his comparatively care-free way, and it was possible that he would be grateful. But what recompense could the years offer her aside from the comfort of knowing that she had done what was best for him?

"I'm glad you can be so cheerful about it," he
flung at her, after what seemed to them both a long
interval. "Personally, I don't see quite where the
comedy comes in."

"Oh, my dear!" She had been standing at the
window with her back to him, staring out at the
whitewashed wall on the opposite side of the court
which alone lighted her small living-room. Even
before he saw the tears in her eyes as she turned and
came toward him the tones of her voice told him she
had reached the limit of her self-control. "Do you
imagine for a moment that I don't--"

She stopped, tried to go on, and stopped again.
Then, with a suddenness which he found appalling,
she dropped on a chair near him, buried her face in
her hands, and began to cry, not hysterically, but
quietly and steadily, as one cries without hope.

For an instant Rand sat still watching her in a dull
misery that offered no comfort for her or himself.
It was her own doing, this thing, he reflected, and
though his hot resentment was cooled by that rain
of tears, he could not yet try to check them. But
at last she uttered a choked little sob, a childish gulp
that pulled at his very heart-strings, and in an instant he was on his knees beside her, holding both
her hands in one of his, while he wiped her eyes
with his handkerchief, abusing himself and soothing
her in the same breath.

"What a beast I am!" he said, bitterly, when she
was calm again. "I can't make a home for you, and

78

I can't stand up under my failure. To be a cipher in business is bad enough, but to know I can't even take my medicine with dignity—that's the turn of the screw."

She put her hand over his mouth. "Don't," she said. "I won't listen. And don't mind me. I'll be all right."

He said no more, and for a moment she studied him in silence, realizing with a pang the changes the last few months had made in him. That he was on the verge of a breakdown was evident. His color showed it, and the look in his eyes and the deep new lines in his face.

"You couldn't possibly support me and my mother, too, as well as your father and your little niece," she repeated, harking back to the discussion her sudden collapse had interrupted. "I won't let you risk trying it. If I could go on with my work after we were married that would make it easier, but they won't keep a married woman—" She broke off suddenly. "But what's the use of going into it again?" she cried. "We've gone over it backward and forward, looked at it inside and outside, and it all comes to the same thing: we can't marry. We've got big obligations in life, and we must meet them. For Heaven's sake, Joe, let us realize that and do it."

"I've saved four hundred dollars, and in a few years—" he began.

She shook her head. "Four hundred dollars builds a very slender plank over the abyss for five

79

persons to stand on," she reminded him. "Things
have grown steadily worse with us. I had almost
three hundred saved. Mother's illness last year
took two hundred of it. No," she ended, abruptly,
"it's fate. We've got to part, for I know—you
can't deny it"—she was speaking solemnly now,
her hands on his shoulder as he knelt beside her, her
eyes fixed on his—"the struggle is breaking you
down. You can go on if your mind is relieved of the
constant thought that you must earn enough to support five of us. If it isn't you'll go to pieces."

He did not deny the truth of what she said. Instead, still on his knees, he bent toward her, speaking
almost as if to himself, in the sudden relief of a
confidence he had not dared to make till now.

"Sometimes I'm panic-stricken," he admitted. "I
wake up at night and break into a cold sweat,
wondering what would happen if I broke down, and
feeling sure I'm going to—"

"I know," she told him. "I've read it all in your
expression and in these new lines around your
mouth."

She traced them with a tender finger-tip as she
spoke, and he kissed her hand as it passed his lips
and uttered an ejaculation that was half a groan. If
there was anything he could do or leave undone, he
told himself, there might be hope for them. But he
had worked with all that was in him for eleven years,
and he was still almost where he had started. That
was because he had started wrong—he knew it now.

But how would his old father and orphan niece live while he started again, at the foot of the hill?

"You see, that's the one thing I can't bear," Evelyn went on, "seeing it break you down. So it's all over. And because if we met we'd keep bringing it up and arguing about it, we're going to part right here and now, like—like—rational beings."

"But I can work better if I have our marriage to look forward to," he protested, reopening the argument at its beginning. "It's an incentive to the best I've got in me—"

She checked him gently. "You said all that before," she reminded him, "and I believed it, because I wanted to. But now I know better. Why, Joe" —she gave him a straight look, charged with meaning—"you know and I know that you'll go to smash nervously in a few weeks more if this strain keeps up."

"And I'll go to smash just as surely without you," he muttered. "That's my situation—the smash is coming, whatever happens. Those tearing pains in the back of my head and the frightful depression I feel are the red lights nature is hanging out. The doctor says that if I could get away and live in the country—" He laughed bitterly.

"I don't think that's necessary." She spoke as his mother might have spoken, with the same comprehending sympathy. "The relief of this understanding between us will help you. You'll be horribly depressed for a few weeks; but underneath it all there will be the inevitable reaction. Then, by and by, you'll get your grip on things again and forge ahead."

"And if I do forge ahead?" he asked, eagerly.

"No." She rose with a quick gesture of decision. "There mustn't be any promise or hopes of that kind. If there were we'd merely be swinging round the same old circle. So it's all settled," she ended, and threw up her head to face a future that did not hold him. "I'm jilting you, Joe. I'm throwing you over. That's what it means. Stand up to it. Take it. Good-by."

She held out both hands. He rose, too, but swung away from her with a brusque gesture of refusal.

"*Now?*" he cried. "But—how absurd! Why, it's Saturday! We always spend Saturday afternoon together."

"Get it over," she said, smiling with lips that felt stiff. "One word and it's done."

"But it's our half-holiday," he protested. "Must we throw that away, like everything else? Why can't we have that, at least?"

He was staring at her now, wide-eyed, incredulous, like a big, hurt child, and she looked at him much as a mother might have looked at a small son who was demanding the impossible.

"What shall I do with you, Joe?" she exclaimed, half in laughter, half in tears. "I hoped you'd understand and help me, but you won't do either."

82

THE FAR-AWAY ROAD

"It's Saturday afternoon," he repeated, as if the simple statement answered every argument.

She reflected rapidly. He must have his holiday, but it should be the last. "Come," she said, "we'll make a bargain. If I go with you up to Bronxville or out on Long Island and we spend the afternoon together, tramping over the hills or through the woods, will you say good-by when you come back, and *keep to it?*"

"Yes," he said, dully. "I suppose I must. You don't give me much choice."

"Then it's settled. Let me see." She looked at her watch. "It's two o'clock. Where shall we go?"

"Westchester," he suggested, still studying her as if he did not recognize the new creature she had become. "It has spots that might be a thousand miles from New York. Let's go to them and lose ourselves."

"We'll find some far-away road," she agreed, "that leads to nowhere. And we'll follow it. Shall we take something to eat?"

"No," he declared, stoutly.

She knew him too well to take him at his word. She went into her small kitchen and made some sandwiches, which she covered with waxed paper and packed in a tin lunch-box, with two cups. Then she filled a thermos bottle with tea, and, carrying both packages, returned to the living-room and handed them to him. He slipped them into the pockets of his overcoat.

83

"We could have got tea somewhere," he remarked, vaguely, as he followed her down three flights of stairs and out of the apartment-house where she and her mother lived.

"On the far-away road?" she laughed. "Never. It wouldn't be a far-away road if it had tea-rooms blossoming along the hedge. Now let's go and find it."

They took a train and rode for an hour, leaving it at a place neither of them knew except by name. The somber lure of a late October day lay over the town, which straggled away from the station as if eager to answer the call of the near-by woods. A main street led to half a dozen nondescript shops, but they rejected its silent invitation and, climbing inelegantly over a rail fence, struck off across a field. As they walked their spirits rose. Nature-lovers, both, they responded at once to the melancholy beauty of the landscape, veiled in its Indian-summer haze, to the pungent smell of burning leaves in a neighboring meadow, to the occasional glimpses of self-absorbed squirrels coming and going on the edge of the wood.

The talk of an hour ago began to seem like an unpleasant dream. With the same impulse they resolutely buried the memory of it and talked of the things around them. In an hour's walk they had come to a region whose narrow lanes, gnarled old trees, and running, vine-covered, neglected rail fences might have been in the very heart of some remote

rural region—a far cry from city streets. Not a
sound of urban life came to them; not even a slow
spiral of smoke floated in the air near them to mark
a spot where some one lived. Their eyes met in a
common flash of delight. Both gloried in the sense
of isolation that wrapped them around and brought
them so blessedly close. And now, final touch to
their supreme content, here at last was the far-away
road, a road of almost obliterated wagon tracks,
stretched at their very feet, as if to make their day a
perfect thing. They took it, with a boyish shout
from Rand, and followed its erratic twists and turns
across more fields, through a friendly wood, and
along a short, almost hidden stream, buried deep in
the long grass of a neglected meadow.

Suddenly they noticed that the sky was growing
dark and that a cold wind had come up and was
sweeping through the branches of the trees around
them, hurling its hostage of leaves at their feet.
Then the rain began to fall, at first in light, scattered drops, soon steadily, and at last in a relentless
downpour that threatened to continue for hours.
Laughing, yet anxious, they ran for shelter, seeing
on all sides only sodden fields and writhing branches
in which the wind was beginning to whine with a hint
of anger in its voice. Rand seized Evelyn's hand.

"Let's keep to the far-away road," he said, as
they raced on together. "There's no building behind us, and this must lead somewhere."

It did. Within a few minutes they came in sight

of a house, closed and strangely desolate, seen through the blur of the autumn rain. Rand pulled back a broken gate, which creaked protestingly on its rusty hinges, and they hurried along a neglected garden path to temporary shelter under a sagging veranda roof. Here, protected from the worst of the storm, they stared around them.

The place bore the look of one that had been deserted for years. The garden was a mere tangle, while the fence that had guarded it, Rand said, was now only an impressionistic sketch. Here and there were great gaps showing where pickets had been torn out and carried away. The building, originally an old colonial farm-house, had been restored perhaps twenty-years ago, and apparently deserted about ten years later. Half a dozen windows were broken, and several shutters sagged spinelessly from solitary hinges. Over the veranda, whose rotten wood, soaked by years of rain and snow, cracked under their feet as they moved, crept tangled vines, bare of leaves. The veranda itself extended across the front and around the left side of the house. Rand followed it eagerly, going from window to window, his hands close to his eyes, peering into the dim interior. Standing where he had left her, Evelyn wondered for a moment at his interest, then told herself that he was trying to find a way of getting inside, to give her better shelter than the rain-swept veranda afforded. He had tried the doors in vain; they were securely bolted. But now, from a side window, she heard his voice and went to him.

"I can get in here," he told her. He had thrust his arm through a broken pane, found and released the catch, and was raising the sash as he spoke. An instant afterward he was inside, holding out his hands to help her.

"Aren't we better here?" she asked, hanging back. "It's sure to be musty in here, and horribly dirty."

"Can't be very musty with all those broken windows," Rand thought. "But wait a minute. I'll take a look."

He disappeared; then she heard an exclamation from inside, and almost immediately he was back again.

"By Jove! Evie," he said, "there's a fireplace in here and some wood. I believe we can start a fire. Come along. It's clean as a whistle, too," he added, reassuringly, as he helped her over the sill.

The living-room in which they found themselves was large and low-ceilinged and, notwithstanding its emptiness and dilapidation, it had an air of recent occupation. There were andirons and ashes on the hearth of the great stone fireplace, and a pile of wood was neatly stacked against the wall. A comfortable old wooden settle stood near it, its venerable back raw with newly cut initials.

"Picnic parties," explained Rand, briefly, as they looked around. "Some of them evidently make a

7   87

point of coming here regularly and building a fire. Not a bad idea. They've cleaned it up, too. Sit down and watch me start a blaze." He swung the settle forward and urged her into it. "Wait a minute," he promised her, "and I'll show you what authors call 'the leaping flames.'"

He set about his task with brisk efficiency, making sure that the kindling he found was dry, and building his fire according to the cherished traditions of that art. As he worked he whistled under his breath. Evelyn watched him in silence, feeling as if each step he took was on her aching heart. Apparently he was absolutely care-free—yet they were to part forever in a few hours.

"What an infant he is!" she told herself, and brooded over him with hopeless and forgiving tenderness. Rand drew out his match-box with a little flourish.

"Now, if I hadn't acquired the vile habit of smoking, where would we be?" he boasted, as he lit the waiting pile of wood. The kindling caught, a thread of flame reconnoitered lazily and decided to spread, the dry wood snapped responsively. In a few minutes the dim old room was transformed. Evelyn felt a strange peace stealing over her. She put her feet on the fender, turning the wet soles of her boots to the comforting heat, and Rand came and sat beside her, his stout shoes close to hers, looking at his fire with proud proprietorship.

"Comfy, isn't it?" he asked, and turned on her the

eyes of a happy boy. "Homelike, too. Jove! how good this is—just the two of us here alone in front of our own fire!"

Evelyn did not answer, except by a pressure from the hand he had taken into his. She was not yet wholly under the spell of the illusion which held him. She still heard the rain and wind of the outer world to which they must soon return. That Rand could find "homeyness" in this decaying structure merely because it held her and a fire caused her an almost unbearable pang. She knew so well the kind of home he needed. In fancy she had constructed it a thousand times. But now at last she knew she could never have it ready for him, nor see him in it.

"This room isn't half bad," he mused, looking around. "It's wider than it's long. It must be— let me see—fully thirty feet, taking in the whole width of the house. And I should say it's twenty-five feet long." He measured it with a calculating eye. "They threw two rooms into one, I suppose, when they remodeled the farm." He loved a big living-room wherever he found it, but he had never owned one.

"There were window-seats in those windows," Evelyn said, partly to humor him, partly because her fancy was at last beginning to picture and people the place at its best. "The view from those two windows is charming even through the rain—see, down the hill and along that old road." She looked around. "There was a writing-desk

89

over here," she added, indicating a point, "and low bookcases between those windows, and a grand-father's clock in that corner, and spindle-legged tables standing there and there."

Rand looked at her curiously. "How do you know?" he asked.

She laughed. "I don't—I merely feel it! But you can see the marks of the bookcases and the clock on that faded paper." She jumped up, regard-ing her steaming shoes with satisfaction. "Now we're going to have tea. Can't you find a soap-box or a chair or something so we can have it elegantly?"

While she unpacked the sandwiches he went into the cellar and over the house, poking into corners, opening doors, and returning at intervals with the spoils of his expedition. By the time she was ready to pour out the tea he had set before her three chairs, one old table very wobbly as to legs, the top of which he covered with his copy of an evening newspaper, a small box that made an excellent footstool, and a china plate and tin pail, both in a high state of preservation.

"Picnic parties left 'em," he explained. "Don't know what we'll do with them, but they'll help to make the table look pretty!"

She added the plate to the decorative scheme, and set the table before the fire, propping its insecure leg with friendly logs. Then they drew up their chairs and attacked the tea and sandwiches with appetites unimpaired by sorrow. As they lingered over the little meal he chatted about his jaunt through the house.

"There's a fine, dry cellar under here," he said. "The place was well built originally. Look at that beamed ceiling. The dining-room's back of this, with a fine view over the country. The kitchen had running water in it, and there are four bedrooms up-stairs, and a bathroom, and a little sewing-room. The wing has a laundry and a woodshed. Evie," he laughed, boyishly, "let's play it's ours."

She looked at him with shining eyes. "It is ours," she said. "Nothing can ever take this hour in it away from us."

When they had finished their tea he led her back to the old settle with knightly courtesy and seated her on it, the soap-box under her feet as excess of comfort. Then he sat down beside her and looked at her adoringly, while she leaned back, giving herself up wholly at last to the sweetness of this game they were playing together. The firelight glinted on her brown hair, and now in her eyes, as she turned to him, was the mischievous spark he loved to see there. But even as he looked at her his heart ached mad-deningly. Here was the one woman in the world for him—the woman he loved and who loved him; yet he must lose her because he could not supply her with the bare necessities of life. The thought was intolerable to him. He rushed into speech.

"It's ours," he began, briskly. "I've just come out from town," he went on, drawing closer to her, "and it's snowing and blowing great guns. I had a hard tramp up from the station, but when I got here you heard my step on the piazza and you opened the door and kissed me and helped me to take my coat off, and then you brought me in here for tea and to get dry before I went up-stairs. Now I'm going to tell you how things went at the office to-day, and what that beast Jenkins did."

"He's afraid you'll get his job," she said. "That's what's the matter with him. I'm sure," she added, with true wifely complacency, "you ought to have it. You do all the work."

He talked on, keeping to his rôle, and conveying to her a singular sense of reality in an intimate discussion of business and home matters between a husband and wife. She told him the waitress had left that morning because life was not sufficiently hectic in the country. He promised to bring a new one out from town the next evening, and to play bridge with her every evening she remained, her wages to be the stakes. They decided to extend the veranda around the right side of the house, and to take their meals on it during the summer. They also planned several important changes in the garden, and agreed that they needed a new slate roof.

"Wouldn't it be better to wait for the roof until next year?" the prudent housewife wanted to know.

Her lord scoffed rudely at this suggestion. "Play up," he said, dropping his rôle for an instant. "We'll have no economy in this dream."

He ran on, resuming the mantle of the house-holder, and as he talked she saw the pictures he painted and knew the sweetness of them, then sternly pulled herself together, for this was dangerous mental dalliance.

"After we had decided all these things you went up-stairs and dressed, and came down and grumbled about the dinner," she said, briskly. "You said you had eaten chops twice this week, and wanted something substantial."

"Think of knowing you well enough to be cross!" he murmured. "I wonder if I ever could! What did you do when I grumbled?"

"Oh!" She kept to the safe highway of badinage. "I handed you a ham and let you gnaw on it."

They laughed, and for a moment sat silent, peopling the deserted house with themselves and their material belongings. Evelyn had some old mahogany and two good rugs, heirlooms from a maiden aunt. Rand had all the furniture that had belonged to his mother. Oh, they could furnish the place admirably—but what was the use of dreaming? She sighed, and dreamed on. Outside it was growing dark, but Rand had been generous with his appropriated logs, and the firelight searched out each corner of the old room as if it loved them all. In the flicker of the flames Evelyn caught the gleam of her old mahogany and pewter and polished brass. She saw herself coming and going about the place, doing things for Rand. Rand, silent beside her, saw these things and more. And in the hearts of both, far down where they had forced it, memory stirred, while the duty they had forgotten raised its insistent voice.

"Part!" it seemed to say. "Part now! Poor fools, have you forgotten *me?*"

Feeling her courage ebb from her, Evelyn turned suddenly and threw her arms around Rand, pressing her face against his in the most spontaneous caress she had ever given him. It was as if in that moment she felt him slipping from her and by sheer force would hold him back.

"Oh, Joe!" she cried, "it's almost over," and he felt her tears against his cheek. "I'm crying *again*," she admitted, needlessly. "That's twice to-day. I'm a-ashamed of m-myself."

He held her close, and in that moment both went through not only the pain of their immediate separation, but the cumulative, chilling loneliness of the years to come. And while they clung together they repeated once more their old, hopeless discussion, he pleading, she refuting, both knowing their hour was behind them. Once they thought they heard a noise on the veranda, as if some one had stepped lightly across it. When they glanced up, however, everything was still, and they were too deeply absorbed in each other to think of the matter again. But a little later an unmistakable step sounded outside, and they heard a noise at the open window through which they themselves had entered. The next instant a man stepped lightly over the sill into the room and came toward them, smiling, but with an air of assured proprietorship.

He was a large man, they saw, about fifty, erect and handsome, dressed in drenched riding-clothes and holding a riding-crop in his hand.

"Good evening," he said, cheerfully, as he reached them. "I hope I don't intrude. Pretty comfortable here, aren't you?"

He removed his hat as he spoke, shook the raindrops from it, and laid it down on the old mantel. Then, turning from them for a moment, he slapped his gloved hand against his sleeves, scattering a small shower around him. Rand and Evelyn rose in stiff resentment of his unceremonious entrance.

"Good evening. I suppose this house is yours," Rand said. "I'm afraid we're the ones who have intruded."

He picked up Evelyn's coat as he spoke, and held it for her to slip into. The stranger had turned to them again at the same moment, and was studying them both with eyes which, though friendly, missed no detail of their appearance. Now he took the coat gently from Rand's hands and laid it over the back of the settle.

"Please don't go yet," he said, in a different tone. "I didn't mean to drive you away. The place is yours as long as you want it."

"Thank you," said Rand. "It's time we went. It's much later than I thought," he added, looking at his watch.

The stranger looked regretful. "I'm afraid I'm speeding the parting guests," he declared, ruefully. "But I saw the firelight through the window as I was riding by and it gave me a bit of a jolt. I don't want the old place to burn down, though I've neglected it abominably for a good many years."

"We shouldn't have come in," murmured Evelyn.

What he thought, indeed what any one thought, was a matter of entire indifference to her. She felt cold and depressed, and her one desire was to get away. He was spoiling everything, this stranger. Now they wouldn't even have their perfect memory. She packed the cups and the thermos bottle, and gathered in a housewifely pile the remnants of the feast, which she wrapped in the newspaper that had served as their table-cloth, and threw into the fire.

"Please don't go," repeated the stranger. "You look so cozy here. I rather hoped you'd give me a cup of tea," he added, frankly, "if you have any left."

She had, and poured it for him at once, necessarily in her own cup, which she polished conscientiously with a bit of the clean oiled paper. She was glad of the opportunity to make even this slight return for the brief hospitality of his roof. It left them quits. He drank his tea very slowly, and to the last drop, while they chatted about the storm and Rand explained their unpremeditated visit. When he had emptied the cup the stranger hesitated for a moment, then set it down and turned to them with an air of decision in which was mingled a sudden air of constraint that sat oddly on him.

"I feel as if I were the intruder now," he said, with a rather nervous laugh. "But, to tell the truth, I don't want to go. I'm enjoying this. You see," he explained, "I've just got back to America, after fifteen years in Japan. And this is the nearest approach to a home-coming I've had yet."

As if on a common impulse Rand and Evelyn sat down.

"That's good of you," he said, gratefully, observing them. He remained standing, however, one elbow on the mantel, his eyes fixed on the fire.

"Most things have changed in those fifteen years," he went on, slowly. "I've come back alone. My wife died out there."

He said it very simply, but his two hearers realized, without understanding why they did, that the few words described the supreme tragedy of the man's life. There was an unconscious flattening of the voice, a sudden droop of the body, as if he had added, "So everything ended for me." He stopped for a moment, then went on quickly, but with an effort.

"My old neighbors—I live two miles from here— have died or moved, or both. It's really very pleasant, you know, to come into this house and find it occupied. It brings back a lot of memories. It's high time I came, too," he added, looking around; "the old place is nearly done for!"

LOVERS' KNOTS

It was plain to them both now that for some reason he was talking against time—trying to know them, and giving them a chance to know him. They uttered some perfunctory murmurs—neither could remember afterward just what had been said; but it didn't matter, for he was busy with his own thoughts.

"It's hard to believe," he continued, meditatively, "that my wife and I came here for our honeymoon twenty years ago. I must have the house fixed up, if only as a matter of sentiment. I don't suppose it would rent for much, off here, away from the main road. But after we left it, it was a nice little poultry and vegetable farm."

He raised his head as he spoke, and looked at Rand with a singularly direct and meaning look. Rand looked back at him. In that sudden flash of eye to eye both men knew a message had been sent and received.

"Could one raise chickens here now, do you suppose?" Rand asked, slowly. "Have a garden—that kind of thing?"

The stranger nodded, with a smile. "Why not?" he asked.

Evelyn glanced from one to the other, feeling something in the atmosphere, but hardly daring to guess what it was.

"When we left, seventeen years ago," their host continued, thoughtfully, "we lent the place to our gardener and his wife. The old man built a chicken-run and stocked it, and started a vegetable-garden. They made a very good living at it till he died, seven or eight years later. Then his widow went West to live with her married daughter. Since that we never rented the place. We didn't want to. Our baby died here, and my wife didn't like the idea of strangers around. The gardener's wife had been her nurse. But I think—she'd like—" He stopped. "I fancy there's something of the chicken-run left," he went on, after a pause. "There was a very good garden, too. Why?" He asked the leading question at last with an air of brisk good-fellowship. "Thinking of going in for chickens and farming?"

"I might." Rand moistened his lips. "How much would you do for the place?" he asked when he could speak naturally. "And how much rent would you want?"

"Let me see." The owner paused, turning the situation over in his mind. It wasn't business, but he could afford to be unbusiness-like at times, and he couldn't forget what he had heard on the veranda as he peered through those broken window-panes. The traces of tears on the cheeks of the girl on that old settle were still very evident. One didn't often have a chance to do a big thing for others at so slight a cost to oneself. His mind had been made up before he entered the room. He had merely wanted to study this engaging pair at closer range, and now that he had done so he was satisfied. He knew the types—the man, dreamy, impractical, in a way, but

99

hard-working, loyal, and honest; the woman, quick, practical, efficient. "They'll win out," he told himself.

"I'm going away again in the spring," he announced, after this reflection, "so it would have to be done at once. It isn't really as bad as it looks. It needs painting and papering and plumbing and some new floors and windows, and possibly a new slate roof—that's about all. But I'll do whatever needs to be done. Could you move in by March if it's ready?"

"I guess so." Rand looked at Evelyn. "Yes," he said, firmly. "We can."

"All right; that's settled." The stranger picked up his hat. "There are ten acres of ground, so you can have a good garden—and you'll have room for a thousand chickens, if you want to branch out to that extent. Better start with less. Possibly," he hazarded, "you've got a little capital to begin with?"

"Yes, a few hundred dollars," said Rand.

"That's good." The stranger looked relieved. It had been quite on the cards that his philanthropic interest might have necessitated financing the enterprise. He welcomed, as a true business man, the soothing clink of real money. Yes, they'd get on, and they were just the sort Millie would like to have on the old place—Millie, who had been dead three years, yet who always seemed so close to him when he did anything like this. To-night he could almost feel the touch of her hand in his and hear the warm gurgle of her contagious laugh—that dear laugh that was like no other sound in the world.

"I can arrange to have the Country Club near here take a lot of what you raise," he told Rand. "That will give you a good start."

"And the rent?" asked Rand, briskly.

"Oh, the rent!" The stranger flipped his riding-boot with his crop, his eyes on them reflectively. "Well, I'll tell you what I'll do. I'll give you the place rent free for the first year, till you get things going. After that I'll charge you the market price —say—oh, well, say three hundred a year."

Rand crossed the room and held out his hand. "We'll take it for a year, gladly, if you'll let us," he said, gratefully. "The second year we'll pay three hundred. After that we'll pay more if we've made it go, for I know it will be worth more—and we *will* make it go!" he added, with a deep breath.

"Done," said his new landlord, and their hands met. "All this," he smiled, "has been rather casual. But if you'll come to my office to-morrow morning —forty-nine Broad Street—here's my card—we'll fix it up in proper shape. Of course you'll bring your credentials."

"Of course!" Rand smiled back at him, radiant. "I haven't got much cash, but I've got lots of credentials. And don't think," he added, "that we don't know what a big thing you're doing for us. It's—well, perhaps you'll know some day just all it means."

"Possibly I know now," suggested the stranger. He was at the open window now, ready to depart, but he stopped and looked back. "Couldn't marry. Wasn't that it? Wanted a home, and were thinking you could never have it."

"That's it," Rand admitted.

"Were saying good-by, and blue as indigo. Life over before it really began, and all that kind of thing."

Rand and Evelyn stared at him.

"You're right," Rand conceded. "But I'd like to know how you knew it?"

The stranger hesitated, then decided to wipe from his friendly slate its one unsightly record.

"Well, to tell the truth, I've been spying and eavesdropping," he confessed. "I crept up on the veranda to see what the light was, and I stayed there a few minutes, looking and listening while you played your game of home. It hit me rather hard, because —well, you see, I spent my happiest days here twenty years ago. You'll forgive me?"

Evelyn went to him and held out both hands. "How good you are!" she said. "It's like a fairy-tale!"

He pressed her hands and looked down on her, his eyes very kind.

"It's the real thing," he assured her, answering her unspoken question. "This little fairy-tale is all your own. Here's your vine and fig-tree just as you saw them in the dream. Live under them and be happy. Good night."

After he had gone Evelyn turned to Rand. "But *can* we?" she gasped. "I'm not sure yet that we really can. Is it practicable?"

Rand drew her to the faithful settle and sat down beside her. "Yes," he said, "it is. I figured it all out while he was talking, which was exactly what he meant me to do. Here are the details: we can move and stock the place with my four hundred. I can borrow a little more if necessary. I'll keep my job, so we'll have that much income assured. Father and you will run this place. Chickens have no secrets from dad, and the chance to help us will make him happy. I'll find some young fellow around here to do the heavy work. That's sound, isn't it?"

She nodded. "Mother can help in the garden," she reflected, aloud. "She'll love that. Your little niece can help me in the house. And there's plenty of room, so every one can be comfy. Oh, Joe, it will work! It will! It will!"

"Let's give your mother the big front room," suggested Rand, generously, as they were going over the house a little later. "This one, *yours*"—he dwelt on the word—"is almost as large, and has as fine a view."

"Your father can have the big rear room, and Alice will like this little one. And I'll sew downstairs," Evelyn decided, "so we can use the sewing-room as a guest-room."

"Yes, for the present," Rand said, with a canny look into the future.

They could hardly force themselves to leave the house. When they were finally outside they stopped in the garden path and looked around them. It was still raining, but to them the whole landscape was bathed in mellow radiance, out of which rose the dream structure of their future dwelling.

"How happy mother will be!" sighed Evelyn. "She has always wanted a garden. And she lies awake nights wishing she could help. Now she can."

"Father, too," said Rand, loyally. "Those chickens will give him a supreme object in life." He laughed, with a little break in his voice. "He's been worrying about me as much as you have," he added. "But now it's going to be all right."

"It's too good to be true," said Evelyn, as they started back to the village. "I hope it isn't just a dream. I'm pinching myself to see. But, no, it isn't, for here's our darling far-away road! Look at it! Just look at it!" There in the rain she knelt down, traced the dim tracks, and, bending, kissed the unresponsive soil. "Oh, Joe! Who would have thought," she asked him, as he stooped to help her up, "that when we blundered across it, only two hours ago, we had found the road that led us home?"

HER MAN FRIDAY

THE *Stormy Petrel* was not behaving well. Instead of leaving the wharf, as usual, in smooth and purring content, its engine kept up a stuttering protest which developed at intervals into almost human gurgles and gasps. The fair owner, who had been bending over the machinery, surveying it with reproachful eyes, straightened herself and turned suddenly at the sound of a voice on the dock behind her.

"Doesn't seem to work very well, does she?" sympathetically observed a stalwart young man in white flannels.

Miss Holcomb bit her lip, and turned from him to a renewed and greatly intensified interest in the engine.

"Have you tried poking it with a stick?" suggested the intruder.

The heightened color in the girl's face might have been due to her exertions, for she was now oiling the machinery for the fifth time. She did not speak, and the man, after a moment of courteous waiting, carefully selected a clean spot on the wharf and sat down upon it.

"It's very cool and pleasant here," he murmured, dreamily, "and I don't in the least mind waiting. But how soon do you think we'll start?"

Miss Holcomb dropped the oil-can and stood up. Her brow was moist under the loose locks of her curly hair, and an angry light burned in her brown eyes. Her sunburnt cheeks were crimson with heat and annoyance, but she made a charming picture, which the young man in white flannels regarded with evident pleasure.

"Go away!" she commanded, desperately. "Go away this minute!"

The young man surveyed her with hurt wonder. "I only wanted to know," he repeated, "when we are to start—"

"You know perfectly well, Archibald Whitney," remarked Miss Holcomb, slowly and incisively, "that you are not going to start at all."

Mr. Whitney turned sympathetic eyes on the motor-boat. "Is it as bad as that?" he asked. "I thought perhaps you'd be able to make her run in a few hours. You're so clever about boats."

"I shall be able to start in twenty minutes," announced Miss Holcomb in a voice trembling with indignation. "Is that quite clear?"

Mr. Whitney rose to his feet with a sigh. "Why, yes," he conceded, cheerfully. "I hope you'll forgive my interruption."

When the girl looked up again young Mr. Whitney was strolling languidly up the village street, and even as she stared incredulously after him he turned a corner and disappeared.

Fifteen minutes later the motor, apparently reconciled to its rôle in life, was humming contentedly, and Miss Holcomb was about to cast off when a large hamper, lowered from the wharf, landed in the middle of the boat, followed the next instant by Mr. Whitney, who dropped into the seat opposite her with an expectant smile. Under her astonished gaze the smile faded a trifle, but the young man's voice when he spoke had lost none of its confident note.

"Good work," he commented. "Your twenty minutes gave me just time to run back to the hotel and have 'em put up a nice lunch for us. Without your tip I'd never have thought of it," he added, gratefully.

The girl's gaze flashed along the wharf. Several fishermen were lounging about, smoking peacefully. To ask them to forcibly drag the gentleman from the boat seemed too radical a proposition. To personally eject him was impracticable. The only remaining alternative—that of leaving herself—would certainly stir up gossip in a village already deeply excited over the lovers' quarrel which for three days had been going on between these two popular visitors. The line of Anne Holcomb's jaw was admirably defined as she guided the *Stormy Petrel* out into the bay. Her eyes looked past her self-invited guest as if he had not been there; her expression denoted complete detachment from her environment.

"Where are we going?" asked Mr. Whitney, casually.

Miss Holcomb, as if recalling his presence with difficulty, leaned forward. "You have forced yourself on me," she said, "and to avoid unpleasant comment I have to stand it. But I don't have to talk to you, and I won't."

"Oh, but I say," protested her passenger, "I came along to talk to you. I risked my life for it. This little tub may turn over and spill us any minute, and while you could swim to land, I doubt if you could save me. Perhaps we'd have to die together. Perhaps we'll have to, anyway. So before we go I want to say that I'm awfully sorry about that silly row of ours, and I want to explain—"

"If you try to explain anything," interrupted the girl, firmly, "or if you say any more, I'll turn the boat and go home."

Mr. Whitney seemed to experience a degree of surprise which for the moment obscured his interest in the issue between them.

"Does she turn around?" he asked, eagerly. "I thought she didn't. I was watching yesterday when you tried to turn her—"

Then, as the girl made a quick motion, he held up his hand. "Don't do it," he begged. "Life is sweet. I'll keep still."

For almost an hour there was silence, broken only

by the beating of the *Petrel's* heart as she cut her
steady way through the calm sea. Off in the distance—a mere line at first, but growing clearer with
every moment that passed, lay an island, soaking
itself in the light of the setting sun. On one side,
as they drew nearer, it showed a wall of rock. On
the other, trees sloped down to a sandy beach.
Young Mr. Whitney surveyed its austere beauty
with an approving eye.

"Good place to eat our supper," he commented,
easily. "We can have a driftwood fire."

"We are not stopping," announced Miss Holcomb.

"The *Petrel* wants to," observed her passenger.
"Haven't you noticed her gasping for breath? We
must have gone all of ten miles, which is about her
limit, I should say. But of course a few days' rest
here on the island may set her up again."

Anne was not listening. She had sprung up to
make a hurried examination, and now she turned to
him a face whose recent frozen calm was replaced by
a growing consternation.

"The gasoline," she gasped. "We're out of it!"

Her guest looked politely interested. "Really?"
he asked. "Is that what she's sobbing about?"

"It's that wretched Bantley boy!" exclaimed Miss
Holcomb. "He told me he attended to it this morning, but I shouldn't have trusted him. I should
have looked myself. One can't trust any one," she
added, bitterly. "Oh, what shall I do!"

Her companion gave his mind to the problem.

"First of all," he said at last, "if I were you I'd run the *Petrel* up onto the beach and let her lie down and take a nap. That seems to be what she wants. Then I'd have a driftwood fire, and a whole lot of supper, and after that I'd look at the moon and listen to me make love. Something tells me," he added, modestly, "that I can make love well this evening."

"Good heavens! can't you understand? We're—we're going to be stranded here!"

Mr. Whitney nodded. "I know," he admitted. "Cast up by the sea, and all that kind of thing. I'll be your man Friday. I'll build a house for you, and search the beach for tool-chests, and shoot big game to sustain you. How many hams a day does a girl eat?" he added, with sudden interest.

Anne Holcomb's thoughts were intent upon manoeuvering the dying *Petrel* into the tiny harbor that lay before them. In the next few moments she had accomplished it, and a little later the boat was fastened and the castaways were on the beach, where the girl promptly sat down and regarded the indistinct line of the distant mainland with an expression of longing and despair.

"Food first," announced young Whitney, cheerfully. "I'll get the driftwood while you set the table. In a few days I'll develop into one of those brave, resourceful geniuses you read about. When it rains I'll probably discover a rubber-plant and make you a mackintosh. But to-night we'll do with the supplies we've brought."

"But—but—" Miss Holcomb's tone was almost humble. "Don't you see—"

"Yon afterglow of surprising splendor? Of course I do. But I'd rather look at it over the edge of a perfect sandwich, if you ask me. Here's the basket. Suppose you unpack it while I make a fire."

He strolled along the beach, picking up bits of driftwood, which he brought back and heaped together. In a few moments he had started a blaze that grew into long, darting tongues of green-and-amethyst fire, highly effective against a background of rock and sea. Then he unpacked the basket which Miss Holcomb had not deigned to touch, and, after laying a plate before her and another for himself, he sat down on the sand and fell zestfully upon a cold chicken. As he carved he recited the menu in a voice filled with pleasant expectation.

"Cold chicken, sardines, egg sandwiches, pickles, olives, half a pound-cake, and two bottles of ginger-ale," he mentioned, peacefully. "Not bad for the Sea Cliff Inn staff, though they might have thrown in a ham or two while they were about it," he added, regretfully. "However, perhaps I'll have a shot at some hams in the morning."

"Mr. Whitney."

"Yes, Miss Holcomb."

"We must get away from here."

"Assuredly—and before the snow flies. I'll attend to it." He nodded comfortingly, his mouth full. "In the mean time, keep up your strength. Eat."

"You might have some appreciation of my feelings. You might show some—some tact and decency."

The young man laid down the sandwich he held in one hand and the hard-boiled egg he had just raised to his lips. "Am I not showing the most delicate consideration?" he demanded. "Here we are, lovers once, but strangers now, separated for three days by a silly misunderstanding, and then cast together on a desert island smelling of crushed bayberries and bathed in seventeen kinds of sunset effects. What would be my natural impulse? Why, to tell you I adore you, and to keep on telling you till I can't talk, and then to teach the waves to say it for me. To wrap the sunset round you, to hand you the moon and the stars, and tell you I made 'em for you, and why. But am I doing it? I am not. Instead, I'm eating hard-boiled eggs," he added, bitterly—and set about doing so.

"Can't you think of any way we can get home?" urged the girl in a voice that trembled despite her efforts to keep it steady.

"Perhaps a fishing-boat may pick us up, or a submarine, or something like that. But until it comes," he added, firmly, "not one word of love from me—not one plea, not one reproach. I won't even tell you how utterly wretched I've been these last three days—"

"Do you think there's any chance of a boat—"

"Or how I've seemed to see your eyes before me every minute—"

"Be quiet."

Mr. Whitney obeyed, giving his close attention to the repast.

"Couldn't we put up a signal?" asked the girl at last, "so that if some boat did pass—"

"I'll hang up the napkins after we've finished with 'em. Meantime I'm wrapped in discretion. I won't even tell you how I wanted to kill Charlie White yesterday morning because I saw you bow to him, nor how I—"

"Can't we put the signals up now?"

"No. Nor how I got so desperate yesterday, after you cut me dead, that I mooned round your hotel most of last night, watching your light till it went out—"

"You didn't!"

The words came before she realized that they were on her lips. Failing to check them, she stiffened and turned red, but Mr. Whitney went on placidly, speaking, it must be admitted, in tones somewhat muffled by his uninterrupted consumption of sandwiches.

"Sometime I'll tell you about it," he promised. "And how I compared you with all the other girls I know and tried to convince myself that you were not the loveliest, most adored and adorable—"

"You mustn't—"

"I know it. How I couldn't see any one but you, your eyes, your smile— Have some chicken, darling. You're not eating a thing—and the whole blessed sweetness of you till my heart almost broke to think I'd lost you."

"Don't—please don't."

"I'm not—but I'm going to, sometime. And I'm going to tell you how I made up my mind to grovel at your blessed little feet till you forgave me, because I simply dared not face life without you."

"Archie, please—"

"Have an olive. And how you're always right and I'm always wrong, and I'm not worthy to be on the same earth with you, and how my only excuse for being on it is that I've got sense enough to adore you."

"You mustn't—you really must not!"

"Oh yes, I must—sometime—not now, of course. Meantime, try the sardines. They're awfully good."

"It's getting dark. I'm afraid."

"I'll make a cradle for you in the tops of the trees, and swing it with a string from below. I'll have the sea sing you to sleep, and the morning stars get up a special rising hymn for you. I'll buy you a comet to take excursions on."

"You promised you wouldn't—"

"I'm not. This isn't making love. It's just making practical plans for the future."

"Hello, Mr. Whitney! I've put your gasoline aboard."

Miss Holcomb uttered a gasp and then a cry of joy. Whitney turned and surveyed with strong disapproval the grinning youth who stood behind him.

"Confound you, Bantley," he exclaimed, angrily. "You're an hour ahead of time. I told you eight o'clock."

114

"It's after eight now," declared the boy, stoutly. "I been waitin' till you got through talkin' to her. When you said it was all over but the practical plans, I spoke up."

Miss Holcomb's brown cheeks crimsoned to the ears. Mr. Whitney, after a moment of stunned silence, spoke in a voice which lacked its usual note of authority.

"You mean," he demanded, "that you've been listening?"

The boy's wide grin disappeared. "Y-yes, sir," he stammered. "You—you said—"

Young Whitney rose, took him by an ear, led him to the water's edge, and lifted him into the launch in which he had come to the island.

"Get out," he commanded, briefly. Then, as the boy snickeringly started his motor the young man became conscious that Miss Holcomb, already in the *Stormy Petrel*, was imperiously motioning to him to accompany the lad. He ignored the suggestion. "Scat!" he remarked to the boy, and the latter hurriedly obeyed.

Somberly Mr. Whitney rejoined Miss Holcomb, somberly he sat down, somberly he stared toward the mainland. There was a long silence after their boat had started. Then Anne spoke.

"So," she said, deliberately, "it was all a trick. You bribed that boy to put my engine out of order and leave me short of gasoline."

Her passenger groaned. "I did," he admitted.

"I was desperate. I'd do it again in the same conditions. But, like most conspirators, I made one fatal blunder, I neglected to muzzle the young fool. You'd better believe I'll muzzle him when we get back," he added, vindictively.

She did not reply, and there was another long silence, during which the darkness folded itself around them closely and comfortingly, as if to bring them nearer together. The *Stormy Petrel* hummed on her willing way, and with each moment of her progress the heart of Archibald Whitney grew heavier. He had played his last card, and lost the game. Anne might forgive much, but she was not a girl to forgive the man who made her ridiculous. All was over. He'd go back to town the next day and try to pull himself together. Then, out of the starlit gloom, he heard her voice.

"Do you think you can muzzle Bantley?" she asked, hesitatingly. "Are you sure you can?"

On the instant the glorious touch of hope illumined the life of young Whitney. "Absolutely sure," he declared, fervently. "I promise you he shall never repeat one word I said—darling!"

He heard a contented sigh. Then, in a voice so low that he had to lean far forward to catch her words, she spoke again.

"If you're quite sure of that," she said, "you—you might go on now and tell me all the things you didn't say on the island!"

PHILIP'S "FURNIS MAN"

MISS ANITA HOLLOWAY rested her arms inelegantly on her breakfast-tray and frowned
down at the silver coffee-pot, the cream-pitcher, the
two slices of toast, and the pile of letters that met
her weary glance. She was twenty-four. A loving
but candid friend had once said of her that she
looked twenty when she was interested, and thirty
when she was bored. She was not interested now.
Another day had begun, and there was every prospect that it would be very much like the seventy-
eight days which had followed her reluctant return
to New York from her big house in the country.
She had been bored there, but not oppressively; she
was oppressively bored in town, and she fiercely resented the fact.

In twenty minutes her masseuse would arrive, and
the strenuous hour of this young person's visit would
be succeeded by the attentions of a maid, who might
or might not arouse the momentary interest attending the building of a new style of coiffure on the head
of her mistress. After that there would be the
nuisance of getting dressed, Anita reflected, gloomily;
and then a luncheon, at which eight or ten women

would gabble, none listening to any of the others. At five she must go to Harriet Mason's tea, "to meet" a person she had not the slightest desire to meet; and she must get away from that in time to dress for a seven-o'clock dinner, followed by a play concerning which she had heard the most depressing reports.

As to the mail, she knew before she opened her letters about what they contained: an appeal in behalf of the Polish fund; an appeal in behalf of the Servian fund; an almost tearful plea from a local charity organization not to forget the deserving poor at home; several invitations to dinners; five or six invitations to luncheons; four requests that she be a patroness of entertainments for worthy ends, and buy half a dozen tickets at five dollars each; one or two casual notes from women friends as blasé as herself; several notes from uninteresting men, inviting her to see the Russian dancers, when—as Miss Holloway reflected with increasing gloom—one should see those Russian dancers with interesting men or one should not see them at all.

She opened her letters. They realized her darkest forebodings. But at the bottom of the heap, almost hidden under the rim of her plate, was a tiny envelope addressed in sprawling, printed letters; and at the sight of this the charming but cold face of Miss Holloway warmed and brightened as if touched by a sudden beam from the sun of romance. She tore open the envelope, swept an eye past a line of white ducks in a frenzied flight across the top of a blue page, and read the words below:

DERE AUNT NITA,—Mother says I can Ask just the Ones I want for my burthday Partie   it is Thursday so I want You. Mother says Tell you the Rest   so it is Jim who does not belong to eny One.   He sels papers   he is Older than Me.   And my nurs.   And the Furnis man and Carlotta From Sweden   she is offel lonsom.   And my Own dokter and Profeser Gray.   Father says he nos more Than Any one els in the Unervercity but he has not Got eny Litel Boy.   Pleas cum   I kno you wil like The furnis Man.

Yur loving frend

PHILIP

Miss Holloway read the letter twice. Then she threw back her head with a joyous laugh—a sound so unexpected that it had a shattering effect on the nervous system of the maid who was removing the breakfast-tray. Subsequently, as Anita resigned herself to the ministrations of the masseuse, and still later to those of the artiste in coiffures, her lips were curved in a tender and absent smile. She recalled the list of Philip's prospective guests, and they seemed to pass before her in review: Carlotta of Sweden, who sounded like a princess royal, but was probably a cook; Professor Gray, visualized as a dried-up, academic person who had won Philip's heart by showing him a tadpole or a caterpillar; Jim, evidently a pal, near Philip's tender age; and last, but far from least, the Furnace Man Philip was so sure *she* would like. She knew the boy must have met this person in his explorations through the cellar of the great Cameron house. She could picture the big-eyed, passionately friendly child sitting on an upturned box, watching the Furnace Man at his labors, and winning the heart of that sooty individual, as he won the hearts of all who touched his life. Philip was a darling, a very prince of darlings; she had always adored him, and now she was almost passionately grateful to him for giving her a thrill of real interest.

She wrote a personal acceptance of his invitation, and, light-heartedly leaving the remaining letters for her secretary to answer according to the dictates of a somewhat limited intelligence, she went to the gabbling luncheon, which was fully as gabbling as she had expected it to be. In one of the rare intervals in which she herself was permitted to gabble, she mentioned Philip's invitation, and was rewarded by an immediate attention, even from a group which was discussing flesh-reduction at the moment.

"That child will have a lot of money when he's twenty-one," contributed her hostess. "But he'll probably be a socialist by that time and give it all away, because of the peculiar notions of his parents. *Fancy* letting him associate with newsboys and furnace-men!"

"But think of getting Professor Gray!" another breathed in awe. "He never goes *anywhere*, and his books are simply wonderful."

"The Camerons ought to be putting Philip up now for the best schools and the big clubs, so he'll get in when he's old enough," another matron thought. "We entered Billy for Grotch the day he was born."

"Are you really his aunt?" a fourth asked Miss Holloway.

"No," Anita admitted; "only his godmother. But when he was old enough to notice names, and heard his mother call me Anita, he thought it meant 'Aunt Nita,' and so—"

Nobody was listening.

"That luncheon of his will be a weird affair," said a girl who affected offhand speech. "Where d' ye s'pose he'll sandwich you, Nita—between Jim and Carlotta?"

Anita laughed. "I hope so," she declared. "I'd infinitely prefer them to Professor Gray and the doctor."

The same problem was at the same moment disturbing the breast of Master Philip Cameron. Following their usual method with this precocious infant, his parents had thrown upon him the burden of the preparations for his party, as well as of the entertainment itself. They were, they lightly mentioned, at his service as a source of general information; but they expected him to untie his own somewhat tangled social knots. Pale but calm, Master Philip asked a few questions. He learned that the table arrangements of his guests was highly important. Also that there were hosts so given to detail that they actually wrote out a list of their guests and

LOVERS' KNOTS

then made a diagram of their positions at the
banquet-board. His mother seemed to admire such
hosts. Philip disappeared with a wan smile. A
little later he returned with inky fingers and a
blotted list, to which Mrs. Cameron gave immediate
and respectful attention.

> Jim
> Nurs
> Dokter Clark
> Carlotta From Sweden
> Aunt Nita
> Profeser Gray.
> the Furnis man

"How many does that make?" his mother demanded.

Breathing rather heavily in his interest, Philip
counted the names. It was an important matter.
There must be no mistake.

"Seven," he decided.

"Eight would be better," mused the exacting
parent. "Eight is an even number. They could
go into the dining-room in pairs."

"Like an'mals into the Ark," confirmed Philip,
grasping the point.

"Can you think of any one else you'd like to ask?
There really *should* be eight."

Philip shook his head. Then his brow cleared.
"Would I do?" he suggested, diffidently. "You
know I—I—really 'spected to be there!"

His mother laughed and hugged him, hiding in his

yellow hair a conscious face. "I think you will," she conceded.

When the question of the diagram came up after this refreshing interval, Philip drew a circle that bore a depressing resemblance to a leaky egg. A few patient touches gave it better proportions, and then, still following a large general plan, he made crosses at the head and foot to represent his guests, and three marks on each side of the imaginary table. There remained the delicate matter of arranging the guests, and at this point Mrs. Cameron departed somewhat abruptly, murmuring that a lady usually sat between two gentlemen, and that the guests "one most desired to honor" were placed at one's right and left. The hints left Philip rather limp, but that night when he was sleeping—somewhat restlessly, it must be confessed, after his mental exertions— his father and mother found this document in his small desk, and bent reverent heads above it:

Aunt Nita
X

Jim—   _The Furnis
                                   man

Profeser_   _Dokter
  Gray   Clark

Carlotta
  from —   —Nurs
Sweden

X
ME
123

"Couldn't have done it better myself," chuckled the elder Cameron. "Few pictures could be more stimulating to the tired mind than that of Clark between Nurse and the Furnace Man."

"Unless," murmured his wife, "it's that of Nita between Jim and the Furnace Man. Oh, Phil, isn't it an appalling mixture!"

"They'll carry it off," predicted her husband. "Trust Gray for that."

"Nita could swing the thing alone, if she happened to be in the humor," brooded Philip's mother. "But probably she won't be. She almost never is, nowadays. How a girl with money and beauty and position and brains can be so desperately discontented *all* the time is more than I can understand. But about this party— Really—hadn't we better—"

"Not a bit of it," interrupted Philip senior. "Give 'em a good luncheon, and let 'em muddle through. You and I would spoil everything. Moreover, my dear—pardon me for mentioning it—the cold fact is that our son has not invited us!"

On Thursday morning Anita learned by telephone that the time set for Philip's luncheon was one o'clock, a detail her overworked host had omitted to mention. She presented herself at five minutes before that hour, and was escorted to the drawing-room by a servant who appeared to be struggling with abysmal emotions. She was, it appeared, the last arrival, and Philip, his blue eyes

blazing with excitement, shook hands with her cere-
moniously, and hastened to introduce her to his
other guests—an attention complicated by the abrupt
disappearance of two of them. Jim had taken refuge
behind a divan, over the back of which his agonized
red face was sinking with something of the effect of a
setting sun. Carlotta, the Swedish nurse of a neighboring child, had coyly retreated into a corner behind
a potted palm. Three men, however, rose as Anita
entered, and two of these Philip presented in turn.

"This is my doctor," he said. "He's awful busy,
but he came to my party just the same. He's going
to bring me a little brother soon's he can 'tend to
it. And this is the Professor. He knows everything."

The foot of Jim, appearing under the divan at this
point, distracted the attention of the host. He
promptly grabbled it. "We'll go in to lunch now,"
he ended, hurriedly, as he tugged away, " 'cause
we're all here. Jim, you just got to come out and
bring Carlotta, so please do it, quick."

Professor Gray looked very much as Anita had expected him to look. Clark was an elegant person,
with a Van Dyke beard and a manner. Both murmured pleasant phrases, to which Anita replied in
kind. Both were utterly insignificant in the presence
of the third man, a young giant with brown eyes
and the handsomest head and face Miss Holloway
had ever seen. They were almost too handsome;
they rather took one's breath away and made one

125

self-conscious—but the manner of their possessor was extremely simple and natural. His eyes were as brilliant as Philip's; there was an amused tremor in the voice that spoke to her.

"May I take you in?" he asked.

Anita took his arm without speaking, but with an extraordinary feeling of having done so before; indeed, of knowing this young man surprisingly well, though certainly she had never met him until this hour. If she had, she could not have forgotten him. Her spirits rose dizzyingly. This was sure to be an interesting luncheon. The portières leading into the dining-room had been drawn back, and Philip, hand in hand with the beloved nurse who was his guest of honor, was advancing at the head of his short procession. Behind him, Carlotta and Jim, equally out of their native element, dragged reluctant feet; and back of them Gray and Clark walked, arm in arm, exhibiting a surprising gift of airy badinage. Anita and her escort came last; and now she shot a second glance at him, quick but appraising, taking in this time not alone his brilliant eyes and handsome face, but the swing of his big shoulders, his splendid length of limb, the perfection of his carriage, the shabbiness of his clothes. His clothes were very shabby indeed—threadbare, even; and one of his carefully polished shoes showed a break at the side. It was a most incongruous thing that such a man should wear such garments. He was a prince in a fairy-tale, badly disguised.

"Philip does not believe in names," she smiled, "but you are—"

"The Furnace Man? Yes." He smiled down at her from the height of his six feet, and something in the smile moved her oddly. No man had ever smiled at her quite like this; it was exactly such a smile as Philip might have given her, and it matched perfectly the look in this young giant's eyes—the look of a happy boy. Those eyes held, too, something of the sudden intimacy of a little boy's expression when he meets and likes a new friend. "Isn't this a lark?" he asked. "No one but Philip could have thought of it. And see him carry it off!"

They were at the table now, looking for the place-cards that bore their names, Gray and Clark continuing their cheerful talk in an obvious determination to make the affair "go," Philip wholly at his ease, Carlotta and Jim still souls in outer darkness. But a few moments later Anita found herself a sharer of the Furnace Man's theory that Philip would carry his party to a triumphant finish. The strain was already relaxing; the newsboy and Carlotta had forgotten themselves in contemplation of the room, the flowers, the food before them. Not even the presence of two noiselessly padding servants who came and went with the dishes of the first course could hurl them back into their abyss of agonized self-consciousness. Peace fell upon them. They had nothing to do but eat.

At the right hands of Jim and Philip stood tall goblets filled with milk. Near the other covers were bell-shaped glasses which were immediately and expertly filled.

Resting his arms on the table, in the attitude of a Murillo cherub, the host's blue eyes swept the circle of his guests. He drew a breath of deep content. "Ain't it interestin'," he said, "that all of us fr'en's is alone together in this room?"

Doctor Clark replied, digging his spoon into his Casaba melon with the zest of a hungry man. "You'd better believe it's interesting," he said, heartily. "And mighty jolly. I was horribly afraid you were going to forget me, Phil. You're so healthy that I never see you except on gala occasions. Can't we knock him out for a day or two with his birthday cake?" he asked the nurse.

But Philip was seriously explaining. "You see, I had to ask my fr'en's when I saw them," he began; "so I asked Nurse first, and the Furnace Man next, 'cause I see them every day, and 'cause the Furnace Man has so many en—engagements. But he said, soon's I asked him, he thought he could get out of some of them. An' he did."

The Furnace Man dropped a few words into Anita's ear. "The special engagement to-day," he murmured, "was Gray's lecture on pragmatism. You see he has cut it, too!"

"Then you are a university student—of course!"

Anita wondered why she had not realized this

before. She felt a quick relief, a quick disappointment, and swiftly wondered why she felt either.

He nodded. "Working my way through," he
added, cheerfully.

"Hence the furnace?"

"Yes. I've a whole string of furnaces on this
street. That's how I met Philip. He's an early
riser. So am I. I get here at six every morning,
and Philip's about the only person stirring. He
trots down into the basement and we talk things
over. We've settled most of the big problems of
life. A few we've had to leave."

"What were they?"

Anita was interested. Her picture of Philip in the
basement on the upturned box had been surprisingly
accurate, as these sudden visualizations of hers were
apt to be.

"He asked me one day if I didn't think the poor
had too many children. I said I rather inclined to
that theory—I'm one of seven myself—but that I
didn't know what could be done about it. Philip
admitted that he didn't know, either. We don't
often give up like that. But Phil added that he was
thinking about it a great deal. He's a fascinating
little beggar!"

Miss Holloway agreed, with the expression that
so warmed her features. But she had known Philip's charms through five years of close association,
following their first intimate inspection a day after
he had arrived on earth. Those of the Furnace Man

were only now dawning upon her; he suggested hinterlands of possibility. She concentrated on the Furnace Man.

"Do you live by furnaces alone?" she inquired. "Forgive me for asking," she added, hastily, "but you know I'm interested in such things."

The Furnace Man's smile faded and the light died out of his eyes. He had forgotten that she was "interested in such things," and that the name of the rich Miss Holloway usually headed the subscription-lists of big charities he read about. To parade his poverty before her that she might study at first hand the expedients to which university students were reduced when "working their way through" was not among his plans for the day. But he answered her question.

"Oh no," he said. "I get a lot of tutoring from first to last, and odd jobs of various kinds. In the summer I have some surveying."

He did not add that there were two young brothers whose expenses in a "prep" school he was paying in addition to his own, nor did he give those details of daily life for which his neighbor was waiting. Anita bit her lip. She had been stupid. She had addressed him as if he were a "case" in the institution of which she was the youngest trustee. As a result he had gone inside of himself and pulled down the blinds. She felt like one ringing the bell of a deserted house, through whose windows, only a few moments before, she had seen the reflection of the firelight.

But he should not shut her out, she determined. She would get into the house. She wanted to know all about him—this Furnace Man—not because she was especially sympathetic, but—well, for many reasons. Because he appealed to her almost pagan love of beauty. Because he was magnetic. Because—oh, because she had this strange sense of knowing him so well. But he had turned an eager ear to Jim, who, under the skilful guidance of Professor Gray, was brilliantly approaching the climax of a vital personal experience which had begun in halting words.

"So when the ice broke you saw the little girl fall into the water," prompted Professor Gray, "and you got her out, and made her run home as fast as she could to keep from catching cold."

"I run wit her. I made her run like hell," corroborated Jim, eagerly. "I wouldn't leave her speak. We hadn't no time. I dragged her arm, an' we run an' we run—fur miles, I guess. All de time she kep' tryin' to talk, jest like a goil! Den she drops down on de road, sudden, and wot you t'ink she says?" He paused to give his hearers the full effect of his climax. "Says she didn't mind runnin', but she *lived* in de op'site d'rection!" he ended in disgust.

Again Anita's eyes met the brown ones beside her, and she and the Furnace Man laughed together. He had pushed up the blinds. She glanced around with a deep sense of comfort. At the head of the table

Philip was devoting himself to Carlotta, who listened
to him with a smile on her fair, sullen face. Doctor
Clark and the nurse were deep in the animated discussion of "a case." Professor Gray was starting
Jimmy on another reminiscence. The world was
hers and the Furnace Man's. But she must not
make another false beginning. While she hesitated
he spoke.

"We aren't hitting it off as well as we should be,
are we?" he asked, sympathetically.

"No," she admitted, with regret. "Do you know
why we're not?"

"Of course. We live on different planets. We
have different viewpoints. We speak a different
language. It's impossible for you to enter my world.
You don't know the way."

"Do you know the way to mine?"

"Try me. Talk to me not as one of 'the deserving
poor,' but as a man in your own class."

Miss Holloway flushed darkly, and her lips set.
The next instant she had turned to him with a new
expression—a most unusual one for her, apologetic,
even contrite.

"I deserved that," she conceded. "I'm glad you
gave it to me. Now we'll begin all over. Tell me,"
she added, mischievously—"tell me what you think
of the Russian dancers. I know you're longing to."

He told her. He also told her what he thought
of "Treasure Island," and the skating at the Hip-
podrome, and Sister Beatrice, and the Philharmonic's

all-Richard-Strauss evenings, and the latest "auction" rule, and Wilson's Mexican policy, and the mushrooms under glass which he was eating at the moment, and Masefield's poetry, and Bakst's decorative schemes. What he thought was frequently what Miss Holloway herself thought—and she realized this with surprise. Also she experienced an impulse to change her opinions if they conflicted with his—a most unusual impulse. He really talked extremely well, but he left her restless, discontented. He was playing a part. With every word he uttered she felt herself getting farther and farther away from the real man. Again she was outside of his house—a house warmed and lighted now, but still locked. Resolutely she rang the bell.

"But how have you seen and read and heard all these things? How have you found time—"

"And money?" His eyes twinkled. As if he had kept her long enough on the threshold, the door swung open. "Oh, I have friends in your world. Dick Mason and Bert Houghton take me about a good deal—and Dick's extra evening clothes fit me to perfection. Once or twice a month I leave the furnaces and get into the clothes and gad. I feel that I can accept their hospitality because—" For the first time he hesitated, looking self-conscious. "Well, because Bert's mother is my aunt, and Dick's father is my godfather!"

Miss Holloway studied him in silence. To her seeing eyes he was as completely transformed by his last words as if a fairy wand had been waved over him. His disguise had fallen off. He stood before her an enchanted prince, glowing in the reflected glory of the Houghtons and the Masons. She knew all about him now. Harriet Mason talked by the hour of this eccentric young man who was quite willing to accept the affection of the two families, but declined the slightest help at their hands. Of course they loved to take him about and show him off! A hundred half-forgotten details jostled one another in her memory. He was captain of the football team which had defeated Princeton in November; he was the man who had saved Dick Mason's life when he was accidentally shot in the Maine woods two years ago; he was, oh, it made her blush to think of all he was and had been—this youth she had so calmly patronized. And the Masons and the Houghtons allowed him to be a furnace-man! That thought was the worst of all. It made her writhe, but she told herself she was merely resenting that waste of splendid material.

"But how *can* they let you work like this?" she exclaimed, impatiently. "Surely they could find a way to make you see how absurd it is! Grubbing over furnaces and tutoring stupid boys—you, of all men!"

His fine lips tightened. "They have nothing to do with that," he said, curtly. "That's my affair. They can take me about if they like—it's my only chance to see them, for they're never at home.

Besides, it's part of one's education. But that's all I'll let them do. However, it's almost over. I'll take my degree this June. After that they can give me a leg up in starting."

"Will you come and dine with me sometime?"

He glanced at her; then his eyes fell. "No, thank you," he said, slowly.

Miss Holloway stared at him, disbelieving her ears.

"That sounds rude," he conceded, "but of course you understand. I've made it a rule never to accept any invitations but theirs. I will not accept hospitality I cannot return."

Anita gave him her shoulder. A sudden depression settled upon her—a depression as unexpected as it was inexplicable. She felt horribly lonely. The Furnace Man, too, was staring moodily at his plate. The voice of Carlotta from Sweden broke the silence that had fallen upon them.

"I ban go home," she said; "I ban seek for home. I ban so loone-some. It is awful to be loone-some. Yes."

As if swung on a pivot, Anita turned and looked at the Furnace Man. As if impelled by a similar force, he had turned to look at her. For a long five seconds the gray eyes and the brown ones plumbed each other's depths and the abyss of each other's loneliness. Then, without a word, they glanced away.

Anita gave a flattering attention to Jim on her right, to whom, as yet, she suddenly realized, she had given almost no attention at all. Under the warmth of her smile Jim detached himself from a rich salad and devoted a margin of his mind to social intercourse. Jim, it soon appeared, knew all about Miss Holloway. He had read of her in the newspapers he sold, and her name was on the brass tablet at the entrance of the big reading-room in the newsboys' home where he lived. But he had been under the impression that she was "one of dem old dames— de kind wit white coils." It seemed a blow to him to find her less than seventy, and Miss Holloway left him to the force of a shock from which he seemed unable to rally, and glanced at the neighbor at her left. The Furnace Man had been listening and smiling to himself.

"Wouldn't flatter you, would he?" he asked, quizzically. "What a nest of barbarians you've fallen into!"

Anita raised an eyebrow. "Do you call that a barbarian?" she asked, with a glance toward Philip.

The Furnace Man's eyes followed hers, growing very soft on the journey. Philip was again talking to Carlotta, his yellow hair an aureole against the dark wood of the great carved chair in which he sat, his big eyes shining into the somber eyes of the girl, his small teeth showing in his shy, adorable smile. Through the heavy rain of the now general conversation a few of his words pattered down on them:

"An' when the flowers is all out in the gardens, and the birds come, you'll like us better. Then you will be happy."

The cloud passed from the brow of Carlotta from Sweden. "I could not like you no better as I do," she said. "I could not, efer."

Philip's response was as eager as a lover's. "Does that mean you like me *now*—really, truly?" he cried.

Carlotta from Sweden answered under her breath, but both Anita and the Furnace Man heard her. "I lofe you," she said.

"It seems almost indelicate to listen, doesn't it?" commented the Furnace Man. "But I know exactly how Carlotta feels."

"Do you?"

"I love him, too," he said, quietly. "I'm simply devoted to the little chap. Once or twice when he has been a bit under the weather and couldn't come down into the basement, I've been almost as disappointed as if the Only One had failed me."

"Is there an Only One?"

Miss Holloway asked the question without compunction. She simply could not help it. Besides, anything was permissible at this incredible luncheon.

"Of course."

"Tell me about her."

"Thank you. There's very little to tell. It's just a piece of madness on my part. She's in your world. The real reason I go there is to see her sometimes— to live for an hour or two the life she lives, to talk to the people she knows, to look at her—from a distance."

Miss Holloway's sense of loneliness deepened into

gloom. She resented the emotion. She had been so interested, so content, during that first hour of the luncheon.

"And she—" she asked, slowly. "Does she care?"

"She doesn't know. Can you imagine that I would let her suspect? We're as far apart as if she lived on Mars."

"I wonder if I know her?" Miss Holloway was running over in her mind the belles and buds in the Houghton-Mason sets, ready to hate the right one if her face appeared. It was a hopeless task. There were dozens of them.

He looked indifferent. "No doubt," he said, carelessly.

"Do you see her often?"

"No."

"Then how—"

"Love isn't dependent on meetings. Surely I don't need to tell you that. I loved her the first time I saw her, at the opera—two years ago. It was one of the things one reads about. I had smiled over them. I didn't suppose such a thing could come to me. But, Lord, how it came! I was like a palm in a tropical storm. It shook the very soul of me. It's shaking me yet."

The brown hand with which he was fingering his glass trembled, and he hurriedly withdrew it and fumbled with his napkin. Looking at him askance, Anita saw that his face had whitened. She felt an almost intolerable pang of sympathy for him, followed by a shock of anger. What right had the Furnace Man to discuss his love-affairs with her—to drag her into the quasi-intimacy such confidences implied? When she spoke her voice was curt.

"You'll get over it," she said, "especially as you don't know her well, and see her so rarely."

He seemed not to notice her change of mood, but he answered her words. "I don't see her often," he mused; "that's true enough. But, just the same, I think I know her better than most people do. You see, we have a common friend, she and I—some one who loves her, knows her intimately, and sees a side of her she doesn't show to any one else. So I, too, know that side. I've been watching it for a year. I know a thousand wonderful things she has done. I know the real girl."

He stopped with an effect of finality. The conversation, so far as he was concerned, was over. Doctor Clark addressed him, and the two chatted for a moment. Anita looked around the room, and as she looked the familiar weight of depression ominously deepened. The charm of the hour was gone. She felt as if a veil of illusion had been torn from her eyes, as if at last she saw her fellow-guests as they really were—Carlotta, a heavy-eyed, stolid servant; Jimmy, a precocious newsboy, with a face clean only in spots; Professor Gray, an academic mummy; the nurse, a worthy person of her kind, to be reckoned with only when she passed one's line of vision; the doctor, a successful physician, with a too-pervasive "bedside manner." There remained Philip, who needed no veil of illusion to heighten his exquisite personality. There remained also this stranger at her left, this stranger she seemed in that moment to have known for a thousand years. He was smiling at Philip—the boyish smile like Philip's own. Her heart contracted with an actual physical pang. Then she knew what had happened. There he was—the man she had unconsciously been seeking—and in the very hour in which she had found him she had lost him again. She had lost him, moreover, in the most maddening of all ways. Both his pride and his poverty she believed she could have conquered—but not this vision of his dream. He was mooning over an obsession, and his passion was kept alive by some sentimentalist who fed it on shadows. She could have taken him, perhaps, from a flesh-and-blood rival—certainly she might have tried; but against a thing like this she dared not pit herself.

It was Jim who escorted her back to the drawing-room, for Clark had passed a friendly arm through the Furnace Man's and was deep in a confidential chat. Then, with surprising suddenness, the party disintegrated. Professor Gray had his deferred lecture. Carlotta had promised to be home at three. The doctor had calls to make. Jim's afternoon newspapers were ready for sale. The nurse went up-stairs. Anita, Philip, and the Furnace Man were left to their harrowing farewells.

With the departure of his other guests, the slight tension on the nerves of their host relaxed; in the companionship of these two intimates he again became a little boy. Grasping a hand of each, and balancing lightly between them, he unconsciously hurled his thunderbolt.

"You like my Furnace Man, don't you, Aunt Nita?" he demanded.

"Yes, dear—of course."

Philip lifted both feet and swung upon their hands. "I'm glad," he said, " 'cause, you see, the Furnace Man and me we talk about you a lot. We talk about you the whole time we're together. And when you come here I tell the Furnace Man every single thing you do."

A groan burst from the lips of the Furnace Man. His dark, brilliant face turned first crimson, then white.

With a gasp Philip flung himself upon him. "I promised I wouldn't ever tell," he wailed, "an' I forgot! Oh, I forgot!"

From the face of Miss Holloway a sudden radiance flamed. The Furnace Man stroked Philip's buried head with a hand that shook.

"He likes you, though," said Philip, after a poignant silence. "I'm 'most sure he does. But he wouldn't ever say so, 'cause he didn't know you. Don't you think he likes you now? 'Cause I want you to be int'mit fr'en's."

"We're going to be." Miss Holloway drew on her

gloves with the little smile her friends loved but saw
so rarely.

"Are you perfeckly sure?" insisted Philip. "He
didn't say so."

"He will." Miss Holloway looked at the bent
head of the Furnace Man, and her eyes grew soft.
"He hasn't our impetuous temperament, Philip," she
added, cheerfully, "so we must give him time. But
he's going to take me home now—and say it on the
way!"

A READJUSTMENT

THE dinner had been a success; now the evening was over, and all the guests had gone but one. Upon this one Miss Janet Varick, sister of the bachelor host, and shamelessly deserted by that weary gentleman, turned a compelling eye.

"Good night, Bertie," she remarked, allowing a certain drowsiness to creep into her voice. "Don't let me keep you up."

Mr. Herbert Gildersleeve favored her with his most radiant smile—a smile which, to his secret horror, always brought into play a deep dimple in his left cheek. This dimple did not go with his athletic record, but he had been privately assured that the record, so to speak, "carried" it. At least, few mentioned it in his hearing. The unmasculine effect of the dimple was also counteracted by a strong jaw—strong for such a young person—the lines of which were especially firm at this moment, as he settled more comfortably into his chair.

"I'll go in an hour or two," he promised. "In the mean time cast your memory back over the brilliant festivity we have just adorned, and answer one question: With the exception of yourself, who was the most entertaining person at the table?"

Miss Varick's reply was prompt, for she was just. Moreover, she was sleepy.

"You were," she conceded, and turned a yearning gaze upon the clock.

Bertie nodded. "Glad you noticed it," he said. "I noticed it myself. I held them enthralled, without effort. Toward the end I realized that they'd never leave if I kept on, so I subsided, and when they saw it was for good they tore themselves away. I could have kept them," he added, proudly, "till breakfast-time, if there had been any need of it."

"I thought you were going to," corroborated his hostess. "Good night. You've been splendid, but I'm sure you need rest."

"I don't know what we'd have done without me," continued Mr. Gildersleeve, gazing dreamily at her. "The way I rescued you from Arthur Murray's analysis of the political situation was simply masterly. And few things could be neater than the tact with which I kept May Allen from telling that Gilbert story, with Gilbert's first wife at the table!"

"If you call it neat to upset a glass of claret," murmured the listener.

"Better a stain on the table-cloth than a strain on your guests," responded Bertie, oracularly. He studied his well-shaped pumps admiringly, lost in the charm of agreeable reminiscences. "I thought," he added, after waiting in vain for an echo of his tributes

from her lips, "the experience might make you realize how handy I'd be around the house all the time,
and especially at the head of a table of our own.
Did it?"

He studied her expression hopefully for an instant. Then, seeing her eyebrows pucker and her
slipper tap the floor impatiently, he relapsed into
depression.

"It didn't," he murmured. "It's plain that it
didn't."

Her lips twitched a trifle, but when she spoke
her voice held the accents of sustained but sorely
tried patience with which one addresses a refractory
child.

"Bertie," she began, "in five minutes you're going
home. But first I've got to say something. There
aren't many certain things in this world, but one of
the few is this: you must stop telling me you love
me. You must stop urging me to marry you. Because"—she was very serious now—"you don't
really love me, and I don't love you, and deep in our
hearts we both realize it perfectly. And it isn't—
well, it isn't quite nice to go on making a game of
something that is a big and vital interest to those
who take life seriously."

It was not easy to bring out the final words, for
he was staring at her like the small boy of eight he
had been when she first knew him, and his face bore
the same hurt, puzzled look it used to wear when she,
a "temperamental" infant of the same tender age,

had flown at him in one of her sudden childish tempers. It was hard to hurt Bertie, her lifelong playmate, schoolmate, chum, and friend, but Bertie was becoming impossible. She proceeded to make her meaning clear.

"Don't you see?" she continued. "We can't possibly go on like this. You make love to me at all times, at all seasons, and in all places, and you place me in the most absurd positions. I don't think I shall ever quite forget," she added, somberly, "the expression of that conductor's face when you put me on his car yesterday, paid my fare, bade me good-by, and then lingered on the platform to propose to me, while he stood waiting to give the starting signal."

Bertie grinned reminiscently. "It suddenly came over me that trolley-cars are dangerous," he defended himself, "and that something might happen to you. Besides, you had on a new hat, and you looked so sweet—"

Her face softened, but she interrupted him.

"When you proposed at the Philharmonic concert the other night, old Mrs. Hunter, who sat next to me, heard every word. She pretended to be asleep, but she wasn't. I distinctly saw her smile."

"She enjoyed it," admitted the young man. "Told me so afterward. Suggested some arguments I'd left out. She remarked," he added, thoughtfully, "that she didn't see how you could resist me."

"Moreover," continued Miss Varick, ignoring the

146

A READJUSTMENT

interruption, "your habit of sending me five or six postal cards every day, asking if I haven't changed my mind, interests the servants but maddens me."

"Does it, really?" inquired Mr. Gildersleeve, sitting up with sudden interest. "Now that's strange." He leaned toward her eagerly, emphasizing his points with an impressive forefinger. "You see, I've been reading one of those French psychological chaps on love. He says the vital thing is to keep yourself before the loved one's mind every minute, no matter how you do it, and that it helps to have those around her familiar with your hopes because they can mentally assist you. I've had some thought of speaking to Kawa and the cook," he added, musingly, "but I haven't had a really good chance. I suppose I might send each of them a postal," he reflected, aloud.

"Bertie Gildersleeve! If you dare!" Her voice had a razor-like edge to it now, her tired eyes flashed at him. "But I don't think you will, after I've finished," she added, with meaning. "It all amounts to this: I don't want to be unkind, but you're beginning to annoy me. Unless you promise never to speak of love or marriage to me again, I must ask you to—well, to try staying away for a while."

The young man sat up suddenly under the words, the pink of his handsome face deepening to an unbecoming crimson. For what seemed a long time he looked at her in silence. Then, "You mean that?" he asked, slowly.

147

She nodded. "I do," she said, "and it's final. I'm awfully sorry to hurt you, Bertie, but, to be frank, I don't think the hurt goes very deep. If the feeling itself were deep you couldn't make a joke and a game of it as you've done for the last two years, making yourself and me the laughing-stock of every one who knows us."

He rose, a sudden gravity draping him like a mantle. In it he looked strange to her and, for the moment, much older than his years, and unexpectedly impressive.

"I understand," he said. "I didn't before. Naturally, if I had, I wouldn't have kept on annoying you. A man doesn't deliberately annoy the girl he loves. As to not being in earnest, well"—he laughed a little—"you know my fool way. I put my silly nonsense into everything I do, because I can't help it. I'm built so. My love for you is there, but"—he held out his hand and smiled at her —"it sha'n't annoy you any more."

She laid her hand in his, and as he held it the memory of the little boy of long ago swept over her again with a sudden tenderness.

"And you're not cross?" she asked. "It would be horrible to think we weren't going to be friends, after all these years!"

It was the old Bertie who answered her, his new gravity dropping from him as unexpectedly as he had taken it on.

"We'll be friends all right," he said, heartily.

"We couldn't change that, if we tried. This passion of mine is going to go on growing, of course, the way it does in poems. This flame will still consume me. But I can stifle my groans so you won't hear them. Good night."

He was in the hall now, putting on his coat. "Good night" he called again. Then the street door closed after him and she heard his quick step on the sidewalk. For some reason her drowsiness had left her. She stood by the open fire for a few moments, one foot on the fender, watching the dying flames and recalling the details of the little interview. Then, with a satisfied nod, she went up-stairs. She was through with Bertie as an importunate lover, but she had kept him as a friend. That was as it should be, and she was still congratulating herself on the achievement when she fell asleep.

Young Mr. Gildersleeve had been in the habit of dropping into the Varick home three or four evenings a week. It was a hospitable house, and the brother and sister had come to accept him almost as a fixture of their domestic hearthstone. The dinner and his talk with Janet had taken place on Wednesday night. That he did not appear on Thursday did not surprise her. That he did not either call or telephone on Friday was in the nature of a surprise, to which she gave the tribute of a fleeting wonder. Saturday evening, however, he arrived at his usual hour, immaculate, radiant, as of old, and, finding other guests there, resolutely outstayed them, according to his invariable custom. As a small boy, Bertie had never gone home until he had been sent by Janet or her mother. As a young man, he had kept this engaging peculiarity.

"You can't stay any longer, Bertie," she declared now, when they found themselves alone. "I'm going to have a headache if I don't ward it off by a long sleep."

The confession filled Mr. Gildersleeve with interest and sympathy, and stimulated him into the most helpful activity. He advised remedies for the incipient headache. He offered a tablet from a box he carried in his pocket as a souvenir of a headache he had once had last winter. He settled her in the most comfortable easy-chair in the room, and adjusted a pillow at her back—an art in which he had no peer. But all the time it was clear that he had something to say, and that he meant to stay until he had said it. At first she did not notice anything unusual in his manner, but finally she observed on his young face the brooding purpose of a "long talk," shot through with a radiant happiness and a sudden boyish shyness. Anything in the nature of shyness resting on Bertie's features was a strange guest there. Seeing it, she marveled.

"I waited," he said when she was comfortable, "because I have something very important to say."

A sudden rush of anger swept through her. So this was it: he had come with the deliberate purpose of disobeying her—of reopening the subject she had distinctly forbidden him to mention. It was not like him. She was at once disappointed, hurt, and annoyed, and she looked at him with mingled incredulity and reproach. That he would disregard her wishes sooner or later she had felt sure; that he would obey them for at least a week or two had seemed equally certain—especially after his unexpectedly manly acceptance of her words on Wednesday night.

"Oh, how can you?" she exclaimed. "You know what I told you—"

He interrupted her, his eyes shining. "I know I'm a selfish beast," he said. "But I can't help it. I've got to talk to you. It's such a big thing."

She leaned back wearily in the big chair. "I can't believe you're doing this," she murmured. "You seem so different from—"

Again he interrupted. "Am I changed?" he asked, radiantly. "Of course I feel that I've lived a thousand years in the last two days, but"—he laughed buoyantly—"I didn't know I showed it so plainly."

She stared at him. His words were easy to understand, but his tone, his manner—she was so puzzled by these that she missed his next sentence, but the following one reached her ears with great distinctness.

"I want you to be the first to know," he was saying, "that I'm going to be married!"

He had said those words. There was no doubt of it, though at first it had seemed impossible, incredible, that he had. And now, sitting facing her, with ecstatic eyes on hers, he waited for her response. It seemed to her a long time before she could speak, but it was only a second or two that she stared at him, her eyes incredulous, questioning, her eyebrows drawn together in the characteristic pucker he knew so well.

"But I don't understand," she stammered. And then, her mind leaping to the inevitable conclusion, her eyes plumbed his with a flash in their depths that reminded him of the tempestuous little girl she had been at eight. "Unless you mean," she demanded, "that you have been engaged all along and haven't told us?"

He repudiated this charge with vigor. "Of course not!" He waved the thought away. "I've only been engaged since last night."

His voice took on a mellow unction as he spoke. A fatuous smile rested on his lips. "Since last night," he repeated, dreamily, and gazed out of the window at something far removed from the view it afforded. Janet felt the strained muscles of her face relax. For a difficult instant she was not sure whether she meant to laugh or cry. Then both her hands went out to him, while she resolutely assumed the sisterly attitude she knew the situation demanded from her.

"But before I really congratulate you," she smiled, after he had released them, "tell me who it is. Some one I know, of course."

A READJUSTMENT

Her mind was already calling the roll of the girls in their set, examining each, dismissing some summarily, pausing over others, but never pausing long. There was not one girl among them all in whom Bertie had seemed in the least degree interested, and now he was shaking his blond head.

"No one you know," he laughed. "Never met her myself till the night before last. But—well, you'll like her!"

"Bertie Gildersleeve!" Miss Varick might have been her own maiden aunt, so austere was her manner, so suddenly worldly and disapproving her tone. "Do you mean to say you've taken up with some girl we've never heard of—some girl without family or position?"

"She's got family and position, all right," he reassured her. "She's Mrs. Van Brunt's niece, from Virginia, and she's just come here on a visit. Never saw her in my life till Thursday," he proceeded, "but the minute I looked into her eyes I knew it was all over with me."

He was moving around the room now like an exultant boy, his hands in his pockets, his head up, happiness and self-confidence radiating from him.

Janet followed his movements with unseeing eyes, her thoughts busy with the problem he suggested. That he was in earnest seemed impossible. That he could change so suddenly was inexplicable. And that he could come and tell her of the change without a trace of embarrassment or self-consciousness simply could not be happening. Even her unfortunate verbal leap at the beginning of the conversation had not pulled him up; it had, in fact, meant nothing to him. She no longer moved him. He was utterly oblivious to the fact that she had ever moved him. But had she? That seemed now the only question—no, that and one other.

"And you met her Thursday night and proposed to her Friday night?" she asked, suddenly.

"Exactly; and came to tell you about it Saturday night."

He was obviously proud of the expedition witn which the little matter had been concluded.

"And to-morrow," he went on, blithely, "I'm going to bring her here to meet you. May we come to tea? She wants to. I've told her all about you," he added, ingenuously.

"What did you tell her?" she asked.

"Said I'd known you all my life, and that you were the best pal I had," announced the young man, happily.

She dropped her eyes and studied the pattern of a prayer-rug at her feet. For a moment the hope came to her that the episode was a dream—a rather unpleasant dream, she admitted, mentally. To dream of Bertie as the property of another girl was strangely unexhilarating. But the six feet of triumphant manhood before her was not the stuff of which dreams were made. No; this incredible thing was really occurring. Bertie was in love with some

A READJUSTMENT

one else! Had he ever been in love with her?
She didn't know. Had she—and this was the vital
question—had she, despite her coy misgivings, ever
been in love with him? She did not know that,
either—and now it didn't matter, to Bertie, at least.
Under an abrupt jar of the glass in Time's relentless
hand, Bertie had suddenly become an affectionate
brother with a confidence to make, and she, in the
same disturbance, had been transformed into that
greatest need in his universe—a Sympathetic Ear.

"You're not half as enthusiastic about it as I
expected," he told her, ruefully. "Aren't you
glad?"

She accepted her rôle and produced a creditable
smile. "I'm delighted," she said. "But it's so—
so abrupt. Bring her to-morrow," she added,
warmly. "Of course I want to meet her." Then
she rose and gave him her hand. "And now good
night," she said again. "I needn't tell you how
happy I want you to be. Till to-morrow, at five."

"You'll like her," he prophesied, joyfully, lingering at the door. "All I've got to say is, wait till
you see her. She bowls folks over. The other fellows are mad about her. Why, Janet, she's the
most exquisite thing that ever lived—utterly different from our Northern girls. I didn't know girls
came that way. She has bronzy hair with gold
lights in it, and great big brown eyes—"

"Bertie, for heaven's sake go home!" begged
Janet Varick, wearily. "This headache of mine—"

He was all contrition. "I'm a beast," he admitted, abjectly; "forgot all about your headache. I'm an awful muff to bore you about our affair like this. But—well, you know, some way," he finished, with a rush, "when a fellow feels like this he's simply got to talk about it to any one that will listen."

He left her to digest that, and Janet took her headache to bed. It was not easy to dismiss Bertie and his fiancée from her mind, but she did it. The silent watches of the night, she decided, were not the time for mental work over the problem they presented. Nor was it easier to solve when the lovers arrived the next afternoon, on the stroke of five. Until she saw them together she had dared to hope, subconsciously, that there had been a mistake. Was it a joke?—in extremely bad taste, of course, and not at all like Bertie. Still she rather hoped it might be even that. Acting on the maxim that "All's fair in love and war," possibly Bertie had arranged an object-lesson for her that would galvanize her into the knowledge of what she was losing. If he had conceived such a plan it would be quite like him to persuade some girl cousin or friend to join in the game. But one look at the faces of the couple dispelled that illusion. Here was young love, indeed— the real thing, full-born, blissful, exultant. There was no self-consciousness in the manner of the bride-elect, nor any flutter in the presence of this other girl who had known Bertie so long, and who might be expected to be critical. She was sure, quite sure, of herself and of him. To all appearances, the lovers might have known each other since the beginning of time.

Bertie, who had written and produced two plays at college, intended, of course, to devote his life to the inspiring but uncertain field of play-writing. Fortunately, he had an independent income, so the result of his dramatic experiments would not affect the domestic supply of bread and butter. They could be married at once, and Ethel—that was Her name—who was an excellent musician, would write the incidental music for Bertie's plays. It was all planned. They told Janet about it, both talking at once, interrupting each other, apologizing, and doing it again. Neither listened to Janet, who devoted herself to refilling their teacups.

Ethel, it seemed, had already written one bit of music on the evening of their engagement when, for some strange reason, she was unable to sleep. At his urging, she rose and played it—a charming little thing, haunting, melodious, with an originality which Miss Varick at least had not expected to find there. Bertie had seized Ethel's tea-cake while she was away from the table, and she scrambled good-naturedly with him for its possession when she returned. They compromised, at last, by eating it together, in alternate bites, and with much laughter. Watching them, Janet felt a thousand years old.

Bertie left with his beloved, and tenderly escorted her home. It was quite understood, in the final moments, that Janet was always to be their dearest friend and was to come to them when she felt tired, and occupy the room which would be ready for her in their home. Later in the evening Bertie reappeared, the sun of his content temporarily obscured by a cloud of enforced separation. Ethel had a dinner engagement for that night—made before she had met him—and as they had been together all day, her aunt had sternly ruled that she must keep it. Miss Varick, it appeared, was happily disengaged, and Bertie, lounging before her open fire, his hands behind his head in excess of comfort, monologued of the Only One.

"You're quite *sure*, Bertie," Janet ventured to ask, "that this is the real thing—that it will stand the wear and tear of life? You know marriage is important. You've got to spend your lives together. Are you really congenial? Will you make each other happy? You've known each other so short a time, and you're both so young—"

Bertie nodded, his face very grave. *"Don't* I know?" he said. "I'm as old as you are! Since I've met her I've broken into a cold perspiration sometimes over the thought that some other girl might have got me before she came. It often happens, you know," he added, soberly.

Miss Varick favored him with a piercing glance, but it was clear that he was speaking with entire sincerity and with an utter absence of memories which might have checked his artless prattle.

A READJUSTMENT

"A man," he continued, oracularly, "flirts and flutters about a bit, and loses his head a few times, perhaps. But all the while he knows in his heart it isn't the real thing, and if any girl he's flirting with takes him when he's off his guard, you know, why it makes him sick!"

"Really?"

He could see that she was interested.

"Ye-s," said Bertie, impressively. "I know one chap that got caught because he was out walking with a girl and saw a sign advertising a flat for seventy-five dollars a month. They had nothing to do, so for a joke they went in and looked at it. It was a dandy flat—beamed ceiling in the living-room, tiled bathroom, view up the river from the dining-room. Jim was so fascinated by it that he asked the girl to marry him. She took him like a shot, and the first thing he knew he was engaged and had the lease of the flat in his pocket. It scared him frightfully at first, for he didn't really care for her and had never dreamed of marrying her. But he got used to her after a while, and they hit it off very well. He told me the last time I met him, though, that the apartment was a fraud," added Bertie, reflectively. "All the nickel came off the plumbing the very first year."

Janet listened in silence to these revelations. She found nothing to say, but that was unimportant, for it was obvious that nothing was expected. This, she reflected, gloomily, was Man's Love!

"Several fellows I know," continued Bertie, dreamily," are married to girls they proposed to by accident. One of them was a classmate of mine at New Haven. We called him 'Hunks,' because it wasn't anything like his name. Hunks was walking in the country with a girl and she sprained her ankle. She couldn't walk, so he telephoned from a farm-house for an automobile, and then sat down beside her to wait till it came. She was in a good deal of pain, and he was so sorry for her that he asked her to marry him. She accepted him, too," concluded Bertie. "Forgot the ankle, and took him then and there. She had presence of mind."

Still Janet did not speak, and, still unconscious of her lack of response, Bertie continued his recitation.

"Sometimes you propose because you can't think of anything else to say," he pursued, reflectively, "and sometimes because it would hurt a girl's feelings if you didn't. She thinks she likes you, and she thinks you like her. Or a man's lonesome, and hates hotels and clubs and boarding-houses, so he 'marries for a home,' exactly as much as any woman ever does." He shook his head mournfully. "It's an awful thing," he summed up, "for every last one of them, when they do that, miss the biggest thing in life—meeting the Right Girl and getting her."

Janet moved restlessly in her chair. There were several things she could have said, several questions she wished to ask, but any one of them would have broken the spell of the moment and might have hurled into abject embarrassment the young man who now sat beside her, deep in his pet arm-chair, thinking aloud, submerged in the interest of the great question he was discussing. She ventured what she believed would be a fairly safe inquiry.

"When the real girl arrives," she asked, "how does a man know it?"

Bertie regarded her pityingly, as one outside the garden of life. "There's no mistaking it," he declared, positively. "Every nerve, every drop of blood in one's body, testifies to it. Every instinct of one's heart and soul cries, '*She's here at last!*' Jove! but it's great when that happens—simply great! It makes the other little affairs seem like the tuning up of the violins before the orchestra begins."

For a long minute he gazed into the fire, seeing there, no doubt, some dream-picture of his future home. Then he drew a deep breath.

"Think of the chaps it comes to too late," he exclaimed, almost under his breath. "But one mustn't think of that. It's too awful."

She did not speak, for his words had sent her thoughts on a little journey in which he had no part. She hardly heard him, yet, subconsciously, she knew that he was helping her to find an answer to the question in the background of her mind. Her nerves relaxed and she smiled to herself in restored content. Suddenly Bertie roused himself from his brown study, almost with a start, then turned to her with the irresistible boyish smile that revealed the despised dimple in his cheek.

"I'm a chump to sit here, boring you with all this," he apologized. "But, you know, I can say things to you I can't say to any one else."

This was like the old days—the old days of last week. She smiled at him quizzically.

"Why, I can talk to you as if"—Bertie paused for a fitting comparison and found it—"as if you were my sister!" he finished, triumphantly.

She laughed, with genuine amusement, and they sat silent for a moment in the old-time common content in each other's companionship. Yet even as he basked in this, a certain change in the atmosphere attracted Bertie's attention. It was not sudden; indeed, he had been vaguely conscious of it ever since Janet had settled back in her chair and laughed that little laugh that almost held a note of relief. He wondered vaguely why she had laughed that way. Then his eyes, traveling from the driftwood fire to his hostess, rested lightly on her face and clung there, fixed. Was she—no; it couldn't be possible—yet it *was*. She was *almost* yawning! Not openly, of course; but unostentatiously, unmistakably, she was struggling with a yawn. He could even see the muscles of her jaw stiffen as she conquered the dreadful thing. Worst of all, her effort was merely instinctive, for her eyes were on the fire and her air was preoccupied, absent. Had she, he wondered, *forgotten* that he was there? That would be bad enough; but another suspicion, infinitely more harassing, stirred in his mind. He hardly dared put it to himself, but it was there and would not be downed. Was he boring her? He had frequently disappointed her; he had often annoyed her; he had sometimes infuriated her. But never, never, until to-night, had he bored her, and she had often told him that she was sure he never could. Yet now—had he begun to, and why? What had he done? And suddenly he remembered. He had talked to her about another girl!

For a moment he was horror-struck; then he became justly indignant. So this, he reflected bitterly, was Friendship! You come to your best friend; you open your innermost heart to her, in the natural expectation of receiving her understanding sympathy in your happiness, and what happens? Dull-eyed, her thoughts a thousand miles away, she yawns before the fire! His chagrin and disappointment almost found vent in an audible reproach, but before he could utter it the scene changed.

The door of the drawing-room opened, and Kawa, the Varicks' Japanese butler, appeared on the threshold, breathed a name into space, and vanished. But striding across the floor with buoyant countenance came Mr. Arthur Murray, and already Miss Varick was greeting this gentleman with a countenance as radiant as his own. Gone was her drowsiness, gone her absent-mindedness, her listlessness. There was unabashed, open delight in her greeting. She

had always liked Murray, and Bertie had always
wondered why. There was no one on earth whom he
himself disliked so much, and heretofore Mr. Murray
had reciprocated the emotion with almost passionate
intensity. But on this strange night, when so many
singular things were happening, Murray, having
greeted his hostess, came toward Bertie with eyes
alight and friendly hand outstretched.

"I congratulate you, old man," he cried, heartily.
"I've just heard the news at the club. It's simply
great. I can't tell you how delighted I am over your
good luck."

He *was* delighted. There was no possible doubt
about that. He wrung Bertie's hand, and that
young man, thus reminded of his felicity, wrung his
hand cordially in return.

"Thanks," he said, gaily, the warm tide of his
happiness again overwhelming him. "Awfully good
of you—"

He wanted to go on talking, telling Murray about
Ethel, but Murray didn't hear him. He had pushed
a chair between Bertie and Miss Varick, had slipped
into it, and now, very much at his ease, was giving
all his attention to his hostess, who, in her turn, was
obviously and wholly absorbed in him. Bertie,
neglected, alone, studied them in silence, caught at
last a look that flashed between them, felt a moment's pang, and then unselfishly rejoiced.

"By Jove! they've got it too!" he told himself,
and he reflected that he had seen it coming—had

seen it and had refused to admit it. But now everything was different. "Good for Janet!" his thoughts
went on. "But I wish," he couldn't help adding,
"it *hadn't* been Murray!"

"You and Horace are going to the Browns' to-mor-
night night, aren't you?" he heard Murray ask.

Horace's sister admitted that they were.

"May I drop in and go with you?" Murray continued. "At eleven? Thanks. And may I have
all the dances?"

Words of protest suddenly burst from Bertie
Gildersleeve. "Well, I like *that!*" he began. "Why,
Janet, you promised—"

Under the look of mild, almost shocked surprise
in the two pairs of eyes turned upon him, the rest of
his sentence froze upon his lips.

"Oh!" he said, and grinned self-consciously.
"That's so. I must—that is, I—"

But he need not have felt embarrassed. No one
else did. Mr. Murray was explaining to Miss Varick
the happy inspiration which only now had come to
him at the club, to drop in and see if she and Horace
didn't want to run over to Westchester the next
morning in his (Murray's) new car, and see the
prettiest game of motor-polo any one could ask for.
Haskell and Jim Reid were to play. Then followed a
technical description of their game, and of Haskell's
exhibition of nerve, which made Miss Varick gasp in
anticipatory delight.

"I wouldn't miss it for the world," she declared.

"If you will excuse me, I'll ask Horace if he's free to-morrow. He's up in his study."

But Bertie had no yearning for a tête-à-tête with Mr. Murray. "I'm off," he said, easily. "Promised I'd call for Ethel and take her home. See you in a few days, Janey."

Miss Varick looked at him as one looks at a pressed rose in a book and wonders when one put it there. Her expression was reminiscent, affectionate, but vague.

"Yes," she said; "and I'll call on Ethel to-morrow. I want to give a dinner for her, you know, on her first free evening. She and I must arrange that."

Her voice was warm and friendly. Bertie had always loved it. He had told her he would rather hear her speak than listen to great singers. Now he had an odd feeling that her voice was coming to him from a distance. She was here, and so was Murray, and he was outside of their circle—far, far outside it. For a moment he experienced the same pang she had felt as she watched him at the tea-table with Ethel—the pang that comes with the passing of something dear, intimate, and familiar that seemed exclusively one's own.

At the door he turned for the farewell nod she had always tossed him. At first he feared he was not to have it to-night, for Murray, as usual, was talking, and she was deeply interested. But as he crossed the threshold and cast a last glance at her he remembered him. It was a dear little nod she threw him—careless, affectionate; such a nod as a mother might give to a small boy who was going out to play.

Well, he *was* going out to play. He was going back to Ethel, and his heart sang at the thought. Nevertheless, in the outer hall he wondered if she would nod at Arthur Murray that way; and he knew she wouldn't. She would go with Murray to the door. Then, as he went slowly down the steps, he pondered the situation and solved its problem in a flash of insight. He understood, at last, both her feelings and his own.

"It came so suddenly," he told himself, sedately, "that I guess we didn't know just how to take it. We didn't know where we were at."

He looked up at the stars, and their beauty filled him with the triumphant joy of a discoverer. Surely they had never looked like that before!

"Love makes the whole world seem different," he mused. "Of course Ethel and Janey and Murray and I couldn't wake up in a moment to the Big Thing in life without a sort of readjustment of all the little things."

THE GIRL WHO LOVED HERBERT

THE excursion yacht laid its cheek restfully against the unresponsive dock of Monniken- dam, and a lonely sailorman of that dead city of the Zuider Zee made the boat fast with a dreamy de- liberation that would have been trying to tourists more eager to land. These, however, were enjoy- ing a purely kaleidoscopic view of Holland to-day, under the personal leadership of a brisk and blond young man who, having no illusions as to life and little interest in places, made up for these lacks by an exaggerated sense of the value of time. Having torn out the heart of the island of Marken for their inspection in one hour, and that of Volendam in an even shorter period, he was now prepared to flourish the delights of Monnikendam before their greedy eyes in something less than thirty minutes. Their return journey, he explained, must be made on a canal-boat leaving its dock in half an hour. By way of emphasizing the need of haste and of keeping his party together, he delivered a curt but depressing aside on the lack of hotel accommodations in Monni- kendam and the fate of those forced to spend a night there, his remarks being so full of prejudice that the lonely sailorman, who understood a little English, paused in his work to regard him with dark suspicion.

The passengers scrambled ashore good-naturedly, but without enthusiasm. They had not found the vaunted loveliness of Marken women up to the high ideal they had formed, and many of them, the men especially, were turning on the remainder of the day's attractions a bored and suspicious eye. Something of this common feeling was expressed by Mr. Henry Johnson, of Chicago, who coldly withdrew his arm from his wife's affectionate grasp when they started up Monnikendam's one street, and remarked bitterly that he was tired "walkin' on ledges and smellin' fish," and that if the contemplation of beauty was what they were after, he, for his part, would rather "stay on the boat and look at Ruthie." Mrs. Johnson beamed at him, unoffended.

"You come right along, Henry," she commanded, placidly. "Ruth's coming, too. I left her hunting in her hand-bag for another roll of films. She wants to take some more pictures. She'll be here in a minute."

Thus reassured, Mr. Johnson suffered himself to be propelled along the way that stretched before them, but he maintained a disapproving silence as he went. At intervals he turned his head for a long backward look, and one of these was finally rewarded by a glimpse of the object of his search. Calmed at last, Mr. Johnson turned a less prejudiced gaze upon the attractions of Monnikendam and puffingly followed his wife along the narrow old road lined with infants who promptly burst into song at their approach.

"I've got to take care of Ruthie," he volunteered, unnecessarily, sternly disregarding this diversion and the outstretched hands of the children. "I promised her pa I would, and I'm goin' to."

His wife smiled. "I wonder how many times a day you say that, Henry," she said, musingly. "George Stewart's been dead nine years now, and I rather think you've convinced folks by this time that you'll look after his daughter. I suppose," she added, reflectively, "you're so fond of her that you've got to have some excuse for talking about her. But one thing is certain: her own father and mother couldn't do more for Ruth Stewart than we've done, and you know it."

Mr. Johnson paused in his onward way to regard her. "Well, ain't she worth it?" he asked, calmly. "Ain't she the best girl, and the prettiest girl, and the nicest girl you know? Ain't you as fond of her as I am? Ain't every one else as fond of her as we are, or wouldn't they be if they had the chance?"

Mrs. Johnson pressed his arm, as she urged him onward. "Ruthie's our child," she said, with deep sincerity in her voice. "If we had one of our own I couldn't love it more. Only"—she hesitated— "I'm afraid you're going to miss her dreadfully, Henry, and I wish you'd try to get a little used to the idea. You can't bear her out of your sight. What will you do this fall, when we go home and she gets married?"

Mr. Johnson pursed his lips. "I won't be worryin' about her, anyhow," he said at last. "She'll have a fine fellow to look after her. I like Graham first rate. And we can go and see her whenever we want to. 'Tain't as if she was goin' to live away from Chicago. But in these furrin' places"—he turned a prejudiced gaze upon Monnikendam's sweep of sea and sky—"I'm so afraid something queer will happen to her that I have to keep my eye on her. At home," he added, arrogantly, "nothing can happen to her; or if it does, I can handle it."

Ruth Stewart, who appeared behind him at this point, looked surprisingly well able to take care of herself. She was a small and slender and radiant young person, with a fresh, exquisite beauty, and a manner of indescribable charm and camaraderie. As if drawn to a magnet, all the child inhabitants of the dead city swarmed around her with much vitality, ready to pose for photographs, to pipe their little songs, or show any other polite attention to a young lady who looked as prosperous as she was beautiful, and as remunerative. Miss Stewart's apparel was all that her loveliness could demand, and the perfection of her Paris hat was vaguely apprehended even by these innocent eyes which gazed upon it with a content blended with awe. It was not Hollandesque.

LOVERS' KNOTS

Ruth looked the infants over in turn with a practical and critical glance. Then she systematically divided them into units, pairs, and groups, posing and photographing these in turn with a genial interest which overlooked the fact that the procedure interfered with the forward progress of her friends in the rear. She paid the children sinfully well, and then employed her small hand in generously allotting their future activities to the whole wide world, by a sprightly valedictory wave.

"Go away," she said, serenely. "Every single one of you go away, except this little girl. She is going to stay and take care of me."

The words were unintelligible, but the expressive pantomime with which the speaker accompanied them was eloquent. For she clasped the willing survivor to her side with one arm, while the gesture of the other fluttered the rejected away, like apple blossoms in a May breeze. Laughing, they drifted on, eager to compare their fees, and Miss Stewart was left with the escort she had selected—a little girl of ten, whose brown eyes were looking up at her with a dawning admiration in their depths. Like her companions, the child was miserably clothed. Her ragged gown was fastened with one button, and great holes gaped in the sides of old shoes, which were so much too large for her that they had evidently been handed down, holes and all. But her face, which had caught and held Ruth's æsthetic eye, was a singularly lovely one, in which

already the innocence of childhood was struggling
with the force of hunger and unchildlike knowledge
and want. Smiling, she slipped her hand softly
into that of this new comrade. She had been well
grounded in the methods which appeal to visitors.
Proudly, she drew on her English vocabulary at once.

"You 'Merican lady?" she asked, insinuatingly.
"I love 'Merican ladies."

Miss Stewart acknowledged the tribute in fitting
terms.

"You got nice hat," was the next contribution to
the conversation. "That you father? You love
him?" She indicated as she spoke a slender youth
of nineteen in front of them, and Miss Stewart, fear-
ing embarrassing results from this combination of
lingual fluency and ignorance of the elementary
conditions of life, hurriedly entered the conversa-
tional arena herself.

"How nicely you speak English," she exclaimed,
with much animation. "Who taught you?"

The digression was successful. The small Dutch
face lighted with gratified pride.

"'Merican ladies teach me," she explained,
blithely. "Nice 'Merican ladies from boats. You
teach me something. You love him?" Her attention returned to the luckless youth in front, whose
ears were now of a fine purple hue as he listened to
the audible chuckles of his friends. Miss Stewart
mercifully fell behind with her small charge, and
lingered at the rear until the others had passed her,

giving a smiling shake of the head in answer to invitations to join them.

"You love him?" the Dutch maiden persisted, craning her neck far forward to follow her victim with interested eyes. Miss Stewart regarded her thoughtfully.

"No, I don't," she confessed, "if you really must know. Now I will teach you some more English. You must learn very quickly."

. "Yes, teach me," echoed the child, dutifully. "All nice 'Merican ladies from boats teach me. You love him?"

Miss Stewart turned and surveyed her with a growing interest. "What is your name?" she asked.

"Katrina. Who you love?"

Miss Stewart laughed and threw her arm over the ragged little shoulder as the two walked on together. "Really, Katrina," she observed, affably, "your interest in love is almost uncanny, considering your tender years. Still, there is something rather nice and human about it. And, since you insist on my revealing the deepest secrets of my soul, I will admit that I think I am beginning to love *you*."

Katrina caught and understood the last words. Her little mouth curved in an adorable smile. But in the brown eyes above it seemed to lie the knowledge of centuries. She cocked her head on one side.

"You love me?" she repeated. "Yes. Tha's nice. You love him?" Again she indicated the

174

youth, now almost lost in the distance. "Who you love b'sides? Hei?"

Ruth Stewart stood still in the middle of the road and looked down at her.

"Katrina, do I *really* show it as much as that?" she demanded, with sudden apprehension. "Is it oozing out of me at every pore? I knew that every one on the boat suspected it, from the loving sympathy of the women and the knowing air of the men. But is it obvious to the simplest child of nature? Do babes in their mothers' laps read it as I pass them? Tell me, Katrina, how did you find it out in this brief but intimate encounter?"

The child passed lightly over this flood of 'Merican words which meant nothing to her. With fine Dutch determination she stuck to her point.

"You love me?" she murmured, comfortably. "Who you love b'sides?"

Miss Stewart sat down on the upturned bottom of an old boat by the roadside and drew the child closer to her. Her friends had passed on. They were alone, she and the little Dutchwoman, on this enchanted land, where the sky touched the sea like a lover's kiss and the sea murmured the everlasting response.

"You are quite too psychic, Katrina, or I am too open and ingenuous—I don't know which," she said, lightly, looking down into the child's brown eyes with a very soft light in her blue ones. "Perhaps both. In any event, if you will stop asking that parrot-like question long enough I will tell you without further delay the short and simple story of my life. I will open my heart to you the way they do in books. But first, let us look at this."

She raised her hand as she spoke, to close Katrina's parting lips, and that infant, used to the vagaries of 'Merican ladies who liked to sit and look out at water and boats, remained silent. It was growing late, and the sky was taking on the rich, opalescent tones of the late afternoon on the Zuider Zee. Before them the painted sails of a few idle fishing-boats swayed in a soft breeze. The only sound that came to their ears was the lap of the waves against the dykes and the voice of a fisherman calling to his comrade. It seemed to come from a great distance. The other " 'Mericans" had reached the end of Monnikendam's one, long street and vanished in the old church. To all appearances Miss Stewart and her little friend were alone with the water and the sky and the toilers of the sea. The peace and beauty of it swept over Ruth, without that sense of desolation it might have borne with it. Her heart swelled almost painfully. Such a beautiful world, such a wonderful world, such an unparalleled world this was—for it was the world that held Herbert.

"Who you love b'sides?" persisted the small voice near her, when Katrina had remained quiet as long as she could. Ruth recalled herself to the present with a start and a laugh.

"Very well, Katrina," she said, softly. "You shall know, for I see it is hopeless to try to keep it from you. And indeed I couldn't here, if I would. I must tell some one, and it shall be you, Katrina— you and no other. You shall have the deepest pearl in that sea which is my soul. Certainly you have dived for it often enough. Because it is the most wonderful and the most beautiful thing in the universe, I will tell you about it and you shall tell it again. You shall tell it to the sea, and to the sky, and to the fisherwomen, and to their babies. You shall tell it to the old men and tired old women who have forgotten, and to the young men who are lovers, and to the young women who are loved, and to the children who will yet live and love. Yes, and you shall tell the 'Mericans, too. You shall tell it to all your little world, Katrina, for I am proud of it. *I love Bertie.* Say it, Katrina. Sing it, shout it, make a song of it. Teach it to the waves and the wind, that they may say it too, and carry it to the uttermost ends of the earth. *I love Bertie.* Say it, Katrina! Oh, Katrina, *ay it!*"

Katrina said it—softly and tentatively at first, as if trying the flavor of the words; then more boldly, as if liking and accepting them. Ruth Stewart listened, sudden tears in her eyes.

"If Bert could hear it," she murmured. "Perhaps he does, away off in Chicago, high above the roar of the dirty streets. Perhaps we two have a private wireless system which is carrying the words to him now. But whether he hears them from me to-day or not, he has heard them from me before, and he shall hear them from me again—the darling. And, Katrina, dear little parrot that you are, you shall add them to your limited vocabulary, and you shall keep on saying them to the end of time, as I shall be doing on the other side of the world. You shall tell all tourists, and they will wonder who 'Bertie' is, but they will not know. You shall tell the sea, and it will repeat the message. You shall send out countless ether waves from this dead city, and every one of them will widen into circles of love and happiness, till they put a girdle of joy around this sad old earth. *I love Bertie.* Even Bertie himself does not yet realize how much, but he will some day, Katrina—he will."

For a long time she sat silent, alone with the great joy in her soul. Beside her, little Katrina, satisfied now, murmured at intervals her new refrain, "*I love Bertie.*" Oddly enough, she no longer asked "Who you love b'sides," as Ruth had half feared she might do. Her question had been answered, and with the uncanny wisdom of the woman-child she was, Katrina seemed to know it.

Suddenly Miss Stewart sprang to her feet. "Come, Katrina, friend of my soul," she said, lightly. "I'm going to take your photograph. Drape yourself artistically over the side of the boat. I want the 'liniments' of the sweet repository of my heart's secrets. Then, when Bertie and I together look at you in the years to come, we'll know you are still doing your little best to tell the story of our love to the universe. That's right, smile. Now say it! Oh, you darling! Say it again. There, I've got you, smile and all! Now we'll go to your mother and make her a present that will be a fitting souvenir of this new friendship and will leave you unlimited leisure for the glorious career I have marked out for you."

The canal-boat waited half an hour for Miss Stewart, and the attractions of Monnikendam, far from inexhaustible, had palled on her friends long before she rejoined them. Mr. Henry Johnson was loud in his reproaches. "I told your pa—" he began. His wife checked him, and, putting her motherly arm over the girl's shoulder, led her off to a secluded corner of the boat.

"You certainly are dreadfully absent-minded, Ruthie, since you became engaged," she chided, gently, "and I'm sure I don't know what we're taking you all over Europe for when you don't really see anything, anyhow. But there—" she stopped, looked at the girl's radiant face, and drew a long breath. "You're doing a lot for us, dear, just by letting us look at you. There aren't many such glorified faces for tired eyes to rest on."

It was the following October, and Mrs. Henry Johnson, in her Chicago home, turned from an unseeing contemplation of the rain-swept streets before her windows, and restlessly walked the floor. Her face bore the marks of recent tears, and her forehead showed new lines, deeply etched into its smooth surface. She turned with a sigh of relief at the opening of the door. Mr. Johnson appeared, stealing in with the elaborate precaution of a man entering a sick-room, though the patient for whom he came to inquire was far away on another floor. His wife's worn face lit up at sight of him. She slipped her hand through his arm with a gesture that told a beautiful story of wifely love and dependence. Together they walked up and down the long room.

"Just the same," she said, in answer to his unspoken question. "No change."

"What do the doctors say now?"

"Well, they're discouraged, I think. They talk about rousing her—giving her some kind of a mental shock. The new one says if she hadn't gone to the funeral it wouldn't have been so bad. He thinks we could have pulled her up."

Mr. Johnson gazed gloomily at the floor. "You shouldn't have let her go," he muttered. "I promised her pa—"

His wife sighed. "We tried to keep her," she said, quietly, "but you know how strong-willed Ruth always was. She said that going to Bert's funeral was the last time she could be with him. She said she'd have all the rest of her life to take care of herself. She said she'd live a hundred years —that all the Stewarts had except her father.

She said—oh, Henry, I can't tell you half the things she said. I think her mind was beginning to go a little, even then."

Mr. Johnson looked out at the driving rain, listened to the wolfish howl of the wind, and shivered.

"And this was to be her wedding-day," he murmured. Then, with the idle speculation of a wholly absorbed mind, he added, "It wouldn't have been a very cheerful one, would it?"

Mrs. Johnson's voice sank. "She thinks the sun is shining," she whispered, "and that she smells the orange blossoms and hears the wedding-march. And every minute she's expecting Bert to come. She's lying with her eyes fixed on the door."

Mr. Johnson shivered again and sank heavily into a chair. With a sudden gesture of despair he drove the back of one closed hand into the palm of the other.

"Good Lord!" he broke out, "and all those specialists here doin' nothing. 'Ain't they learned, with all their studyin', how to save a girl's mind when her poor heart is broken?"

His wife checked him. "They haven't quite given up hope," she reminded him, quietly. "It isn't gone yet, you know. It's only—going. Every now and then she comes to herself and remembers the funeral and the music and the firing of the salutes at the grave and the sound of the 'taps'; and then she lies perfectly still, with the most awful look on her face. A military funeral is such an agonizingly dramatic and heartbreaking thing, even if one isn't a mourner. And when one is"—she stopped. "If she could *cry*," she began, and stopped again.

Henry Johnson resumed his restless pacing back and forth. In him was the savage revolt of the strong man, accustomed to meet and conquer obstacles, but now confronted for the first time by one he could not overcome. His dead partner's face rose before him, accusingly, almost menacingly. Was he doing everything possible for that dead partner's child, in this supreme crisis of her life?

"I promised her pa—" he muttered, brokenly. His thoughts swung back to the specialists. "Well, get some more of 'em, then," he commanded, almost roughly, answering his own reflections rather than his wife's words. "Ain't there some we 'ain't got yet?"

She shook her head. Then, suddenly, she let it drop, and big tears rolled down her cheeks. "They all say the same thing," she explained. "She's got to be roused."

"Good Lord! Then *rouse* her!"

"Do you suppose we haven't tried everything?" she asked.

He knew they had. Stolidly, inwardly raging, he continued his walk up and down the room, his head bent on his breast, his arms behind him. There was a soft tap on the door and a maid entered. She brought a tray full of letters to her mistress.

"Most of it for Miss Stewart, ma'am," she said, timidly, and then, more timidly, "I—I hope she's better. We—we all love her so, down-stairs, Mrs. Johnson."

"Thank you, Katie." Mrs. Johnson's voice was unsteady. "You may leave the mail on the table."

After the servant had left the room she glanced over the addresses with absent eyes. Letters, telegrams, cables, notes, slipped through her hands one after the other. At the bottom of the pile lay a thick package.

"Photographs," she told her husband, "from Paris. She left all her films there to be developed. She's been so anxious to see them until this happened. They have been due for weeks and she has watched every mail. I wonder—" Her face lit with a sudden hope, then clouded again. "No, of course, she wouldn't look at them now."

Mr. Johnson faced her. "Make her," he said, sharply. "Show her every one. If she was interested, here's our chance."

"I know, but—" Mrs. Johnson hesitated. "It was for Bert she wanted them, you know. She wanted to show him the places she liked best, and now—"

"Try it, anyhow."

Mr. Johnson's tone compelled obedience. Very slowly his wife lifted the packet and walked across the room.

"I'll try," she said, "but I don't think—" The

words were lost in the sound of the door as it closed behind her.

She ascended the wide stairs slowly and laboriously, and softly entered the sick-room. A nurse was there, and two physicians, one of whom had evidently just come. He stood beside the patient's bed, looking down at her, his greatcoat still buttoned to his chin, his wet hat on a near-by chair. At the foot of the bed stood another physician, evidently at his usual post, and ready to answer, so far as he could, the questions of his eminent colleague. But the great specialist asked none. He stood for a moment, silent, frowning reflectively upon the beautiful face below him. Ruth Stewart's blue eyes, wide open, looked back at him unseeingly, with no interest, no speculation, no reason in their depths. They looked like balls of polished agate set in the white face outlined against the pillow. Little locks of yellow hair, as soft as a child's, curled round her forehead, giving her head an indescribable effect of youth and innocence and helplessness. The newcomer turned away, slowly removed his coat, handed it and his hat to the nurse, and drew a chair close to the bed. Mrs. Johnson went forward with the package. Very quietly they exchanged greetings.

"This is a package of photographs," Mrs. Johnson explained as they stood together. "The ones she took abroad. She had been talking about them so much before Captain Graham's death that I thought they might—she might look at them—"

184

Her motherly voice died away under the doubt in the doctor's quiet glance.

He shook his head. "I'm afraid we're past photographs," he said, slowly. "Still, we'll try. It's a case of grasping at straws, Mrs. Johnson. You say she felt some interest in these before Graham's accident."

Mrs. Johnson undid the package, and he took the photographs from her hand. There were dozens of them, neatly mounted, taken in out-of-the-way corners of Europe—quaint cottages, odd craft, picturesque bits of sea and sky, groups of peasants, and children of many lands and climes—laughing children, crying children, even fighting children, for Ruth Stewart had permanently preserved with her camera the record of one pitched battle in Killarney, whose sanguinary memory had already faded from the minds of the participants. The great doctor looked them over slowly. Then he suddenly addressed his patient.

"Miss Stewart," he said, distinctly. "I want to show you something. Won't you sit up for a moment and look at these? They are photographs you took when you were abroad. They are very interesting. They have just come. Will you look at them? See, I will make you comfortable."

He lifted her skilfully as he spoke, and the nurse hastened to make a support of pillows. He had spoken very slowly and distinctly, as if to a child, keeping his eyes unswervingly on the patient's, and

Ruth Stewart had looked stonily back at him, wholly without response. As he seated himself, however, facing her and with the pictures in his hand, she spoke.

"Has Bert come yet?" she asked.

Mrs. Johnson answered. "Bert cannot come, dear," she said, gently. "You know that. But these are the photographs you wanted to show him. Look at them and see if they are all here."

The eyes of the girl Herbert Graham had loved moved toward the package. Its association with his name arrested her attention. She smiled; then for an instant her face took on a look of indescribable horror—the look of one who has gone to the edge of life and looked over into an abyss one must not see. Some memory gripped her. Her eyes dilated.

"He's late," she whispered. "Why—why doesn't he come?"

The physician raised his hand as Mrs. Johnson was about to speak. "She must realize it," he said, curtly; "she must take it in and get hold of it and pull herself up to it. It's the only chance." His cool, professional tones filled the room, but they shook a little, for Graham had been his friend, and this was the woman Graham would have married to-day had he lived.

"Bert cannot come," he said, clearly. "You know that. He cannot come. And because he cannot, it would hurt him to feel that you look for him when you know this. You must not."

She lay silent for a moment. "The orange blossoms," she said, dreamily. "Don't you smell them? The whole world's full of them."

The doctor's face clouded. Aimlessly he picked up the package of photographs and began to examine them at random.

"Graham would have liked this one," he said, clearly. "It's very good of you, for a snapshot."

It was, for it had been taken by a fellow-traveler with some taste for background and posing. Ruth Stewart stood on the bank of a Dutch canal, hand in hand with two picturesque Dutch babies, an effective windmill behind her, and the amusement of the moment in her blue eyes. Her beautiful face was alight with the joy of living.

"Bert would like that," repeated the doctor, slowly, holding it so that she could see it.

She looked. Her features twisted sharply. For an instant, far back in her numbed brain, there flashed a conception of the difference between the girl in the picture and the girl who now looked at it. Some awful abyss lay between the two. She dared not try to cross it. She dared not even look into it. But the doctor had caught the fleeting ray of intelligence. Firmly he grasped and held it.

"Bert would like this one, too," he said, deliberately. "You used to write him about all these places, you know, and the odd things that had happened. He told me sometimes, and once or twice he read me a bit from your letters. You liked Holland especially, I remember. Here are some very good Holland scenes. Graham meant to go there with you next summer. He would have liked these pictures."

As he talked, with an effect of urgently holding her attention, he picked up the Holland photographs at random and held them before her. As if against her will, she looked, and as she looked at one after the other of the familiar scenes her face changed. A mask seemed to fall from it. It became warmer, more human. The others in the room hardly breathed. The great specialist was a silent man by habit, never free of speech, so it was not easy for him to make conversation. But he dared not stop talking now. She must be held some way, any way, for this was a crisis.

"Here's a pretty one," he cried, enthusiastically. "A little girl, and an old boat, and a stretch of sea and sky. Such a pretty little girl, too, with an uncanny wisdom in her face. *She* knows things, that child. By Jove! how artistic the whole thing is!" He paused, in genuine admiration. "Bert would have liked *that* immensely," he added, holding it up before his patient.

Arrested by something in his words, Ruth Stewart looked, looked again, tried to pull her eyes away, found them dragged back irresistibly, and then let them rest on the picture with an awful fixity.

It was Katrina, the woman-child, Katrina of Monnikendam, Katrina, the soul confidante. Katrina, who knew that Ruth loved Bertie, and was to tell it to all the world. Ruth Stewart looked into the brown eyes, looked at the smiling mouth, looked, looked—looked again, and *remembered*.

The wave of memory was black and unspeakably terrible. It rolled toward her, lifted her up, swept her onward, bore her through storm-swept seas, and finally cast her on the indescribably bleak and desolate shore of a burned-out world—for it was a world without Bertie. He was gone and she was left. Yes, that was it. And the scent around her was the heavy scent of the flowers of death—not that of orange blossoms, and the music she had heard was the sound of a dirge—not the triumphant peal of the wedding-march. Herbert was gone and she was left. That's what it had all meant—the tramping of horses' feet, the regimental music, the "taps," and the silent, observant men and women around her. Herbert was gone and she was left. Others were left, too, and they were expecting something of her, some action, some service, perhaps— what was it? She was left. Sometime, perhaps, she would know what they wished her to do. But now—oh, little Katrina, far off there in Monni- kendam—you have come to-day with a different message to your friend, and it is well. Again and again you might repeat your lesson. Again and again the sea and the sky might hear it. Again and again others might listen—but because it can never reach one pair of ears it is all lost and the world lost with it. Oh, dear little Katrina, with your shy smile and your tragic eyes, have you been sent to help and comfort? Would you be sorry if you *knew?*

Ruth Stewart dropped the photograph, threw out her empty arms, fell forward where she sat, and burst into wild weeping. The tears rained down her cheeks. The eyes of those around her were wet, but their faces shone. Mrs. Johnson had fallen on her knees at the foot of the bed. The great specialist drew a long breath, and nodded at her with contained satisfaction. Hearts might be broken. Time was the best, sometimes the only, specialist for them. A shattered mind, however, is sometimes like the jumbled pieces of a picture puzzle. If they are reassembled, it has a meaning. Association is the key to that reassembling. He had placed a piece that led to reconstruction of the whole.

"That's all right," he said, comfortably. "She'll do now."

TO MEET MISS POMEROY

MR. ARCHIBALD HIBBARD restored the
season's prettiest débutante to the shelter of
her mother's wing and thanked her for the pleasure
she had given him, gallantly concealing the fact that,
incidentally, she had reduced him to a physical condition approaching collapse. As he turned away he
was suddenly caught up and buffeted along the
floor of the ballroom by several pairs of determined
dancers, who showed their further disapproval of
his presence by treading severely upon his feet.

The experience, added to what he had already
undergone, embittered Mr. Hibbard. He received
their light-hearted words of apology with an in-
articulate mutter, and, feeling very much like an
unwilling child on a merry-go-round in full swing, he
plunged wildly off into a recess in the wall that
looked like a shelter. His instinct had been right.
It was a shelter, and in the next instant he was out
of the crowd and resting on a wide window-seat.

The retreat was empty, and though it was also
very small, it seemed to the appreciative young man
to offer all that for the moment he asked of life.
Thin silk curtains protected him from the unsym-

pathetic gaze of his companions in pleasure, and a potted palm suggested mutely but eloquently that the spot was designed for a sentimental tête-à-tête, and not as a hiding-place for a guest deaf to the call of duty. But Mr. Hibbard ignored this intimation and set about the rehabilitation urgently required after three hours in a crowded ballroom. He pulled at his waistcoat, smoothed his hair with his hand, and straightened his tie; and, after somberly regarding what he mentally classified as "the well-defined footprints" on his patent-leather pumps, he removed these blemishes with a leaf from the potted palm.

After this he noticed that the musicians were playing the opening bars of the next dance, and, with the deep sigh attending an unwillingly awakened conscience, he took out his dance-card and looked at it. His brow cleared. Fate has its moments of softness: the space opposite the next dance was blank. For a few care-free moments he need not wedge himself into the overcrowded ballroom. Of course, what he should be doing, as he instantly realized, was joining in the attack on the buffet and bringing glasses of punch and plates of chicken salad to yon distant frieze of purple dowagers. But Archie dismissed this reflection as soon as it was born. He had firmly decided never, under any circumstances whatever, to attend another dance, so it really did not matter what his fellow-guests thought of him. As for his sister Mollie, who had

dragged him to this affair, in the warm month of
May—a hideous time to have a dancing-party—he
would have a few words to say to her in the morning
about the things that are worth while and the things
that are not, pointing out that if she cared to waste
her life— It was at this precise moment in his
reflections that he discovered Her.

She was a girl, and a very young girl, probably
not more than eighteen., He had never seen her
before, and yet why hadn't he? Why had she not
been among the dozens of débutantes with whom,
during this season, and especially during this evening,
he had tangoed and fox-trotted and hesitated? Was
she a stranger in New York? Had she just come to
the ball? Surely she could not have been here all
the evening without bringing the dancers to her feet
in an ecstasy of admiration. Beyond question she
was the most beautiful thing he had ever seen, and,
safely hidden behind the silk portières, Archie stared
at Her through their narrow opening with his heart
in his eyes. She was small and slender and dark,
with wavy, blue-black hair, and blue-black eyes, a
complexion like white velvet, and an expression of
proud dignity much older than her years, an expression saved from hauteur only by an adorable dimple
at the corner of her mouth. She was not dancing,
but was the heart of a little group of men and girls,
all strangers to Mr. Hibbard.

Suddenly Archie blinked and drew a quick breath.
He had been staring at her movelessly, almost

breathlessly, for some time, five minutes, ten, fifteen, he had no idea how long. He knew only that during the interval, however long or short, he had been in a trance. He, the level-headed, the unromantic, the unassailable; he, who had never been in love and abysmally was beginning to fear that he never would be, had been bowled over utterly, had lost his head completely after one long look at a girl he had never seen before. She smiled, and at the smile Archie's heart stopped, leaped, then beat suffocatingly. Again he drew a quick breath, and his blood seemed to sing in his ears.

Unconsciously he spoke aloud, a little thickly: "Great Scott!" he muttered. "What's the matter with me? It—it doesn't come this way!"

But it does, sometimes, and in the next instant Archie knew it. He knew it by the panic which filled him with the discovery that she was moving, going out of his range of vision, that he was losing her. He pulled the curtains apart with a jerk and started toward her, only to collide with a man he knew who was plunging in the opposite direction.

Archie caught this victim by the arm. "Haxton," he cried, "wait a minute. Who's that girl over there, the one with the hair? Do you know her?"

Haxton stared around stupidly, like the ass he was, Archie reflected. As if there were more than one girl in the place to look at! Then, following the direction of Hibbard's eyes, Haxton's expression brightened. "Oh, that one, yes!" he said. "Rippin', ain't she?"

"Who is she?" Hibbard's tone held a warning to stupid young men.

Haxton lost it, however. "Nice girl. Friend of my sister's. Pretty," was his calm reply.

"*Who is she?*" Archie spoke through set teeth.

Haxton recoiled as if the other had made a threatening advance on him. "Say, what's the row?" he stammered.

"What's her name, you chump? Who is the girl?"

"Oh-h-h!" Haxton's comprehension now was too complete. He grinned widely.

Archie felt his face grow red. "Will you introduce me?" he asked, more quietly, pulling himself together.

"Surest thing you know. Wait till I get this stuff down the throats of the McCreedy twins," agreed Haxton.

Haxton, Archie now observed, was laden with two plates of sandwiches and salad, on each of which a glass of punch trembled precariously. "They've been waitin' an hour," he explained as he turned away. "Frightful crush out there. Right back." He elevated his plates above the throng and shouldered his way ahead after another meaning grin at Archie and a soothing injunction to "keep cool."

Archie remained where he was, hot with impatience. She was still in sight, and that calming fact enabled him to wear a deceptive air of self-control.

He watched the crowd round her, searching vainly for a face he knew, and at intervals he plucked a friend from the dancing throng in the hope of finding some one else who could introduce him. But evidently she was a stranger, for none of the men he held up had met her. He was capable of anything by this time, and, as Haxton did not return, he was thinking of dragging his hostess away from the supper-room to make the presentation, when a familiar face smiled up at him, and Betty Corson, his sister's dearest friend, laid a hand on his arm.

"Don't be embarrassed," she announced, sweetly. "The fact that it is our dance, and that Mr. Kirby has escorted me all over the place to find you, doesn't matter in the least."

Archie greeted her with pleasure and lent himself to gallant lying. He liked Betty Corson, largely because she had no sentimental nonsense about her. "I've been looking everywhere for you," he declared. "Thanks awfully, Kirby. By the way, do you happen to know, either of you—"

He had turned to face Betty. Now he looked around to find the object of his dreams, and suddenly the universe grew black. Incredulously, and struggling with a tendency to rub his eyes, he stared at the spot where she had been. She and her little group had disappeared as completely as if they were part of a fairy pantomime and a trap-door had opened beneath them.

The look of consternation on Hibbard's face was

so unmistakable that Betty Corson sympathetically clutched his arm. "Why, Archie," she gasped, "what has happened?"

Again Archie pulled himself together. Strange things were occurring, but he could not discuss them, even with Betty Corson. Had he fallen asleep and dreamed the girl? For a moment he almost believed that he had.

"It was the fear of losing you," he explained, with recovered assurance. "It just swept over me how easily we might have missed each other in this crush!"

But all the time he was dancing with Betty his mind was full of the other girl. Had he lost her forever? But of course he had not. He did not know her name, but Haxton did, and Haxton should make up for to-night's fiasco by bringing them together within twenty-four hours. When he had turned Betty over to her next partner, he sought Haxton.

That gentleman was refreshing himself with a cigarette in the smoking-room. "Awfully sorry, old chap," said the culprit, as Archie appeared. "Couldn't possibly get away, and now she's gone. 'Fraid it's all off, too, for she's going on a yachting-trip to-morrow. Jove! there's my dance with Miss Carey!"

He darted for the door, but Archie, too quick for him, jumped forward and stood with his back against it. "Who is she, and whose yacht is she going on?" he demanded.

"The Wetmores'. You know 'em. So long."

Haxton jerked open the door and fled, leaving Archie wearing a seraphic smile. This was luck. The Wetmores were among his best friends, and his sudden determination to be a guest on their yacht was based on the pleasant certainty that they would be glad to have him. Just the same, he would make sure of it: he wasn't leaving anything more to chance. Escorted by an over-eager servant, he hurried to his host's telephone and called up Mrs. Wetmore.

"Hear you're off for a cruise to-morrow," he said, after a preliminary greeting. "I'm a bit under the weather, and I wondered if you—"

"Oh, Archie, will you come?" Mrs. Wetmore's voice as well as her words breathed hospitality. "Jack will be enchanted, and so shall I."

The matter was arranged in the next two minutes, and Mr. Hibbard hung up the receiver with a look of triumph. There were business reasons why he should not leave town at present, but he ignored them all and gloried in the wonderful new impulse that was driving him on. A week on a yacht together, a whole week of moonlit nights and sunflooded days, of deck-walks and talks! It was ideal! He couldn't possibly have planned it better; it would give her several days to get acquainted with him before he asked her to marry him, and there would be several more, in the same ideal setting, after she had accepted him. Archie did not stop to analyze his conviction that she would accept him. He had found her, and she was his, which was all that counted.

The Waterfowl sailed early the next morning, and young Mr. Hibbard, despite his love and longing, was the last guest to arrive. He had not slept at all until five in the morning, and then he had over-slept. His host, convinced that he would not appear at all, was about to give the starting-signal, when the young man hurried on board; and the jocular greetings he received from his fellow-passengers were mingled with the farewell whistle of the yacht as she cast off her moorings and slipped out into the river.

Archie's eyes were very brilliant, and his heart pounded against his side as he waited for Her to appear. She was not in the little group that greeted him, but he knew girls well enough to realize that she was probably fussing in her cabin, getting into ship-togs. He was glad to find Kirby on board, and Betty Corson's mother, though without Betty; also the Blinns, a delightful pair of "newly-weds" he had recently met and liked. But She remained invisible, and at breakfast, before *The Waterfowl* was an hour on its way, his hostess awoke him from his second dream.

"We had hoped to have two delightful Southern girls with us," she told her guests, blithely, with no idea of the blow she was directing at one buoyant heart, "but late last night they telephoned that they could not come. The mother of one of them was ill. It's a pity," she added, sympathetically, turning to Archie, "they would have played so prettily with you and Mr. Kirby!"

Archie agreed that it was a pity, and his voice sounded strange in his ears. Sick despair had overwhelmed him. Here he was, cooped up for a week, while She, the wonderful, the indescribable, the unapproachable She, was in New York, where he might have remained to meet her to-day if he had not acted like an emotional idiot. After breakfast he retired to his state-room to think things over, and, though his first audible reflections were of a nature to blister the finish of *The Waterfowl's* excellent woodwork, he grew calmer as he reviewed his situation. There was, he realized, a way of escape. The yacht stopped at several ports, and at the first of these he would find a telegram demanding his immediate return to New York by rail.

This plan was shattered, however, when, late that afternoon, his hostess again prattled of her missing guests. "I did so want you to meet Miss Pomeroy," she said. "She's a Southern girl, from Tennessee, and one of the prettiest creatures I know. Her sister, who married Dick Edington, was a classmate of mine at Farmington."

"Miss Pomeroy's dark, isn't she?" asked Archie, with deep guile.

"Very, and very lovely, in an unusual fashion. By the way, she was at the Van Vleits' dance last night. Didn't you meet her there?"

TO MEET MISS POMEROY

Archie shook his head. "I saw her, though," he admitted. "Is it her mother who is ill?"

"No, her cousin's mother. But both the girls went home. They all live together in Nashville."

"Oh, then Miss Pomeroy's on the way to Nashville now?"

"Yes."

Archie did some rapid thinking. By leaving the yacht the next day he could be in Nashville the following morning with a letter of introduction to Miss Pomeroy from Mrs. Wetmore. Thus managed, the thing would be pretty raw, but he was desperate. His only course was to confide in Mrs. Wetmore, who was a good sort and would understand.

She did understand, so well that, thirty-six hours later, Mr. Hibbard found himself waiting for Miss Pomeroy in the big living-room of an old Southern house, all wide halls, family portraits, and cut flowers in bowls and vases. It seemed so fit a setting for her, and he was so certain of seeing her in it, that when he rose and faced a girl he had never seen before, a dark, pretty, slender girl, who held his letter of introduction in her hand, he stood before her stunned into speechlessness.

Little by little, as she talked on, he grasped the situation. It was so pleasant to meet a friend of Mrs. Wetmore's, she said; Mrs. Wetmore had been so sweet to her and her cousin Eleanor. They had hoped to come South in *The Waterfowl,* but a letter from her mother, who was not well, had made the speaker anxious to return to Nashville at once. Eleanor had decided to go on to Chicago to visit the Rexfords. Charming people; possibly he knew them? He did? Then he knew how delightful they were. Kitty Rexford was Eleanor's dearest friend, and as mother was not seriously ill, it had seemed better for Eleanor to make her visit now instead of later. Oh yes, Eleanor's name was Pomeroy, too; their fathers were brothers.

As one in a bad dream, Archie drank tea and ate tea-cakes, talked small talk, and finally got away. As he passed down the great hall on his way to the front door he caught, through another door, a glimpse of Her, and stopped. It was her portrait, full.length and extraordinarily vital.

Seeing him hesitate at the threshold, his hostess hospitably urged him into the room, babbling explanation. "That's Eleanor," she explained. "You see, this is her home as well as mine. Sargent painted the portrait in London last year, and it made a sensation at the Academy this spring."

If it had not been for the portrait, Hibbard might have abandoned what he mentally called his "wild-goose chase"; but, looking into the painted eyes, it seemed to him that he had met Eleanor, after all, and the encounter was fuel to the flame of his purpose. Beyond question he was a fool, but there was something divine in such folly and in letting it have its way. He was going on to Chicago, he told his hostess, and if she would give him a letter to her cousin, he would be glad. Of course he would see the Rexfords there. Possibly there was some commission?

He carried the letter to Chicago in his breast pocket, and sent it with his cards to his hostess and Miss Pomeroy.

"Why, Mr. Hibbard, how perfectly delightful this is! It's ages since I've seen you. Wasn't it at the 'Senior Prom' the last time, five years ago?"

The voice was the high-pitched but agreeable voice of Mrs. Rexford, and she had shaken hands with him and asked a dozen questions before he found it possible to remind her that he had hoped to see Miss Pomeroy, too. The corners of Mrs. Rexford's pretty mouth drooped mournfully.

"Why, you know, she didn't come," she explained. "At the last minute she decided to stay out the week with some friends in New York, and come here later, as originally planned. How long shall you be in Chicago, and won't you put up with us?"

But it became evident that Mr. Hibbard's visit in Chicago was the briefest episode, merely a touch on a branch in his flight back home. He was returning to New York that day, on the limited— and he did so, though unsustained by any fair prospect, for Mrs. Rexford had not given him the names of Eleanor's new friends.

Archie was in a very bad humor when he reached his New York house the next morning, and he was not soothed by the butler's obvious pleasure in his return, nor by the welcoming joy of the sister and the elderly aunt who made up his domestic circle.

"You've only got twenty minutes to get into fresh clothes for luncheon, Archie," Mollie reminded him. "I'm so awfully glad you're home again. It's horrid without you. Besides, I want you to do lots of nice things in the next few days."

He gave her shoulder an absent pat and went to his room, where he dressed gloomily, feeling horribly let down and depressed. All the savor had gone out of life. True, he could chase up Haxton again, but Haxton had proved a broken reed, and he was beginning to fear that a malignant fate had taken a hand in his affairs. Perhaps, after all, She was not in the world for him. If he could accept that idea and realize that he had struck bottom, as it were, perhaps he'd come to his senses again and think of something else. But he did not want to come to his senses again. He did not want to think of anything else. Before his eyes he saw Her constantly, saw the poise of her proud little head, the dimple at the corner of her adorable mouth. Jove! how empty life would be without her! No, it should not be passed without her. He'd follow her to the limits of the earth, if necessary, but he would have her in the end!

With the calm of that decision still resting on his brow, he descended the stairs and opened the door of the living-room. As he did so, his aunt and sister came forward to meet him, and, hanging back a little shyly in the first moment of this family reunion, was another figure which suddenly, inconceivably filled the room with glory.

To Archie all the trumpets of the earth seemed to be acclaiming his triumphant entrance as a victor in the arena of life, but what his ears really heard were the quiet tones of his sister's voice: "Eleanor dear, may I present my brother? Archie, I persuaded Miss Pomeroy to spend this week with us when her cousin went South."

Archie bowed. He simply could not speak; the thing was too overwhelming. Mollie and his aunt prattled on while his thoughts whirled in a delicious chaos.

This week was almost gone. It was already Friday, so there would be only one day more of her visit, or two days, if she remained over Sunday. But Archie, listening to the voices of morning stars singing together, paid little heed to that reflection. Masterfully he drew Miss Pomeroy's arm through his and led her to the dining-room, seating her at his right. The chair opposite his, which his aunt now occupied, would be her place in the future, when they two were married. She could make the house over to suit herself and get a new staff of servants. Aunt Bertha and Mollie would be delighted to have some one else take on the responsibility which they had always shirked. He and She could spend some time each year in that jolly old place at Nashville.

Probably Eleanor would want to. Eleanor! He liked the name, but one would need some tender abbreviation. Not Nora! Not Nell! Not Elly!

That left corner dimple was the most wonderful thing he had ever seen. It was made to hold a kiss, to hold a man's heart, a man's very soul! How soon could he tell Her so? After luncheon? That might be rushing it a bit, but too much time had already been lost to make delays possible now. And wasn't her being in his home all the time a sure proof that she was his? Yes, certainly, after luncheon he could get rid of Aunt Bertha and Mollie on some pretext, and make love to Her. The thing to do with a girl like that was to sweep her off her feet if one could.

There was a look of fixed determination on Mr. Hibbard's handsome face when, an hour later, he followed his guest to the living-room. In ten minutes more he had persuaded Aunt Bertha to take her daily nap a little earlier than usual, and had convinced Mollie that a theater-party for that night was the best possible form of entertainment. With Mollie safely anchored to her desk and the telephone for half an hour, he drew two easy-chairs close together and established his guest in one of them. Then, sinking into the other, he gave himself up to the deep delight of this first tête-à-tête in his own home.

"What kind of a proposal of marriage," he asked, gently, "do you like best?"

TO MEET MISS POMEROY

Miss Pomeroy's blue-black eyes, which had been glancing absently out of the window, turned and swept his face. She seemed surprised, but not greatly interested, and she did not answer.

"I mean," he continued, "is there any special wording you prefer?"

"No," said Miss Pomeroy, calmly.

He sighed. "I'm sorry," he said. "I rather hoped there was. It's nice to know one's taste in such things, don't you think?"

"No," said Miss Pomeroy, again. "I don't think it matters very much."

This was discouraging, but the young man persisted. "But the manner and the method make all the difference," he urged. "Now, suppose, just suppose, that I proposed marriage to you. If I said: 'I love you. Will you marry me?' what would you say?"

"I should say, 'No, thank you,'" declared the lady.

"Exactly. Of course you would. And why? Because the question was too cold, too formal. But suppose I said this: 'Darling, I adore you. You haven't been out of my thoughts for one instant since I first saw you, five days ago. You've made the whole world look different to me. You've given life its meaning. Trust me, love me, marry me!' What would you say to that?"

Miss Pomeroy reflected. "I think," she said at last, "I should say, 'What an extraordinary person you are!'"

Mr. Hibbard's face fell. "Would you?" he asked, disappointedly. "I hoped you'd say something shorter. Just, 'Yes,' or, 'Of course,' or simple, easy words like that. But it proves what I claimed: there's a right and a wrong way."

"It proves that there's a wrong way," admitted Miss Pomeroy.

"So we'll try another. How's this? 'You can't care for me yet, because you don't know me. I don't know you, and still I adore you; but that's different. It's my nature to give freely. If you knew me, you would love me. I've got stunning qualities, lots of 'em. I'll make you love me. I'll make you the happiest woman in the world. I'll give you everything life can offer. I'll tear the stars from the sky and make them into a diadem for you. If there's anything you want, you have only to mention it.'"

"I've always thought," mused Miss Pomeroy, "that I'd like to be a widow."

For a moment Mr. Hibbard seemed staggered, but only for a moment. "All right," he said, "be my widow. I'll make you a widow in fifty or sixty years."

Miss Pomeroy shook her head. "I want to be a *young* widow," she declared, firmly.

"But don't you want a lot of beautiful memories to cherish?" urged her host. "Say, twenty years of marriage, and then romantic widowhood?"

"No!"

TO MEET MISS POMEROY

"Ten years?"

"No!"

"Five?"

"No!"

"One?"

"No!"

"One month?"

"No! And really, Mr. Hibbard, don't you think we've been silly long enough?"

"Why, no; we haven't been half as silly yet as we're going to be," he explained.

An hour later Mollie Hibbard met her brother in the hall, and, according to her custom, promptly buttonholed him.

"How handsome you look, Archie," she exclaimed, admiringly. "I'm glad you're in good spirits, too, for I want to ask a favor of you. It's this: I want you to be especially nice to Eleanor Pomeroy. Will you?"

Archie frowned. "I'll be nice to her, all right," he promised. "But you'd better get after her and make her nice to me. Why, Mollie, that girl swears she simply will not marry me till June!"

"W-h-a-t?" gasped Mollie.

"June!" grumbled her brother. "A whole month off!"

BILLY BATES, PREFERRED

"AFTER mature deliberation," remarked Billy Bates, pensively, "I have decided to raffle myself off!"

The group of girls to whom he spoke glanced at him with the weary indulgence shown by a mother to a trying child, and, without perceptible pause, continued to discuss their plans for the day.

"Osaki will row me over to the Point," said Isabella Branch, "and I'll join the Winthrops there, and 'do' the Indian Trail. I'll be back for luncheon."

"Kittie and I are going off in the *Petrel*," explained Harriet Beardslee. "We—"

"And I," repeated Billy Bates, raising his voice a trifle, "am going to raffle myself off, as I was remarking when I was rudely interrupted. And I'm going to do it now."

The girls turned to him, regarding him with a doubt that deepened into a faint interest.

"But why, and, as it were, wherefore?" demanded Miss Beardslee. "What's the idea?"

Young Mr. Bates stretched himself out more comfortably in the reclining-chair he occupied on the camp veranda, and clasped his hands behind his head. He was sure of his audience now, and very much at his ease.

"Because," he explained, affably, "it's the only way to meet the embarrassing situation in which I find myself."

Two of his hearers looked puzzled. Four looked annoyed.

"Meaning—?" interrogated Kittie Noyes, who had looked puzzled.

"Meaning just this," continued young Mr. Bates. "Here I am, the only unattached man in camp, among six charming girls. What is my natural impulse? To spend the happy hours with all of you. But how the deuce can I do it when every one of you has a different taste? I long to hike with Isabella along the Indian Trail, but my heart also pants to be with Harriet and Kittie in the motor-boat, and with the others, wherever they're going. It's a frightful situation. I'm feeling the nervous strain of it, so I intend to settle the thing once and for all."

Miss Beardslee, who had been standing with one foot advanced in the direction of the anchored *Petrel*, withdrew it, and sat down on the top step of the rustic porch.

"It sounds very interesting," she drawled, with an edge on her voice, however, which would have carried a warning to the youth. "How are you going to do it?"

"I've told you twice." Billy spoke without re-

sentment, but a trifle wearily, as one who addresses
a slow-moving mind. "The girl who wins the raffle
has me for the week I'm here. She has an escort
for all occasions, and I'm saved the mental and
emotional strain of deciding every morning what girl
I'll spend the day with. Great scheme, isn't it?"
he finished, with a cherubic smile which made him
look about four years old.

The girls glanced at one another, flushing; a message flashed from eye to eye.

"Well, of all the conceited, insufferable—" began
Kittie Noyes, hotly.

"The trouble with girls," murmured Mr. Bates,
addressing space, "is that they're ruled by their
emotions. Try to appeal to their reason, and they're
furious."

Harriet checked Kittie's retort with a warning
gesture. "No one pays any attention to anything
Billy says," she reminded her friend. "What he
does is different. As the nephew of our hostess, he
is, in a way, our host! If he wants to plan a new
game, let him do it. I rather like it. Then one of
us will have charge of him, and the rest of us will
have him off our minds." She turned to Billy.
"But," she added, "suppose none of the girls cares
to take a chance. What then?"

For a moment the young man looked dashed.
Then his brow cleared. "Oh, but you'll have to,"
he said, airily. "You see, the proceeds will go to
charity—starving Belgian child, or something like

that. Six tickets at one dollar each. Within the reach of all." He sat up in his chair to emphasize his next point. "First I thought I'd sell stock in myself," he went on, cheerfully. "Bates Common and Bates Preferred—that kind of thing, you know. Then the largest stockholder, of course, would own the most of my time. But—er—there are disadvantages to that—there would be jealousies and rival claims. The raffle is better. Settles everything."

Miss Beardslee rose, and with a nod signaled her friends to follow her. "We'll talk it over," she said. "It won't take more than five minutes. Then," with a glance at Mr. Bates, "we'll let you know whether we care to invest."

It was more than five minutes before the girls returned, and to the young man in the reclining-chair the interval seemed even longer. Moreover, the expression on their faces when they finally appeared was not especially reassuring. Billy, though a law unto himself and a thoroughly spoiled youth, was no fool, and the glint in the eyes of several of the girls did not escape him when he rose to hear their report. Most of them, moreover, were giggling. Miss Beardslee alone was serious and purposeful of mien. She wore the air of one assisting at a ceremony.

"It's all right," she announced, briefly. "We agree, but we want you to sell seven tickets instead of six. The seventh is for Helen Wickersham, who is coming to-night for a week's visit. She must be in this, too."

"Oh, of course. Just as you please."

Mr. Bates was fumbling in his pocket for his note-book. When he found it he proceeded to tear out a page, which he divided into seven strips. On one he wrote two words, and showed them to the girls. "*Bates Preferred*," they read in chorus, and again they giggled.

Mr. Bates folded the strips with great solemnity, dropped them into the crown of his Panama hat, shook them violently, and offered the hat to his audience. Miss Beardslee was the first to draw.

"I'll take two chances," she explained as she did so, "one for Helen."

When the others had drawn, there was a moment of suspense.

"Now open them," commanded Mr. Bates.

A suggestion of interest was in his languid voice, and a little stir of expectancy was perceptible among the girls as each unfolded her paper. With an odd smile, Miss Beardslee held up one of the two slips she had drawn.

"Helen's!" she murmured. "She has won!" Then she burst into helpless laughter. "And, oh, Billy," she added when she could speak, "you *are* in for it."

Mr. Bates turned an anxious eye upon her. "I don't know Miss Wickersham," he admitted, un-comfortably, "but she's a good sort, isn't she?—and

you all like her, don't you? You've done nothing
but talk about her since I came!"

"Of course we like her. But she's deep, Billy,"
Kittie Noyes warned him. "You'll have to watch
her!" And they all laughed again.

An expression of almost fatuous content over-
spread the ingenuous boyish countenance of Mr.
Bates. "Oh, if that's all!" he exclaimed, with such
artless relief that another gale of laughter swept over
the girls.

Upon his own invitation, Billy accompanied Miss
Noyes and Miss Beardslee on their motor-boat excursion, cheerfully explaining that he did so because
two pretty heads were better than one; and during
the boat's humming progress over the sun-touched
sea he succeeded in extracting from them some interesting information concerning Miss Wickersham.
It seemed that they knew her well: indeed, had been
her classmates in a New York school for two years.
Her home was in Alabama, and this would be her
first experience of camping in the Maine woods.
How old was she? About twenty-three. Pretty?
Y-e-s. Small, dark, brown eyes, brown hair. It
seemed clear that as usual young Mr. Bates had
fallen on his feet, and he plumed himself so openly
on the coming of the figure draped romantically in
the veil of the unknown that his two companions
exchanged a glance of heartfelt understanding.

He was impatient to meet Miss Wickersham, and
distinctly annoyed, as well as disappointed, when

15   215

Harriet, now the appointed Mistress of Ceremonies, declared that the introduction must not take place until the next morning.

"She gets in late," she explained, "and she'll be tired and want to go to bed. But to-morrow morning we'll meet here on the veranda before breakfast, and turn the prize package over to her with due pomp. Would you mind," she added, wistfully, "if we did you up in ribbons?"

Billy decided light-heartedly that he did not mind, and his serenity remained undisturbed when Harriet explained that they had to do something to make the gift acceptable. In the evening he went for a moonlight sail with Kittie and the Sheldon twins, and was many miles away from camp when the exhausted Miss Wickersham arrived and was tenderly escorted to her room, from which waves of laughter rolled at intervals for the next hour.

Billy was up early the next morning, and as he dressed he observed with satisfaction that the day was glorious. On the canvas walls of his tent lay the shadows of the surrounding pines, and beyond the drawn flap at the entrance he saw and heard the sea, singing to the sun. He was a satisfying young figure in white as he bounded across the narrow stretch of woods that separated his sleeping-quarters from the dining-tent, and when Harriet hurried down the path to meet him, carrying several bolts of brilliant-colored ribbons, he greeted her with a smile as jocund as the morning, and lent himself cheerfully to the decorative scheme she at once began to carry out. He was festooned like a Christmas tree when she finally led him in triumph to the veranda where the girls were waiting.

In the center of the animated group they made he caught a glimpse of a stranger, and he was wholly on his guard as he approached. What he was not prepared for was the perfect naturalness of the girls, the ease of Harriet's presentation, and the extraordinary appearance of the little figure before which he found himself bowing. Helen Wickersham was all her friends had claimed for her—small and brown, and, y-e-s, pretty. She was no doubt intelligent. But her clothes, her carriage, her manner, and the general effect she presented were wholly different from anything Mr. Bates was accustomed to in what he loftily called "our set." As he would have put it, she looked "disgustingly thrown together."

Her wavy brown hair was pulled back from her forehead and fastened on the top of her head in a relentless little "pug." A brown-flannel shirtwaist, bulging in the back, eluded by two inches a safety-pin that sought to confine it to a shabby brown-tweed skirt which dragged on one side and pulled up on the other. Serviceable gray stockings ended in a pair of large tan walking-shoes with extension soles and worn rubber heels. Every girl at the Bateses' Camp wore serviceable shoes and rough tweed outing clothes, but, compared with their trim effect, with

the perfection of colors, pins, and belts, Miss Wickersham looked like a bedraggled little brown hen among
a group of peacocks. Not that the effect was exag-
geratedly bad. Met on the road, she might have
seemed a self-respecting country schoolma'am with
a mind above the trivialities of dress.

Her mind seemed to be above other trivialities
as well, for when Harriet presented the bedizened
Mr. Bates with a laughing explanation, she seemed
neither amused nor impressed. Indeed, Billy was
quite sure she did not wholly realize the situation,
and with a wild grasp at his vanishing self-confidence
he buoyantly addressed her.

"What shall we do to-day, Miss Wickersham?"
he asked. "What sort of thing do you like best—
riding, swimming, sailing, rowing? It's for you to
say, you know."

Miss Wickersham regarded him with a pair of
brown eyes whose expression was kind, yet incredibly remote. "Why, I don't know," she said,
vaguely. "I — haven't thought about it." She
was not self-conscious, but it seemed clear that
she was shy.

Billy watched her carefully. "Then let me do
the thinking," he suggested. "We'll go for a sail,
and we'll start as soon as breakfast is over. The
wind's just right."

Miss Wickersham looked around the little circle,
with the same vague uncertainty in her brown eyes.
"Are we all going?" she asked, doubtfully.

"Great Scott, no! That isn't the idea," Billy broke in, airily, upon the sentence Kittie had begun. "They all have different tastes. Sailing makes most of 'em sick."

"It makes me sick, too," murmured Miss Wickersham.

Billy was disappointed—and showed it. With a good boat to manage, and a splendid breeze, he could have had a glorious morning, with or without a companion.

"Row, then?" he asked.

"Mercy, no!" with a shudder. "That's worse."

"H-m-m! Swim?"

"I don't swim."

Harriet came to the rescue. "We'll go in to breakfast," she declared. "After that you can decide what to do. We've made all our plans," she added, graciously.

She led the way into the big dining-tent, and Billy followed, feeling rather foolish; but he dutifully seated himself beside Miss Wickersham, and attended to her wants with care. The figure he presented in his fresh white flannels and colored rosettes and streamers was such a contrast to the girl beside him that the others seemed unable to keep their eyes from the pair. Miss Wickersham was increasingly shy at the breakfast-table, and had to be "drawn out," but Billy was relieved to observe that she had a good appetite. At least she was not "delicate." She confessed to some fatigue after her journey, and when breakfast was over she announced her determination to unpack.

"Then Billy can wait on the veranda until you're ready for him," suggested Harriet.

Miss Wickersham signified that this arrangement would be satisfactory to her, and Mr. Bates agreed to it perforce, but the look he gave Miss Beardslee as she started off an hour later should have disturbed that young lady's subsequent dreams.

He made himself comfortable, however, in the hammock with a book, and he was so lost in the interest of the story that he failed to hear the happy band of his friends returning at lunch-time. At the table Miss Wickersham apologized palely. The unpacking had taken her longer than she expected. If she had unpacked her wardrobe, she had put it carefully away, for she was still clad in the nondescript garments of the early morning. After luncheon she declared that she was tired, and suggested that, as Mr. Bates seemed fond of reading, he might read aloud to her. Her taste in literature, it appeared, differed from his, and she regarded with distaste the light novel he suggested. Instead, she offered him his choice between Haeckel's *Riddle of the Universe* and Rodin's *L'Art* in the original French, and after one awestruck glance at the latter he opened the *Riddle* and read until his throat ached. Subconsciously he experienced a horrible fear that Miss Wickersham was a "high brow," but this lightened somewhat when he discovered that she slept peacefully through the reading, though she always stirred restlessly if he stopped.

That night there was a dance at the next camp, and Miss Wickersham permitted Mr. Bates to escort her there. She appeared dressed for the festivity in a badly made white frock, a worse made blue-ribbon belt, and a sprawling blue bow pinned against the side of the unrelenting "pug." After one glance at the ensemble, Billy decided that he liked her better in the brown things. It appeared that she did not dance, but she evidently expected Mr. Bates to sit out all the dances with her, and after one effort to escape he did so, not caring to subject himself to another rebuff such as the one Miss Beardslee gave him when he asked her for a waltz. She had looked at him with eyes brimful of horror and incredulity.

"And take you from Helen?" she gasped. "Why, *Billy*."

Billy returned to Helen, murmuring something for Harriet's benefit as he did so. At the end of the evening he mentally counted and classified the remarks his charge had made to him. There were five in all—two about the weather, and the others covering such miscellaneous interests as the fox-trot, which she thought ungraceful; the supper, which, to Billy's anguish, she declined; and—this in explanation of a slight yawn—the soporific quality of the pines. Altogether she was a rather heavy and drowsy young person, shy, unsophisticated, as out of place in the gay scene as a "bouncing Bet" in a vase of orchids.

Mr. Bates, on the other hand, talked steadily, until, as he later expressed it, his "tongue ached." He outlined in detail the joys of camp life, described the surrounding region for a hundred miles, made elaborate plans for the coming days, monologued on athletics, and praised the progress of the moving-picture drama, throwing in for good measure a story or two as revealed by the films. He made a gallant showing, and a hint of appreciation touched his companion's eyes once or twice as they rested upon him.

As he jumped into bed that night he smiled to himself in the darkness. The situation was becoming extremely interesting. They were not going to get a "rise" out of him. As for that girl, he'd give her the time of her life. He'd show her.

"Can you walk?" he asked her the next morning.

She did not seem to know, and gazed at Isabella for inspiration.

"Because we're going to walk," continued Billy, lightly. "You and I are going to do the Indian Trail. Be ready right after breakfast, please. I'll have Osaki put us up half a ton of luncheon."

She was ready on time, and appeared still wearing the brown skirt and bulging flannel blouse, with an added horror in the form of a mustard-colored blazer that set Billy's teeth on edge. But she could walk—

he soon discovered that; and to-day she seemed to know him a little better and to have lost some of her shyness. Once she spoke impulsively, and then, seeming to regret it, sank into a depressed silence, followed by a resolute effort to find out how much he knew about trees. Discovering that he knew nothing except that they were pleasant things to sit under, she told him all she knew, which took some time. It seemed that she loved to be among them, preferably alone. But not even this admission, for which she hurriedly apologized, not the relentless "pug," nor the prosaic shoes, could check the exhilaration that swept over Billy as they ate their luncheon together under the dim arches of the cathedral woods. Resolutely dismissing the subject of trees, he began to talk of life, of what it meant to a fellow just starting out—with ambitions. Of what girls could do to help him, especially the right kind of a girl; most of all, The Girl.

Miss Wickersham seemed interested. There was a more human look in her brown eyes. It appeared that society girls were mostly dolls—Billy had observed this. What a fellow needed was the home type of girl, the girl whose thoughts were not on clothes and parties. Could she, Miss Wickersham, cook? Billy asked the question with pathetic hopefulness, and Miss Wickersham seemed dazed. When she admitted that she could not, he turned away as if he had received a blow, and the lady regarded the back of his Norfolk jacket with a puzzled frown.

There was something about Billy she did not understand.

For three days he swept her out of camp immediately after breakfast and kept her all day long upon the sea or in the woods. They ate their luncheons beside driftwood fires, and in the evenings they sat out on the rocks, watching the moon, which posed for them esthetically in a fleckless sky. The third night they studied it until it was the only light in camp save one, and again Billy discoursed of life. Cooking, it appeared, was not important, after all. He dismissed it with the assurance of one who had recently eaten an excellent dinner. There were other things—inspiration, for example, and being understood! To be able to look past externals and know what a man or woman really was! To read the human heart and soul! For example, Billy was sure he could read her heart. He was equally sure she could read his. Hers was an unopened flower, waiting for the sun. Miss Wickersham gazed on the path of the moonlight, leading far out to sea, and coughed restlessly. Billy Bates was setting a pace she could not follow.

The interested Miss Beardslee was waiting for her when she returned to camp, and after a somewhat lingering good night to her escort Miss Wickersham entered the big living-room and turned fiercely upon her friend.

"I'm going to stop this nonsense," she said. "It's silly. And he's—he's rather wonderful!"

"Wonderful! *Billy?*" It would have chastened Billy to hear those two words as Harriet Beardslee uttered them.

"Yes, wonderful. He—well, he has found me, the real me, and I haven't made it easy."

"*What?*"

Helen nodded. "He has," she declared. Her voice softened. "He has," she repeated, dreamily.

Miss Beardslee shook off the spell that seemed settling upon them both. "You mean he's been making love to you," she said, with frank scorn. "Billy would do that to a wooden image. It doesn't mean a thing!"

"Oh, Harriet!"

"Do you *want* it to?"

"N-no. Of course not!"

"Well, then, play the game to the finish, as you promised. He is fooling you, and he'll have the laugh on his side yet if you don't watch out."

Any one but the irrepressible Billy Bates would have thrown up the sponge during the next two days, and it must be admitted that even Billy had moments of depression. One of these came when, after ten minutes of impassioned love-making on the sand, he discovered that Miss Wickersham had reverted to her former distressing habit of going to sleep. He stared at her incredulously. Was she pretending? If she was, she was doing it remarkably well. Nothing could have been more unstudied than her ungraceful pose and—he looked again and sighed; yes, her mouth *was* slightly open!

When she deigned to keep awake and to talk she expressed views that wounded Billy's sensibilities. Her interest in life was on a far higher plane than his, and as to men— It seemed that her ideal man was the brawny son of toil, the diamond in the rough, such as the cowboy of fiction. She admitted regretfully, when pressed to do so, that she had never met one in real life, but intimated that she still had hopes. She considered the Brotherhood of Locomotive Engineers the finest body of men in the world, with the possible exception of New York's mounted police. She liked big men. (Billy was of medium height.) She liked men who wore flannel shirts. (Billy dressed with unusual care.) In short, she was for brawn and simple hearts. It had taken two days to draw these convictions from her, and at the end of that time, when Billy began to talk, she had gone to sleep!

It was on the same rocks, two nights later, with that night rover, the moon, still chaperoning them, and the love-song of the sea in their ears, that Billy asked Miss Wickersham to marry him. For a long moment she stared at him without speaking. Then at the look in his eyes a big sob burst from her.

"But you don't really love me!" she cried. "You can't. You only love what you think I am."

The next minute she had gone, leaving Billy staring after her. Five minutes later she had hurled

226

herself into Miss Beardslee's tent, and was sobbing violently in the arms of that dazed young person.

"I won't go on with it another minute," she cried. "I won't! I won't! I don't care what I promised. I'm going to pack to-night and go away on the five-o'clock boat in the morning. You've got to explain everything and — and — t-take all the b-blame!"

Harriet grasped her shoulders and shook her. "Good heavens!" she cried in exasperation, "the blame for what? It's all a silly joke. Don't you realize that?"

"But he—he loves me," sobbed Miss Wickersham. "I mean he loves what he thinks I am. When he finds I'm different it will b-break his heart."

Miss Beardslee laughed, then hastened to apologize. "Billy with a broken heart is something I just can't see," she admitted. "But did he really ask you to marry him?" she added, incredulously. "*Really?*"

Miss Wickersham's face flamed into a white anger. "Yes, he did, *really*," she said, "and he meant it. I could tell by—by the look in his eyes." Her voice trembled. "But it isn't really me he loves," she repeated, miserably. "It's the girl he thinks I am. When he knows the truth he'll hate me. O-h-h-h!"

Under the force of that final wail Harriet's eyes widened. "Helen Wickersham!" she gasped. "You don't mean that in these few days you—you—" The thing was too incredible. She stopped.

"Yes, I do," flared her friend. In the next instant her resentment died. "But that's all the good it will do me," she added, dully. "He won't *look* at me when he knows the kind of girl I really am!"

Miss Beardslee's lips set. "You leave this to me," she said, and walked out of the tent.

She found Billy high on the rocks where Helen had left him. He volplaned down to meet her, with the shining eyes of a little boy.

"Harriet!" he jerked out, breathlessly. "Isn't it wonderful! She will take me, won't she? She's only a little frightened, isn't she? I was too sudden. I ought to have known better. Girls often rush off like that, don't they? But it can't mean that she won't—that she doesn't—"

Harriet drew a deep breath. "Billy," she said, imploringly, "tell me the truth. Are you in earnest?"

His eyes answered and she hurried on.

"What is it you see in Helen? She's so different from all your friends."

"That's it!" Billy's words leaped at her. "That's what I see. A fellow likes to play with society girls. But when he marries—"

Harriet felt herself skidding, and wondered wildly where she would bring up. "But she's bound to change, and—and—take her proper place," she urged. "You want her to be different, don't you, and develop—"

Billy shook his yellow head. "Not on your life!" he declared. "I don't want a single thing about her changed. I couldn't stand it. I want," he ended,

228

sentimentally, "I want the little brown wren I've been looking for all my life." At something he saw in Harriet's face he turned away hastily, as if to hide his emotion. "Send her here to me, Harriet," he urged in a choked voice. "That's a dear. Make her come back. Tell her I *must* have my answer to-night."

With reluctant steps Miss Beardslee returned to her tent. Of all the hideous mix-ups! Never again, she decided, would she take part in playing a practical joke. When she reached the tent Helen was still there, and she turned her out into the night with a friendly push on her shoulder.

"He's waiting for you," she said, somberly. "I —I—guess you two can fix it up together. If you can't, I'll try again."

Billy was still gazing out over the sea when Miss Wickersham reached his side, and he turned on her a face transfigured by the moonlight. Without a word he took her in his arms and held her there, and after a long interval she gulpingly began her confession, her wet cheek still against his.

"Oh, Billy," she cried, "I'm—such—a fraud! You won't—love—me—when—you—know."

Billy drew away, took her face between his hands, and looked into her wet brown eyes. "What do you mean?" he asked.

"You love me because you think I'm quiet and— and don't care for clothes or—or for society, but —but—I do. *I do!* I've been deceiving you, Billy, and I'm—utterly—wretched! I—I dance, and I run a motor, and—I—I do all sorts of things. I'm not a bit quiet or domestic."

"Anything else?" asked Billy in a strange voice.

"Yes. I—I wear good clothes, too!" she wailed.

Billy laughed. Then he kissed her. "I know you do," he said, comfortably. "I've seen you in them. I've seen you in the other kind, too! In short, I've seen you do 'The Country Mouse' before!"

"Wh—what!" This time it was she who drew back to stare at him.

He nodded. "Yes; I was in the audience when you did it in New York at the Belgian benefit. I recognized the 'make-up' the minute I saw you in it the morning we met here."

"Then you knew—all along—that I was—"

"Masquerading? Of course. It's been lots of fun! And *what* a rise I took out of poor Harriet just now! It was simply great!" Billy chuckled.

Miss Wickersham turned pale. "You mean—" she faltered.

"I mean," said Billy Bates, fervently, "that I adore you. I've been in love with you ever since I saw you in the play. And this raffle of mine was just a little scheme to get you all to myself this week. I knew the girls would swallow the bait, but I didn't think they'd gulp down the hook, too!"

And he kissed her again.

THIRTY-THREE CENTS, PLUS

A YOUNG man strode briskly along a highway of Westchester County. As he walked he whistled, and as he whistled he swung his stick ineffectually toward the swaying purple asters and the goldenrod of the hedges at his right and left. Around him hung the soft mists of an autumnal twilight, and in his ear the tinkle of a near-by cowbell and the honk of a distant automobile horn blended pleasantly. One spoke of the rural delights he was leaving—the other of the urban joys to which he was so soon to return. Also, and almost simultaneously, another sound reached him—the creaking of a weather-beaten signboard, swinging lightly in the evening breeze. Stopping short, he read it:

```
+-----------------------------------------+
|                                         |
|             Yᵉ Wayside Inn              |
|                                         |
|  Offering Comfort Alike to Man and Beast|
|                                         |
+-----------------------------------------+
```

Appreciatively his eyes traveled from the sign to the gate below it, then up a garden walk to a brown cottage over whose latticed veranda the vines of a morning-glory climbed. For a moment he regarded the place with pleasure, his elbows on the gate-post, an anticipatory smile on his lips. Then, on a sudden reflection, his brow darkened. He stepped back from the gate, thrust his hand into the right pocket of his trousers, and drew forth its contents—subsequently regarding with severe disapproval the varied collection of articles that lay upon his open palm. It comprised a silver quarter, a five-cent piece, three pennies, a match-box, and a two-cent stamp, the freshness of the last being considerably dimmed by intimate association with its neighbors. Still cherishing these articles, he set his lips and plunged an eager hand into the left pocket of his trousers, producing a silver cigarette-case which seemingly dwelt there in a splendid isolation.

The young man returned it to its place and muttered something under his breath. It sounded like a rude word, wholly out of harmony with the brooding peace around him. Hurriedly he went through the pockets of his coat, even through the tiny one over his heart. He found a silver key-ring with keys, a newspaper clipping, and a letter addressed to Mr. George Eddington, 147 East Seventy—— Street, New York. With another word, expressing even more untrammeled emotions than the first, he thrust these objects back into their original shelter. "By Jove!" he muttered, plaintively. "And I'm hungry!" Again he surveyed the collection of coins in his right hand. "Thirty-three cents," he muttered. "What a chump I was to leave myself so short."

THIRTY-THREE CENTS, PLUS

He recalled his balance at his banker's and a recent flurry in stocks, which had been to his advantage at the time but failed to cheer him now. Even for a walking-tour, he bitterly reflected, a man with forethought would have been too well supplied with cash to find himself reduced to thirty-three cents when still twenty miles from New York. He had bungled his tour, just as he bungled everything else that was really worth while. Resting his arms on the gate-post, he gave himself up to meditations which he imagined were philosophical, but which were merely the results of a growing impulse of hunger.

What had life given him, anyway? Thirty-three cents, plus sixty thousand dollars or so, and a good appetite which he was for the moment unable to satisfy. Nothing else—at least none of the big things other men had. No wife, no children, no love, no prospect of any. It was quite too harrowing—he dared not let his thoughts dwell on it further.

"Wonder how much comfort for man they give for thirty-three cents?" he mused, aloud. "I'll find out."

Restoring the change to his pocket, he opened the gate and strolled up the garden walk, looking around admiringly, smelling the mignonette that edged the path, and stopping to nod at a row of dahlias that seemed coyly bowing to him a few yards away. Just such a row had graced the back fence of his mother's garden when he was a little boy. "About

a thousand years ago," reflected Mr. George Eddington, drearily, "or was it twenty?"

Yᵉ Wayside Inn seemed strangely deserted. No
bustle of footsteps was heard inside as he approached
it, no voice was raised to greet him. But the big
front door was half an inch ajar, and the young man
pushed it open and entered.

He found himself in a tiny hall. At his right was a
closed door. At his left, through an arch, lay an old-
fashioned dining-room, long and wide, its beamed
ceiling dark with age, gay rag rugs upon its floor,
the blazing logs in a huge fireplace offering its sole
illumination. Half a dozen small tables stood
around the room, set for the service of afternoon tea,
and at one of these—the only person visible—sat a
girl in a brown golf costume, eating toasted muffins and jam and drinking tea. She wore a small,
close brown hat with a hint of red in it; and a golf-
bag, bulging with clubs, leaned against a chair behind
her. She made an attractive picture, and Mr. Eddington paused to regard it with approval. Then, as
she paid no attention to him, he walked into the
room, passed her with a slight bow and his cap in his
hand, and carefully selecting a near-by table from
which he could keep her in full view, sat down, and
waited for his tea.

In the fireplace a log broke and a shower of sparks
flew up the wide chimney. The girl, whose charming
profile was toward him, drank her tea with her eyes
fixed in an abstraction which probably had to do

with her excuses for missing that last putt. Mr. Eddington looked around for a bell or a bell-rope, and, not seeing one, coughed restlessly. Nobody came. He rose and started toward the girl in the golf costume. Without giving him time to speak she addressed him.

"If you clap your hands," she said, gently, "the Ogre may come."

Her voice was contralto, with really beautiful modulations, but under the force of her simple words the young man stopped and gaped at her.

"I—I beg your pardon," he stammered. He had a momentary but strong impression that he was asleep and dreaming a fantastic dream. But the liberal allowance of strawberry jam the girl was spreading on that muffin was reassuring. There was nothing dreamlike about her appetite, nor in the pang of hunger her chance companion experienced as he watched her.

"The Ogre," she repeated, patiently, with a courteous but impersonal glance at him. "If you clap, he may come."

Eddington clapped, feeling rather foolish. The Ogre did not come.

"Perhaps," suggested the young man, diffidently, "a loud cry of hunger might bring him. Do you mind if I try it?"

"Not in the least," said the girl, selecting another muffin and dipping anew into the pot of strawberry jam. She really had a very good appetite, Eddington reflected, with one hungry eye on the jam. He hoped it was not the last pot of jam in the place; and then he remembered that it didn't matter, anyway, as his thirty-three cents would hardly run to jam. Tea, toast, and a microscopic tip to the waiter seemed to be his program—assuming, that is, that the waiter, or the Ogre, ever came.

"You might beard him in his den," suggested the girl. "Through the door behind you, down that long hall, then to the right. Enter calmly, and keep your eyes on his while you speak."

"Thanks very much. Any password?" asked George, briskly, starting for the door.

"None. You must quell him by the power of the human eye."

Following her directions, Eddington found himself walking along a narrow and very dim corridor, and eventually standing before a closed door, which he opened without ceremony. He was in a small, clean kitchen, lit by a kerosene-lamp which stood on a table; and in the next instant he was confronted by the largest and most unprepossessing man he had ever seen.

"Six feet five at the least," George reflected as he unconsciously gave way a step before the figure that rose from the table and towered above him. The giant's breadth was in proportion to his height, his coarse thick hair stood up in a forbidding pompadour, and a deep scar furrowed one side of his face from temple to chin. He wore black trousers tucked into

high boots and a gray-flannel shirt with a turned-
down collar. Also, and this detail impressed his
caller more than any other, he seemed extremely
annoyed by the young man's appearance. The
guest found himself apologizing, as if he were an
intruder.

"E-excuse me," he began, uncertainly. "I'm
looking for the waiter or the proprietor."

"What you want?"

The Ogre's voice was as unattractive as his face
and manner—harsh and guttural; but by this time
the visitor had recovered his nerve. Also he remembered the instructions of the girl in the dining-
room. He gazed steadily into the Ogre's small
black eyes, and the Ogre returned an unwinking
stare.

"Oh, lots of things," said Eddington, airily. "A
waiter first, a menu next, and then things to eat."

"There iss no menu."

"Oh," muttered Eddington, rather blankly. He
had planned to cast a piercing glance at the menu
and to select those dishes that lay within his humble
means. He still clung to the Ogre's eyes, but there
was a growing uncertainty in his own. It was hu-
miliating, but he must ask a question.

"How—how much is tea and toast?" he inquired.

"Twenty-fi' cen's."

"All right. Tea and toast—and quick, please."

He threw out the last words with a forced im-
periousness, designed to cover his embarrassment of

the moment before. "I've been waiting fifteen minutes already," he added, as he turned to leave the room.

A quarter for his tea left five cents for the Ogre's service, and three cents for the journey to New York —hardly enough, but for the moment Eddington ignored that trivial detail. He was about to be fed, and he was returning to the girl in brown. Both were pleasant reflections. He found her pouring out her last cup of tea. The muffins and jam had disappeared. She *had* an appetite! He approached her with easy camaraderie.

"I found him," he told her, "thanks to you."

"There are two candles on the mantel," she remarked. "Would you mind lighting them? I have no matches."

A friendly darkness, he now observed, was folding itself round them. He found the brass candlesticks on the mantelpiece, and lit the half-burned wax candles they contained. The illumination merely emphasized the dimness of the room by throwing up its shadows. He threw another log on the fire and returned to her side.

"May I ask you a few questions?" he suggested, "about this place? I feel as if we were meeting in a dream or a fairy-tale."

She smiled. "Poor Alexis," she said. "It is no fairy-tale for him. His employer, who is a Russian woman, opened this place four years ago, and succeeded very well. When the war began her two brothers were wounded, and she returned to Russia to look after them. She left Alexis in charge, and Alexis is very honest but very stupid. He thinks every one who comes here is trying to rob his absent employer—so he has driven most of her customers away. When she comes back I'm afraid she'll find nothing left but her sign, swinging in the wind."

"She'll find her Alexis swinging in the wind," predicted Eddington, darkly, "if he doesn't bring me something to eat pretty quick. By Jove! I never was so hungry in my life—and I haven't even a cigarette left."

He drew out his empty case and surveyed it bitterly. She looked at it, too—casually at first, then closely and with a sudden gleam in her eye which in his abstraction he failed to observe.

"I'm sorry I've nothing left to stay you till Alexis comes," she murmured, a more cordial note in her voice than it had yet held, "but I'll give you this comforting knowledge: what Alexis deigns to prepare is really good. Your meal will be delicious."

"I'm not going to have a meal," said the young man, with unconscious pathos. "I'm going to have tea and toast—and save my appetite till I get back to town," he added, hastily. Then he leaned toward her with an appealing, boyish smile.

"May he serve my tea here?" he begged, "at your table? Say yes. It wouldn't be fair to cast me into the outer darkness of a table alone, would it now?"

For a moment she studied him without replying, but with a faint smile. Under its encouragement, he went on.

"Besides, I've got to save you from the Ogre. At exactly the right moment, *after* I've had tea, I shall do it—in the showiest manner."

"Remain then," she said, "on the distinct understanding that you will die for me."

"If *necessary*," corrected the young man, dropping into the chair opposite her, "and preferably after a lifetime of service and devotion." Seeing her eyebrows rise, he rushed into generalities. "The dramatic value of these hasty, messy deaths," he added, "has been greatly exaggerated."

Alexis brought the tea, excellent tea, as the girl had predicted, and thin slices of delicately browned and buttered toast.

"The strawberry jam," she recommended, "is excellent."

"None for me," said her companion. "I'm positive you haven't left any in the place. But if you would only pour my tea, and share it—"

"I will pour," she agreed, beginning the task, "but not share. I have had two cups already."

"Four," corrected Eddington, incautiously.

She ignored the word.

"Do you like it weak or strong?" she inquired.

He told her, regarding with delight the picture she made. It was a wonderful experience to be sitting with her in the dim old room, in this companionable way. His heart was beating a little faster than usual.

"Sugar?" she asked, "and cream?"

"Yes, thanks. But you really ought to know," murmured the young man. "You have poured it for me every day for the past ten years."

She stared at him.

"In my dreams," explained Eddington, cheerfully, as he took the cup.

"Oh!"

For a moment she seemed at a loss, but her brown eyes still shone at him out of the firelit room with a soft brilliance in their depths, and in them lay something else, a gleam of tolerant, friendly understanding. Her face, Eddington told himself, was really beautiful. Gazing at it in rapture over a slice of buttered toast, he went on.

"Yes," he mused, "I've seen you every day for ten years, looking exactly as you do now—the same deep, wonderful brown eyes, the same beautiful mouth—"

"And I hope," she interjected, "the same expression of disapproval at this point. Really, you know—"

"Not at all," interrupted Eddington. "You're always heavenly kind—in my dreams. The same brown hair, too, with the same wave in it, and the same hint of red—"

"Life," she mused, "must be difficult for an impulsive temperament like yours."

"But it isn't impulsive," he protested. "I've never been impulsive before—except in my dreams."

"Because one day," she added, following her own train of thought, "some girl will take advantage of your absent-mindedness, if you prefer to call it that. Then, before you know what has happened, you will be assuring some clergyman that you *do*."

"There is exactly one woman in the world for whom I would make that promise," murmured Eddington, beginning on his last piece of toast.

"Ah, really!" She seemed interested, and also relieved. "You have found her, then."

"Of course I have," explained the young man. "I've already mentioned that to you. But," he added, hurriedly, as she was about to speak, "of course I realize that as I know her so slightly I must not alarm her by being abrupt. I must proceed cautiously and slowly and tactfully."

"She will, no doubt, appreciate your consideration," murmured his companion, without interest.

"Naturally," added Eddington, offering her his cup to be refilled, "a man knows the One Woman the first time he meets her. He doesn't always tell her so; he cannot always get her (two lumps, please); but the alarm-clock of his life strikes twelve the minute he sees her. (Yes, a little more cream.) It's his warning to wake up and win her; and if he's a man he drops everything else and, as we Americans say, 'gets busy.'"

She gave him his tea in silence, and he drank it

slowly while she settled back into her chair and began to search the pocket of her tweed skirt. Eddington's heart sank. Had he offended her? She was about to pay her bill and depart, and he could think of no good excuse for detaining her. However, and his spirits revived at the thought, considering the lateness of the hour, he could surely escort her to the station or to her home, if the latter happened to be in the neighborhood. He swallowed the last of his tea, and as if in response to his frantic mental summons, Alexis now loomed darkly at his elbow, presenting his bill.

Eddington gave him the silver quarter, unostentatiously adding the nickel. He observed that Alexis was still waiting, his heavy gaze fixed on the lady's charming face. That face was now flushed and anxious, and the girl in brown was plunging her hand excitedly into the side pockets of her coat. A small collection of feminine possessions lay on the table before her—a handkerchief, a score-card, a note-book, a gold pencil. As Eddington surveyed this she turned to him, her cheeks flushing more darkly, all her self-possession gone.

"Do you know," she gasped, "I haven't my purse with me! *What* shall I do? I've been here several times, and Alexis knows me—but he'll never let me go until I pay."

Eddington's lips curved into a reassuring smile, which suddenly froze upon them. His heart dropped a beat. He had remembered his three pennies and his postage stamp. His stupefaction, however, was but momentary, and her own excitement made his companion oblivious to it.

"Leave that to me," he said, reassuringly. "I will attend to the matter."

"But—" protested the lady.

"I beg of you." Eddington silenced her with an eloquent wave of the hand. He was glad of her protest. It gave him time to think. Alexis was still standing beside him. He appeared, under the combined effect of the situation and the darkness, to be about ten feet tall. The young man had a wild thought of taking him out and slaying him and hiding his body in the cellar; but after one glance at the huge figure that seemed to fill the room he abandoned this plan. The girl in brown was murmuring something.

"It's horribly embarrassing, but if you will be so kind—and let me send you the amount by mail—"

With set teeth Eddington plunged his hand into his left pocket. It was an instinctive gesture, made to gain time. The fingers close on his heavy silver cigarette-case. He leaned forward and picked up the lady's check. Seventy cents! No wonder, he reflected, bitterly—all that strawberry jam! She must have eaten jars and jars of it. And buttered muffins, too—such extravagance!

Slipping the cigarette-case under the check, he handed both to Alexis, firmly closing the latter's huge hand over them. "And keep the change, Alexis," he added. He rose, and, taking the arm of the stunned Russian, whose mental operations seemed to have stopped, led him firmly into the hall. "Keep your mouth shut," he hissed when they had reached that refuge. "The cigarette-case is worth fifty dollars. I'll come back and pay the bill to-morrow, and give you five dollars for yourself." He thrust the Ogre into the kitchen and returned hurriedly to his lady's side. He was anxious to get away, and it was a relief to find her standing ready, with her golf-bag in her hand. Taking this from her, he led the way down the garden path, haunted by fears that even yet the Ogre might pursue them. Outside of the gate he paused and looked at her. "Which way?" he asked.

"Why, New York," she told him. "That is," she added, consciously, "if you'll add to your kindness by getting me a ticket!"

Under the horrible shock of her words Eddington stood still. He had three pennies and a stamp, and with this he was expected to get a lady and himself back to New York! Then he found his voice.

"Splendid!" he cried. "I'm going back to town, too."

He strode beside her to the station, his mind working feverishly while he lent an absent ear to what she was saying. What should he do? An impulse to return to the inn, on the pretext of having forgotten something, and wrest the money from Alexis, died under a sudden appreciation of the difficulty of that enterprise. Then, like a lightning flash in a storm, the thought of his silver match-box came to him, and he walked on with a lighter step. Also, he was able to smile and make an occasional coherent remark.

He had planned his campaign by the time they reached the station, and on entering the waiting-room he led his companion, with much care, to that end of it which was out of view of the ticket window and the young person in charge. Having seated her, he retraced his steps and confronted a languid youth in the ticket-office. At his first words the youth's languor disappeared and he eyed Eddington with dark suspicion. The silver match-box lay on the wooden ledge between them.

"Will you give me two tickets to New York for this?" asked Eddington, flushing a little.

"No, sir," said the youth, promptly. "I won't."

"Why not?"

"Because this is a cash business."

The youth grinned at his own humor, and Eddington, slightly encouraged, forced himself to grin back.

"I'm in a hole," he said, frankly. "The details wouldn't interest you, but I've got a lady with me and I haven't a cent. The box is worth twenty times the price of the two tickets. Can't you take a chance?"

The youth stared at him and he stared back at the youth, with more appeal than he had ever thrown into his eyes before. The ticket-seller picked up the

match-box and looked at it. It was a handsome
box.

"I'll come back to-morrow and redeem it," urged
Eddington, "and pay for the tickets. Come, help
me out—like a good fellow."

The youth dropped the match-box into his pocket,
and from another pocket drew a small handful of
silver. Rather too ostentatiously he counted out the
price of the tickets and dropped the money into his
cash-drawer. Then he stamped the tickets and
thrust them toward the would-be traveler. Picking
them up, Eddington saw that they had a little companion—a silver ten-cent piece.

"What's that for?" he asked, turning redder.

"Car fare," replied the youth, laconically. "Got
to get her home, 'ain't you? But you can spend it
for a wine supper, if you'd rather," he added. Then,
repressing his tendency to levity, he went on, grimly:
"This is a pers'nal matter. Understand? When
you settle, if you ever do, you settle with me."

"I'll settle with you to-morrow. Thanks," said
Eddington, conquering with difficulty an impulse to
take the lad by the collar and shake him. Indeed,
his resentment of the other's manner was so keen
that he spent the ensuing ten minutes over a time-
table in preference to asking an entirely proper question as to the departure of the next train.

"We leave in a quarter of an hour," he explained,
as he rejoined the girl in brown, whose solitude had
been disturbed by the arrival of a fretful baby and its

tired mother, and a young woman who was chewing gum with an energy out of all proportion to the importance of the occupation. Having surveyed this person with disfavor, he suggested that they stroll on the station platform.

Night had fallen and the stars were out. The rising autumn wind was soft and cold. It ruffled the brown hair of his companion, bringing out a curl or two from under the shelter of the little hat.

"And now," began Eddington, "now that all the sordid details are settled, let us resume our interrupted conversation. When did you say you would marry me?"

She smiled into the darkness. "What an extraordinary person you are!" she murmured.

"I know my own mind," he admitted, complacently.

"Perhaps—though I doubt it. But you don't know me."

"We're even on that score."

"Indeed we're not. I know you quite well."

He stared at her. "You know me?" he stammered.

"Of course. If I hadn't, do you suppose I would have let you talk to me, pay for my tea and my ticket—"

"We've never met—"

"No."

"Nor seen each other—"

"No. And yet I know you."

248

"Some one," mused Eddington, "has described to you a superman, and quite naturally you think you recognize him now. But I am not Adolphus Cadwalader Blinks, or whatever the phenomenon's name may be."

"You are George Eddington," she said. "And it was not you I recognized, but something about you."

"Something about me? What?"

"Oh, I mustn't tell you that. It wouldn't be kind!"

"Why—what—Great Scott! What d'ye mean?"

The headlight of the locomotive shone out of the darkness. When the train stopped he helped her on board in a daze, and during the short journey back to the city he tried in vain to solve the puzzle she had offered him. To all his questions, his guesses, she responded only by a shake of the head.

"I won't discuss it," she declared. And she repeated, darkly, "It wouldn't be nice of me."

At the New York station she insisted on being put into a taxicab. "You will kindly *not* pay the driver," she directed, with a gleam in her eyes which he did not see. "My debt is too large already. Once home, my family will come to my rescue."

"And the address?" demanded Eddington, hopefully.

She mentioned it, and he repeated it to the driver. Then as he stood with his hand on the door he had just closed, gazing at her through the open window, something in his expression touched her.

"Good night, Mr. Eddington," she said, gently, offering him her hand, and she added, with an adorable smile, "Give my love to Ollie."

"Olivia? You know my sister?" he cried.

"Very well. So well that we often go shopping together. I was with her last Christmas"—she hesitated—"when she bought a present for you?"

His eyes shone as he leaned toward her. One thought filled his mind, to the exclusion of all others.

"Then it's clear sailing!" he cried. "You must be Ruth Crowell. Ollie's been trying to bring us together for months. Will you go out to Westchester with me to-morrow? It's perfect weather for golf!"

"To-morrow? But your work—"

"Is it possible you have forgotten so soon?" he demanded. "The only work for a man to do when the One Woman comes—"

"To-morrow, then," she said, hastily. And just as the cab started she added, wickedly, "And while we're there, we'll redeem the cigarette-case Ollie gave you!"

The taxicab hummed away. Eddington stood still, staring after it until it was out of sight. Then he looked up at the stars and drew a deep breath. Two hours ago he had been a lonely man, whining mentally over a few coins in his hand. Since then those coins had opened a new world to him—a world in which existence was a wonderful, an indescribably beautiful experience.

"Thirty-three cents," he mused, "plus love! What a difference! By Jove! it's great to be alive!"

AN INTERLUDE

M ISS JESSICA GIBSON stood at the extreme
right end of the veranda that ran the front
length of the Gibson home. Mr. "Ben" Van Allen
stood at the extreme left end of the same veranda.
Between them stretched a gulf of despair, a valley of
humiliation, and a mountain of misunderstanding.
For they had quarreled. At Ben's feet, tossed with
unexpected accuracy of aim, lay the ring he had given
Jessica the month before. He spurned it with the
toe of his tan shoe, and the diamond in the ring
winked at him as if in sardonic understanding.
Stiffly, and with the awful dignity of twenty-three,
Ben stooped and picked it up.

"Then this is final?" he asked, the chill of an autumn wind in his boyish voice.

"Absolutely."

Jessica thought the word sounded very well as it
fell from her lips. She had heard it frequently, for it
was a favorite with her mother—a lady of positive
expression. Jessica had never expected to hurl it
into Ben's ear in an interview like this. But she was
glad she had thought of it, for Ben's actions immediately proved he had got its full effect. With his

head very high and lips tightly set, he dropped the ring into his pocket and turned on his heel.

"Then good-by," he said, and walked quickly down the veranda steps and toward the gate.

Jessica regarded him with eyes widened by surprise and pain. Obviously, since they were to part forever, Ben's cue was to go, as hers was to remain. But she had not expected to get this appallingly final effect from the lines of his back and the set of his shoulders, while the very gravel in the path he trod seemed to cry out against the decision of his footsteps. He was half-way to the gate; now he was at the gate; now his hand was on the latch.

"Ben—"

Jessica's cry died before it was born. Her mouth, opened to emit it, closed self-consciously. Her mother's decided voice was in her ears, and that stout and majestic lady was just stepping, not without difficulty, over the low ledge of the long French window opening from the living-room to the veranda.

"What's the matter with Ben?" she asked when this manœuver had been safely accomplished and she was at her daughter's side.

"Nothing."

Jessica's tone was that of one deeply injured and unforgiving, but much of this feeling was directed toward her mother, whose inopportune appearance had checked her appeal to Ben. To call to Ben in another's presence, and have Ben ignore the cry, would have been too horrible. Mrs. Gibson favored her daughter with her close attention.

"For a young man who has nothing the matter with him," she remarked, tersely, "he exuded a surprising amount of gloom and resentment. Have you two been quarreling?"

Jessica did not reply. Her mother's eyes traveled from her flushed face to the bare finger which Ben's ring had so recently adorned, and her eyebrows mounted toward her gray pompadour in sudden understanding.

"So it's as bad as that?" she mused, and asked, abruptly, "What did you quarrel about?"

"Pl-*please* don't ask any questions, mother," begged Jessica. "I don't want to talk about it. I—I *can't*."

"Don't you think your mother ought to know what has happened?"

Mrs. Gibson was becoming more majestic. She was a frequent speaker before women's clubs, and something of her platform manner occasionally appeared in her home circle when she was facing a domestic crisis. It appeared now, and Jessica, an exquisite, tiny, fragile thing, usually easily swayed, instinctively started to respond. Then, on a sudden reflection, her manner stiffened.

"Please don't ask me to talk about it, mother," she said, resolutely. And she added, dropping into a chair and burying her face in her hands with a shudder, "It's too dreadful!"

Her mother followed her and looked down on the bent figure, a gleam of tenderness coming into her shrewd eyes.

"Very well, my dear," she said, kindly. "Keep your own counsel. The quarrel probably doesn't amount to much, anyway." Then, because to give advice was a law of her nature, she added: "Write Ben a little note and tell him you're sorry. He will be back in half an hour."

But at this Jessica's spirit flashed up again.

"Write him a note!" she echoed, fiercely. "Well, I guess not. If any notes are written, Ben Van Allen will write them, and I won't forgive him unless he takes back what he said. Why, mother, it was dreadful. I never dreamed Ben was like that." And she added, solemnly, "It's a matter of principle."

Mrs. Gibson's smile faded. "Of principle?" she asked, severely. "Of what principle?"

"I can't explain, and I wouldn't, anyway," said Jessica. "It hasn't anything to do with any one but Ben and me, but it concerns our whole future. I can't change my con-convictions for any man," she sobbed, "not even for Ben. And—and no one can help me, because no one can possibly understand."

Mrs. Gibson's somewhat austere features relaxed. That serious thought of any kind was going on in her daughter's head was sufficiently surprising. Others had thought for Jessica ever since her birth, eighteen years before. That an actual conviction had now found lodgment in her soul was a phenomenon almost too startling to contemplate. No wonder it had upset Ben. No wonder it was causing the poor child herself considerable discomfort. But Jessica must be encouraged to endure these psychical growing-pains. Mrs. Gibson had moments of insight, and this was one of them.

"If it's a matter of principle, my dear," she said, gently, "that's quite different. You are right to stand up for your convictions. I'm sure Ben will realize this when he has had time to think things over. Give him a chance; and meanwhile, don't worry about it."

She went into the house, and Jessica, about to follow her, was checked by the sight of her father, walking slowly up the long path from the gate. She would have preferred not to see him just then, but she had no choice, for he had already seen her. Slowly she went to meet him, and without a word raised her face for his usual kiss. When he had given it he held her head between his hands, looking at her with eyes that held a steady twinkle, softened now by quick concern.

"You've been crying," he exclaimed. "What's up?"

Jessica twisted her face out of the encircling hands, took his arm, and led him slowly toward the house.

"Nothing," she said again. "That is, everything's all right at home. It's nothing to worry you."

LOVERS' KNOTS

Her father turned off the path and toward a rustic bench under his favorite elm. There he made her sit down, and, seating himself beside her, took off his straw hat and fanned his heated face with it. "Whew! it's hot!" he said, and chatted a moment casually, giving the child time to collect herself. Then he returned to the vital topic.

"Anything that worries you worries me," he reminded her, gently; "so let's have it out. About Ben?"

She nodded, speechless.

"Anything he has done?"

She shook her head. "Not exactly anything he has *done,*" she admitted. "It's worse than that. It's—it's something he said. It disappointed me horribly. It showed me he isn't the—the boy I thought he was. So our engagement's b-broken o-off!"

The last words came out in a mournful gurgle as she turned suddenly and buried her head in her father's shoulder. He let her cry while he patted her cheek, thinking rapidly. This was the worst, he reflected, of an engagement between a pair of kids like Ben and Jessica. Their little difference might mean nothing at all—the spilling of a few grains of sawdust, perhaps, out of their doll—or it might mean the upsetting of the whole apple-cart.

"Tell father all about it," he invited, guardedly.

A negative shake of the hidden head was his answer.

"But I can't advise you till I know what has happened," he persisted.

Jessica found her voice, wiped her eyes, and brought forth her heavy reserves, remembering their effect on her mother.

"It's a matter of principle," she told him, and went a step further. "Ben's principles are not what I thought they were," she added.

"But how do you know this? How can you be sure?" Her father was patiently groping in the dark.

"He—he—admitted it. He—he—confessed it to me to-day," gurgled Jessica.

Mr. Gibson frowned, then hurriedly smiled, for Jessica's eyes were searching his face.

"I guess it wasn't a very startling confession," he remarked, comfortably, though his heart sank. "What did he say?" If the boy had foolishly sown some wild oats at college, and had confessed it, there was no telling to what lengths Jessica's inexperience might carry her.

"Now come," he said, cheerfully; "I think we can fix this up. I'll have a few words with Ben as man to man, and you'll trust your father's judgment as a court of appeal, won't you?"

He pulled a curl as he spoke, but again Jessica revealed an unexpected obstinacy.

"Father," she said, firmly, "all you and mother can do for me is to leave this matter alone. It's my affair and Ben's, and no one else's. And it would

make us both very angry if any one interfered.
I want you to promise me not to do a single
thing."

Mr. Gibson promised, with inward reservations.
He decided, comfortably, that he'd "leave the thing
alone for a day or two," giving the children a chance
to come to their senses and fix it up themselves.
But at the end of a day or two matters had passed
far beyond the stage when tact and judicious inter-
ference might have saved the situation. For Jessica
had admitted to her best girl friend that her engagement was broken. Ben had made a similar confidence to one of his friends, both friends had told
others, and the little summer resort was humming
with gossip which grew with each tongue that turned
it over. No one knew the cause of the quarrel between the lovers, but quite obviously young Van
Allen was the person in the wrong. He was almost
a stranger in Broxton—this was his first season there
—whereas the Gibsons had been residents of the
place for the past ten summers and Jessica was very
popular. Within a week after the quarrel half the
citizens of Broxton were looking at Ben askance,
to that youth's great mystification. Soon several
of the rumors which were floating about reached
Mr. Gibson's ears. In some consternation he addressed his wife when he got home.

"Exactly what was it that Ben confessed to
Jessica?" he asked, in what he hoped was an offhand manner. Mrs. Gibson looked worried.

"I don't know," she admitted. "Jessica wouldn't tell me. She said it was too horrible."

Mr. Gibson pondered this in silence for a moment.

"There's a good deal of talk about it," he told her then. "In their efforts to explain the break people are telling one another all they have heard or can imagine about Ben. Some of it"—he hesitated—"some of it's not pretty," he concluded at last.

"What are they saying?" demanded his wife.

"Well, all sorts of things. That he's a perfect young Nero, for one thing; has a temper that makes him act like a madman at times—oh, a lot of stuff. I never suspected anything of that kind. Did you?"

Mrs. Gibson avowed promptly that she had not, but she looked very thoughtful.

"Perhaps that is what he admitted to Jessica," she reflected, aloud.

"I guess Jessica Gibson's well out of that engagement with Van Allen, after all," the brother of Jessica's closest girl friend told his sister. "I never knew Van Allen till this summer, and he's seemed an awfully decent chap. But, from all they're saying, I'm afraid he has fooled us, Minnie. Don't see any more of him than you can help, will you?"

"But what are they saying?" demanded Minnie Cary, resentfully. "I'm not going to cut Ben Van Allen till I know what he's done. I think he's a perfect dear."

Her brother regarded her disapprovingly. "Why can't you girls learn to stand by one another?" he demanded. "Look at the way he's treated Jessica. Isn't that enough for you?"

"It might be if I knew what he had done," persisted Minnie; "but she won't tell me."

"Then I guess you'd better follow her example and drop him," said her brother. "She wouldn't do it without good reason. Besides—well, 'knocking' people isn't much in my line, but they say Van Allen is an awful brute under that candy-angel outside of his. Edwards, that Boston chap who's visiting the Wallaces, was his room-mate at New Haven in their Freshman year. The two don't even speak now, and Edwards refuses to talk about Van Allen at all. But they say he knows things that would shut Van Allen out of decent society if he told of them."

"Jessica," mused his sister, "*did* say something about Ben's being the brute type."

"Then that's it," decided her brother. "She's heard something pretty bad. That must be it, or there wouldn't be all this talk about him."

In the next few weeks Minnie Cary heard many additional surmises about the breaking of the Gibson-Van Allen engagement. Jessica Gibson had found out "something horrible" in Ben Van Allen's past. Every imagination in Broxton had promptly set itself to work on a conception of what this horrible thing could be.

AN INTERLUDE

Realizing the seriousness of the situation, Minnie flew to Jessica, but Jessica refused to discuss Ben with any one. Indeed, the only time she listened to anything that was said about him, and showed any feeling over it, was when her father drew her to his side one day, a month after the breaking of the engagement, and said, quietly:

"I'm afraid you were right about Van Allen, dear. I didn't think so at first. But from all I've heard since, it's pretty plain he's not the man for you."

Jessica's pale face grew a little paler. The big brown eyes, which of late had held an expression her father could not bear to meet, filled with tears. But she made no reply. That Ben Van Allen was supremely and ideally the man for her her hungry heart was assuring her every minute of the interminable days that had passed since their parting. But she could not talk about him, even with her father, and she could not talk to Ben, either, for she had never caught a glimpse of him since the morning when she had thrown her ring at his feet. She declined all invitations and drooped mournfully at home.

Ben, on the other hand, tried to live his life as if nothing had occurred, the only difference being that he sought diversion a little more strenuously than ever before. But, as time passed, all the forces of local society seemed arrayed against him. His acquaintances, cool from the breaking of his engagement, finally vouchsafed him only a curt recognition.

Any group he joined at the Country Club or the Boat Club guiltily ceased talking when he appeared. It did not require much intuition to realize that they were talking about him.

Entering the Country Club one Saturday morning, nobody seemed conscious of his presence. Everybody he approached was hurriedly going somewhere else. Not an eye met his, not a hand was extended in greeting. The thing was so marked that even through the clouds of his enveloping gloom Ben perceived it. With the compression of the lips characteristic of him in moments of emotion, he pursued and caught by the arm one of the men he knew best after his two months' sojourn among them. It happened to be young Cary.

"Jack," he said, quietly, "what's the meaning of all this?"

"All what? What are you driving at?" Cary was flustered, and showed it.

"What's the matter with all you fellows? Why am I cut dead?" persisted Ben.

Cary hesitated. Ben looked him straight in the eye.

"Come," he said, imperatively; "out with it, please. What's up? It isn't quite a square deal to act like this and then refuse to explain."

Cary stuttered a little. He was having an unpleasant five minutes.

"Why," he said at last, "there's—there's a lot of feeling against you, Van Allen. Surely you realize that."

Ben kept his steady eyes on him. "What are they saying?" he demanded. But Cary broke away from the hand that held his arm.

"Oh, come now," he exclaimed. "Don't try that. You know what started it."

"Yes," said Ben, "but a whole club doesn't cut a fellow dead because his engagement is broken. What's up?"

"Why," hesitated Cary, "it's the kind of thing they're saying about you. I'm not going to stand here and repeat the stuff."

"But you must believe it," said Ben, quietly, "or you wouldn't act as you do. So out with it. Give me a fair deal."

Cary looked around wildly for reinforcements, but no one approached the two men, and Ben had him backed into a corner from which he could hardly get away.

"It isn't any one thing," he said at last. "It's dozens of things."

"Oh, it's dozens of things, is it? Well, let's have a few dozen."

Ben's pink face had gone white. His clear blue eyes held a strange glitter. Looking into them, Cary experienced a sudden pang of sympathy.

"Look here, old chap," he said. "It's hard luck. I don't believe 'em—all," he added the last word rather lamely. "But where there's so much smoke there's some fire, and if half they say is true, it's a pretty big indictment against you."

"Give me a few specimens."

Ben's voice was very steady. Cary, after an instant, obeyed him.

"Oh, it began," he said, lamely, "with what Miss Gibson said."

Ben whitened a little. "Yes," he said, quietly. "And after that—"

Cary reflected. "The first definite thing after that," he went on, reluctantly, "was Edwards's story about the saddle-horse you killed. He said you rode it to death in one of your black moods."

"Yes," said Ben. "Edwards! I see. Go on."

"Why—why, after that," stammered Cary, "everything came out. You see," he added, "when a man's room-mate 'knocks' him, and his fiancée throws him over, everything is bound to come out."

Ben laughed a little, an odd laugh which Cary didn't like.

"So that's what I'm up against," he said, quietly. "It all came out, and I guess the truth is that it all came out of Edwards." He turned to leave the club. At the door he paused. "Can't you tell me anything more definite about what else came out?" he asked.

"No," said Cary, with recovered assurance. He believed now that Ben was fully as black as he had been painted. "You've got enough to go on, haven't you?"

"Yes," said Ben, gently, "I've got enough to go on."

And he went. During the day he went among his club acquaintances, getting from each of them some part of the general arraignment against him. Also, he sought Edwards, but Edwards was singularly elusive.

Ben left Broxton early the next morning, vastly interesting several citizens who recognized him as he got on the train. That day the little town buzzed louder than ever. Ben Van Allen had found the place too hot to hold him, so Ben Van Allen had fled. The new friends Ben had made during the summer days sighed and tried to forget him. Edwards and his set openly exulted.

Both friends and enemies were surprised, five days later, when Ben Van Allen returned to Broxton and walked straight from the station to the Gibson house, carrying a small leather bag in his hand. It was five o'clock in the afternoon. Mr. Gibson was resting comfortably in his library, with his daughter near him, when Ben's card was handed to Jessica. She uttered a little gasp as she read the name, then rose. Looking up, her father caught her expression.

"Who is it?" he asked, quickly.

"Ben," said Jessica. "Oh, dad, it's Ben!" Her face was radiant; her heart was in her voice as she started toward the door.

"Hold on a minute," said Mr. Gibson, rising hastily. "I'm going with you."

She opened her lips to protest, but he silenced her with a motion of the hand.

"My girl," he said, "I'm going with you. I ought to go alone," he added, "but I'll compromise by letting you come, too."

After that there seemed nothing for Jessica to say. Together she and her father went to their guest. Ben, sitting in a corner of the large, shaded living-room, rose as they came in. He came forward to meet them, but did not offer to shake hands or to put down the bag. His face was very pale, and he looked thinner and older than in June.

"Jessica," he asked, without taking time for any greeting, "do you know what they've been saying about me in this town?"

There was neither resentment nor appeal in his voice. It held, instead, a certain flatness, as if he were very indifferent or very tired. Jessica looked at him, and at the changes she saw tears filled her eyes.

"About—about our engagement, do you mean?" she faltered.

"Yes," said Ben; "of course that started it. And about my character. Haven't you heard the gossip?"

Jessica shook her head. Ben turned to her father.

"You haven't told her?" he said, dully. "That was good of you. But I want her to know now." He turned to Jessica before her father could speak. "I'm an outcast," he added, in the same flat tone; "a pariah. I want you to take that fact in, please, before you interrupt."

266

He told the story of his experience at the Country Club, and his interview with Cary and the others, dispassionately, as if what he said concerned some one else. Then he hesitated for a minute and started to open the black bag. But before he could do so something soft hurled itself into his arms, while something damp and infinitely tender lay against his cheek.

"Oh, Ben!" sobbed the girl who loved him. "You poor, poor boy! To think they've dared to say such things about you! How perfectly horrible this world is!"

She put both arms around his neck and held him close, as if in doing so she could shut away from him all unkindness, all criticism. For a moment he remained silent in her embrace. Then he put his hands on her shoulders, held her off, and stared at her as if he could not believe his eyes.

"Then you don't—you don't *believe* the stuff!" he stammered.

"*Believe* it! Ben Van Allen, how silly you are! I could slap you for even asking that."

Jessica's tears had stopped flowing. Her wet eyes flashed at him. "Do you think I'm *crazy?*" she demanded. "I'd just like to hear any one *dare* to say anything about you to me."

"But—but they're saying," gasped poor Ben, "that you broke our engagement because you knew I was that sort—a perfect beast, you know."

"It's lucky for them they didn't say that to me,"

exclaimed Jessica between small, clenched teeth. "I'd like to see any one dare to attack you to me!"

A great gulp, like the sob of a little boy, wrenched Ben Van Allen's throat. He swallowed it, and bent his head to hide the tears in his blue eyes—the first tears he had shed since he had been a very little boy indeed.

"Then it's all right," he said at last, brokenly, "and these things aren't as important as I thought they were."

As he spoke, and as if partly to hide his agitation, he stooped and picked up the black bag which now lay on the floor at his feet. With hands that shook he opened it, revealing a formidable mass of letters and documents with impressive seals.

"You see," he explained, as he handed a bundle of these to Jessica's father, "there was only one definite charge, and it's perfectly true. I did give a terrific thrashing to one of my classmates at New Haven when I was a Freshman. The man was Edwards, and every one in college knew he deserved what he got. But he never forgave me, and this summer gave him his chance to get even. All the other stuff about my ungovernable temper and my brutality grew from that episode which Edwards described without admitting that he was in it. The rest he helped along by nods and hints, and the damned thing grew and grew till it blotted out every friendship I had made in Broxton. Shows what a thin crust we stand on, doesn't it? To clear my record I've got letters here from my professors at New Haven, from men in my class, from Prexie himself, who knew all about the Edwards fracas. The whole business was so silly that I'd have cleared out of this gossip-ridden little hole without giving it another thought, except for Jessica. But I couldn't let her think the man she had been engaged to—"

"The man I *am* engaged to," corrected Jessica, firmly. "Ben Van Allen, where's my ring?"

Again they were in each other's arms. Mr. Gibson observed them with pleasure for a moment, then dropped the documents on the table and tactfully left the room.

Ben stayed to dinner, of course. Late that evening, when he and Jessica had talked it all out on the veranda, and while Jessica was admiring the effect of the restored engagement-ring upon her finger, her father joined them.

"Got it all settled, have you?" he inquired, jocosely.

"Of course," answered Jessica, without raising her head.

Mr. Gibson lingered. "There's just one thing I'd like to know," he remarked, apologetically. "It's this: if it wasn't something in Ben's past that caused your quarrel, what was it?"

His daughter looked at Ben; her brow perceptibly darkened. "It was something very serious, papa," she said, sternly. "I hate to speak of it,

because Ben and I have just decided to forget it
forever. But—Ben—confessed—to—me"—she drew
the arraignment out with solemn severity—"that he
simply *hated* suffragettes; and he said that if I ever
made a suffrage speech he'd die of shame."

With great difficulty Mr. Gibson kept his face
straight. "Ever expect to?" he asked her.

"Of *course* not! The idea!" His daughter looked
shocked beyond expression. "But I have to feel that
I can if I ever want to, don't I?"

"Certainly," agreed her father, seriously. "And
Jessica's suffrage convictions disturbed you?" he
asked the boy.

Ben blushed like a girl. Then his young lips set.
"Why, no," he said. "What bothered me was that
Jessica said if I felt that way I was the kind of
brutal tryant who would grind a woman under his
heel. That hurt my feelings," he added, sedately.

Without replying, Mr. Gibson surveyed the pair.
Like a pleased child of four, Jessica was playing with
her diamond ring, turning it in the moonlight to
make it flash. Ben's head was close to hers as he
bent adoringly to study the beauty of the ring restored to its rightful place. His fluffy yellow hair
was ruffled at the back by the evening wind, as a
little boy's is sometimes rumpled by a mother's hand.
He looked about as tyrannical as a newly hatched
yellow chicken. At Jessica's feet her pet white
kitten riotously chased its little tail. There was
about as much chance of Jessica's ever making a

public speech on any subject, her father reflected, as there was of that kitten's breaking into an impassioned oration now.

"Good Lord!" he exclaimed, in frank disgust. "Do you mean to tell me that the row which has set this whole village by the ears for the last two months started with such idiocy as *that!*"

But the reunited pair didn't even hear him.

MR. WALDO AMUSES THE BABY

MR. GERALD WALDO, stretched at full length in a hammock on the veranda of the Evans' camp, was lost in the oblivion of slumber. Seated a dozen feet away, Miss Virginia Evans, the daughter of his host, restlessly fingered the pages of a new novel, and cast upon him an occasional glance of heartfelt disapproval. At her feet a chuckling bundle was intrenched behind blocks, rag picture-books, and vividly colored rubber balls. It was incased in blue rompers, from the top of which a pink-and-white head emerged, crowned with down strongly resembling the covering of a newly hatched yellow chicken. From the bottom of the rompers appeared a pair of small, fat legs wearing blue stockings and ending in minute white rubber-soled "sneakers." Two tiny and extremely active hands arranged blocks in piles and then swiftly demolished the piles. In short, Master Robert Grant, aged twenty months, son of the proprietor of the nearest neighbor's camp, was making an afternoon call on Miss Evans.

Unlike her house guest, Mr. Waldo, young Robert was very wide awake; but, like the older gentleman, he offered little companionship to his hostess, being wholly absorbed in interests in which, for the moment at least, she had no part. On his arrival, and with great directness of purpose, he had gone to her room, where, from the box of toys she kept there for his delight, he had selected his favorites and brought them forth. The rest was happy murmuring, broken occasionally by a yelp as the blocks fell, or a word or two from his small but expressive vocabulary.

Virginia Evans turned her brown eyes first on one guest, then on the other, and her lips drooped in self-pity. This, she reflected, bitterly, was a nice sort of an afternoon for a girl who had refused half a dozen invitations that morning. There were so many pleasant things she might have been doing—sailing, fishing, motor-boating, "hiking" along the Indian Trail with the Winslow party—and here she was, with nothing to engage her attention but a sleeping man and an absorbed though adorable baby. As her reflections reached this mournful stage, the infant looked up and met her eye.

"How-do," he remarked, affably.

"How do you do?" responded his hostess, with some reserve. "I'm glad you've remembered at last that I am among those present. Of course you know perfectly well that you ought to be sitting on my lap, hugging me hard and giving me a kiss a minute, instead of seeking your own amusement. But you're selfish, Robert, like all your sex."

Robert caught the vital word of this address and his brow clouded. Why the otherwise agreeable persons around him were incessantly demanding to be kissed was the hardest problem in his little world, but already he had learned the one effective way of solving it. His not to reason why; his to do the job at once and have it over. With an unconscious sigh he rose, came to the side of his hostess, raised a face like a pink morning-glory, touched his lips to her cheek, and returned briskly to his toys. He was gratified to observe that the bridge he had made of two blocks had not fallen during his absence.

"Thank you," exclaimed Virginia, pleased by the unexpected attention. "That was a very sweet kiss —a trifle too perfunctory to satisfy my emotional nature, I admit, but distinctly better than nothing."

"How-do," murmured Robert, in preoccupied recognition of anything the lady said. He was not to be outclassed in the amenities of life, but he had just put a wobbly humpty-dumpty on top of the bridge, and his attention was centered on the experiment.

"Heaven help your wife, Robert," mused Miss Evans, aloud. "You'll be the kind of man who reads the newspaper at the breakfast-table—or," she added, with penetrating clearness, "sleeps on the veranda in the presence of ladies."

The words followed Mr. Waldo out on to the sea of slumber where his soul was rocking, and upset his cradle. His eyes opened, at first reluctantly, then with horrified contrition. He sat upright with a jerk.

"Great—great Scott!" he stammered, "have I

been dozing? I beg a thousand pardons! I—I—thought I was alone!"

"You were when you fell asleep," his hostess deigned to admit. "But when Robert and I joined you we naturally expected that you would wake up and do something toward our entertainment."

Leaning forward, Mr. Waldo surveyed the absorbed blue bundle.

"Hello!" he exclaimed, glad of the excuse for a change of topic. "What a jolly little beggar! Where'd he drop from?"

"The next camp. His mother is 'doing' the Indian Trail and has lent him to me for the afternoon. She doesn't like to leave him alone with the servants, and we love to have him here. We all adore Robert, from mother down to Kawa."

Hearing his name, Robert looked up and met the eyes of the big young man who was smiling at him from the hammock.

"How-do—by-by—dada-mum—i-keem—ou-do — mon—bo!" he remarked in a burst of cordiality.

Mr. Waldo regarded him with increased interest.

"It seems awfully rude not to reply to such a flow of conversation, old man," he apologized, "but I haven't got the cipher."

"He has generously bestowed upon you almost his whole vocabulary," explained Miss Evans. "It is a little overwhelming at first. He says, 'how—do—you—do—daddy—mother—ice-cream—outdoors—come on—boat!'"

Mr. Waldo jumped up. "By Jove!" he cried, enthusiastically, "I don't know when I've heard a more intelligent and timely suggestion. Let's come on and go outdoors in a boat. I'll row you over to Lobster Cove." Then, seeing her hesitate, his manner changed. "You know," he reminded her, "this is the day you're to give me my answer."

"Yes," admitted Miss Evans, coldly. "And you were so anxious about it that you went peacefully to sleep in the middle of the afternoon."

"And slept exactly fifteen minutes, while I was waiting for you to appear," corroborated Mr. Waldo, glancing at his watch, "to make up for three sleepless nights of agonized uncertainty. 'Mon,' as Robert so wisely remarks, let's take a row. We can't waste a day like this on land. It's glorious."

Uncertainly, Miss Evans surveyed her younger guest. "But Robert—" she objected.

"Has four able-bodied, highly intelligent persons here to look after him," the young man reminded her, "beginning with your mother and ending with the Japanese butler, who, you say, adores him. Get your hat."

Miss Evans got her hat. As she emerged from the house, wearing it, Robert dropped his blocks and scrambled to his feet.

"Mon!" he chirped, joyously. "Bo!"

Miss Evans gazed at the expectant baby face and wavered. Her mother, who had followed her to the veranda, filled a pregnant interval with alluring cluckings, directed to the younger guest.

"Won't Robert stay with Grandma Evans?" begged the girl, "and have a beautiful time with his toys? Grandma will make all Robert's tops go round."

Robert glanced at Grandma Evans and his mouth set. "No," he remarked, with finality.

Ignoring this decision, Virginia and Mr. Waldo passed him and hurried along the veranda. The next instant an anguished and resentful howl shattered the peace of the atmosphere, and, looking back, they observed that young Robert had hurled himself upon his stomach and was rapidly following them, crab fashion, down the steps. His small mouth was forming a very large letter "O." Big tears rolled down his cheeks, and his wet blue eyes held an expression of furious incredulity. With a gurgle of remorse, Miss Evans flew back to him and clasped him to her breast.

"Of course he shall come, the blessed baby," she cried. "Of course Aunt Virginia wouldn't leave her 'wonderfulest' boy behind. He shall go in the boat, so he shall! And if he gets restless," she added, wickedly, turning to her protesting mother, "Mr. Waldo will amuse him."

"I'll catch him a whale, or something," promised Mr. Waldo, lightly.

The yells of young Robert ceased. He drew one long, deep, quivering breath, and then dismissed

from his mind the memory of their attempted per-
fidy. An adorable smile revealed his entire collection of teeth. "Mon," he murmured, contentedly.
"Bo."

"Let me carry him." Without comment on the
vagaries of his lady or the infant, Mr. Waldo held out
his arms, but already young Robert was indicating to
Virginia his desire to be put down on the ground.
To be ignominiously carried was no part of his plan,
and his absurdly small rubber "sneakers" were as
much at home on the rocks of this particular bit of the
Maine coast as were those of Miss Evans herself.

"He'll walk," she explained, "and he won't be the
least trouble. He's been used to the water all his
little life. His father and mother practically live in
boats, and usually he's with them."

"He has such an understanding air," murmured
Mr. Waldo, "that he embarrasses me. I'm afraid,
if you turn me down, he'll laugh at me."

"He understands every word one says to him,"
corroborated Virginia. "And he'll listen to stories
for five minutes at a time—if they're very exciting!
Robert, what does your hippopotamus do?"

An appalling chasm split the features of the baby
as he opened and shut his mouth in an impressive
imitation of the mechanical toy.

"He does seem to take it all in," marveled Gerald.
"I didn't suppose babies heard or saw anything till
they were four or five years old!"

This exhibition of masculine ignorance received

the tribute of a moment's silence. Then Miss Evans
mercifully went on:

"I must hold his hand every minute on the pier,"
she said. "He's as quick as a lizard. He would slip
over the side and be down in the water in half a
minute if we didn't watch him."

Accompanied by a very small boy at peace with
the world, they made their way across the rocks and
out on the long, narrow pier leading from the shore
to the deep-sea float to which the Evans' boats were
fastened. The tide was high and the supporting
trestles, which a few hours later would stand up tall
and gaunt against the water-line, were now almost
concealed by the encroaching waves. Tied to the
bobbing float was a rowboat, bearing on her stern
the name Miss Evans had given her—*The Banshee*.
Gerald unfastened the painter, while Virginia gave
her attention to the impatient Robert, who seemed
to be experiencing an impulse to hurl himself head-
long into the waiting craft. Then, seated in the
stern with the child beside her, she steadied the boat
with a casual hand on the edge of the float as the
young man prepared to step in after them. He had
one foot on the seat and the other on the float when
young Robert, who had suddenly discovered a jelly-
fish near the surface of the water, leaned far over
the side of *The Banshee* and made a swift grab for it.
Virginia caught him instinctively and pulled him
back into place, but the effort had called for the
quick use of both hands. *The Banshee*, released,

swung away from the float, and Mr. Waldo, after balancing for a precarious interval with legs wide apart like a human Colossus of Rhodes, leaped for it, missed his footing, crashed down in the boat, struck Virginia in his fall, and felt her go backward. In the next moment the little boat had tipped and filled. A high, trembling wall rose before him and fell upon him. *The Banshee* had gone down. They were all in the water.

For an instant more he saw nothing. Then, in the swirl around him, he had a glimpse of something blue —caught at it, missed it, clutched again, and secured it. Simultaneously, he heard himself speaking.

"Catch the float," his voice cried. "Got it? That's right. Hold on!"

Thus far he had acted automatically, with no consciousness of any mental process whatever. Now, suddenly, his brain cleared after the shock, and with every faculty alert he took in the situation. He himself had been drawn, feet first, under the float, in the narrow space between the two pontoons used as its foundation. With one hand clutching a slippery, canvas-covered edge, he was, for the moment, secure, though a strong current was doing its best to loosen his hold. Directly above him, near the same edge of the float, but seated safely upon it, a blue bundle sputtered and reassuringly yelped— the blue bundle he had thrown there. Quite near him was, must be, the One Girl in the World. He could not see her, but he had heard her speak.

"Virginia," he gasped.

"Yes."

Her voice, too, was a gasp. The whole incredible episode had occurred with such inconceivable suddenness.

"Are you all right?"

"Yes."

"Thank God!" A rapture of relief surged over him.

"And you?" she asked, quickly.

"All right, too. What hold have you?"

"The wooden peg we tie the boats to," she told him. "I've got a firm grip."

"That's fine! That's great!"

It meant that she was near the end of the float, safely away from the danger-point where he was, and that she was probably head and shoulders above water and braced almost upright by the pontoon's deep, protecting end.

"And the baby?"

"In front of me. He's not afraid. He has never learned that there is anything to be afraid of; but he's mad clear through. Hear him yell!"

Master Robert had found his breath and was using it in vociferous protest that should have carried half a mile. He did not cry often, but when he did he gave himself wholly to his grief; and this new game of being abruptly pitched into cold water with all his clothes on was not at all to his liking.

"I've got to join him in that," explained Gerald.

He spoke with difficulty. An occasional wave swept over his face. He had to watch for it and hold his breath when it came. He did not intend to startle Her by gasping and strangling. "I'll have to yell for some one to come and get us out," he added. "You see, dear"—the humiliation of the confession scorched his soul—"I can't swim!"

"Oh-h-h!" It was an instinctive wail, which she checked as soon as it had begun. But he heard it and set his teeth. "Neither can I," she added, in a voice from which the vitality had gone.

His heart sank, for this was a blow. He had hoped that she could swim at least enough to reach the shallow water barely a hundred yards away.

"And no one can climb up on this high float from the water," she added. "The young fishermen have often tried it, as a 'stunt,' but it can't be done."

"I know," he said, quietly. He knew it too well. The muscles of his back were strained by the futile efforts he had already made. Twice his hold had slipped and, as if by a miracle, he had recovered it. "But there's no danger," he added, "it's merely a question of holding on till some one comes, and some one will come soon. Sure you and the boy are all right?"

"Quite sure."

He shouted with all the strength he could put into the sound, and the cold, wet baby on the float above him stopped crying, intrigued by the interest of this new distraction. Thus far he had sat still,

MR. WALDO AMUSES THE BABY

giving his whole attention to the expression of his
self-pity. Now he intended to discover the source
of the entertainment so unexpectedly furnished him.
With a crow of interest he fell forward on his
stomach and crawled nearer to the edge of the float.
A cry from Virginia warned Gerald of the new peril.

"He'll fall in!" she gasped. "And what would we
do? Oh, how can we keep him quiet!"

Again Gerald tried to draw himself from under
the float and up over its side. That he risked his
life in the effort was a detail to which he gave no
thought. If only there was something he could get
hold of—anything; but there was only the elusive
side of the wet canvas padding. His hand slipped,
lost its grip, caught, slipped again. His nails dug
desperately into the edge of what appeared to be a
small break in the canvas. The head of a nail tore
his fingers. Desperately they closed upon it. It
moved, but held.

"Robert," he commanded, "be quiet! Sit still!"

The baby, checked in his journey toward the edge
by the unexpected shock of the words from an unseen
source, obeyed them. He uttered a surprised gulp,
pulled himself upright, and sat quiet, staring with
wide blue eyes in the direction of the voice he had
heard. Raising her free hand with some difficulty,
Virginia clutched one of his fat, wet legs. Instantly
and fiercely the baby resented the indignity, kicking
himself free with unexpected strength.

"He won't let me hold him," panted the girl, "and

if he gets on his feet he'll toddle out of reach and fall over. Oh, I can't bear it!"

It was plain that her whole thought was for the child. Again Gerald lifted his voice and shouted—again and yet again. There was no response, no sound of life from the rock-bound shore that was so near and yet so tragically distant. The thing was becoming a nightmare. One could not keep a restless baby indefinitely quiet on a bobbing float six feet square. Well, if the youngster went he would go after him—that much was certain. He could not save him; but he could at least make the effort. Then—what would become of her? How stunning she was! She hadn't given a thought to herself. And he couldn't save her! He set his teeth. God! what a useless thing a man was who could not swim! He himself hardly deserved to survive. But the Only Girl! And the baby!

Again he shouted, and again he was answered by the mockery of silence and sunlight and blue sky and the brooding peace of a summer afternoon in a world that seemed somehow to be slipping away. Less than a quarter of a mile distant lay the Evans' camp, containing four persons, any one of whom would cheerfully risk life to save Virginia Evans. An equal number were ready to die, if need be, for little Robert. Yet no instinct warned these unconscious persons of the peril of the two they loved. There must be woodsmen at work in the forest around the camp. But they did not hear. No one heard.

And she was growing tired. He knew it. And that blue bundle on the float above him was beginning to move about again, and the small nail was looser, and his hand and arm were numb—and he could not hold out much longer!

That was the cold truth of it. That was the thought he had not been allowing to take form, though it had crouched at the gate of his consciousness for the past ten minutes.

"All right?" he asked her.

"Yes. And you?"

"All right. Getting"—he hardly dared put the fear into words—"getting tired?" he brought out at last.

"No."

It was a gallant lie, but it did not deceive him. He knew she was getting tired. He knew it by the quality of her voice.

"Cold?"

"N—no!" Her teeth were chattering. Above him, the baby had begun to wail.

"Mum—mum—mum—mum," he reiterated.

"He wants his mother," said Virginia.

Afterward, as he recalled it, that seemed to Gerald the most poignant moment of the whole episode, but at the time he was merely conscious of a deepening of the sense of unreality which he had felt from the first. The thing *couldn't* be happening, simply couldn't be—it was a dream, a nightmare. But waking or sleeping, living or dying, he must do his

best for Her and the baby—his miserable, contempt-
ible, helpless best. Again he lifted his voice. It
was not as powerful a voice as it had been at first.
Again there was no response.

"Can you see any one on shore?" he asked the girl.
"See anything moving?"

"No. Oh, Robert, Robert! *Robert!*"

The last word was a shriek. Evidently the tired
baby, thoroughly weary of this strange game the
grown-ups were playing, was again scrambling away,
still wailing his monotonous "Mum—mum—mum—
mum." Waldo lent his voice to the din.

"Robert," he shouted, "stop! Sit still!" A half-
memory leaped into life in his brain. What was
it She had said? Oh yes. "I'll tell you a story,"
he added, desperately.

There was silence on the float.

"Is he quiet?" he asked the girl. The tide seemed
to be pulling at his shoulders. The numbness in his
hand and arm was spreading to his neck and back.

"Yes," she said; "he's looking where he thinks
you are."

"All right! Here goes!" A wave washed over
his face. He waited until it had gone, then drew a
deep breath. "I'll shout again. Then I'll tell the
story." He shouted. The rocky shore flung back
the echoes with cold indifference. Above him, the
blue bundle stirred. "Once there was a little boy,"
he began, hurriedly, "and his name was Robert.
And Robert lived in a big camp near the water,

And Robert had lots and lots of toys. Robert had a duck that said 'quack, quack,' and a cow that said 'm-o-o-o.' "

The opportunity offered here was not to be neglected. Gerald sent an appealing cry out over the water, and a pleasant echo of it floated from the blue bundle above him.

"M-o-o," chirped the baby, charmed by the duet.

"And Robert had a dog that said 'bow-wow-wow!' " On this excuse another cry rose to the contemplative heavens.

"Bow-wow-wow," repeated the baby, forgetting all his troubles in the joy of this recital. Here was a man who could make a real noise—the first man who had ever made a noise loud enough to suit a somewhat exacting specialist in the art. It was really most entertaining. Robert's blue eyes glowed. He experienced an exhilarating sense of participation. "Bow-wow-wow," he yelped.

"And Robert had another big, big animal that said 'H—e—l—p!' "

The word rang far out across the sunlit water that merely sparkled in response.

"E-e-e-p," echoed the fascinated baby.

An unseen wave approached and passed. Gerald gasped and strangled.

"Now Aunt Virginia will make the noise like the big, big animal," he stuttered, when he could speak.

Aunt Virginia made it. But soon the child began to weary of the pastime.

"Oh, he's crawling round again!" cried the girl. "Robert! *Robert!!*"

"Sit still. Another story!" promised Gerald. Could he last five minutes more? And could he— oh, *could* he go down without making any noise those two could hear? Could he do that?

"One day Robert came out on the float," he continued, "and all the little birds up in the air said, 'Hel-lo—see Robert!' And Robert sat very still, so that all the little birds could look down and see him."

There was utter silence on the float.

"And the fishes down in the water said, 'Hello, there's Robert. Hel-lo! H-e-l-lo-o!' (This was another cry.) 'Let's go and take a look at Robert,' said the fishes. And Robert sat very, very still, so that all the little fishes could come up to the top of the water and see him."

To Gerald, his own words seemed to come back to his ears from a great distance. Could he go down without making any sound—*could* he?

"He's like a tiny statue," reported Virginia, "and his eyes are sticking out of his head." She spoke with a little gasp, half a laugh and half a sob.

"W-a-ll, m-y suz!"

The voice was a new voice—the sharp, high-pitched voice of a Maine woman. "I heard some noises from the shore, an' I says to m'self—"

Some one had come—at last.

"Pick up that baby!" commanded Gerald. "Carry him up to the Evans' camp. Send the butler and any other men you can find to Miss Evans's rescue. Quick! Run! It's life or death!" He heard a gasp from the woman, a sputter of protest from Robert, and then the sound of swiftly running feet. "All right now," he told Virginia. "Help—coming —in—a—minute."

"Yes, I know."

He said no more, but saved his strength. Later he heard men's voices from some remote point at the top of the world. It was glorious to know that— what was it?—something glorious was happening. She—she—yes, she was being saved. And—and— what else? Oh—yes—the youngster was all right. That—was—all—that—mattered.

The rise and swirl of the water caused by pulling Miss Evans up on the float had loosened Mr. Waldo's frail grasp. He went down, but Kawa dived for him, secured him with considerable difficulty and the assistance of two woodsmen, and subsequently gave him some violent and extremely disagreeable treatment on the float, after which Gerald revived sufficiently to walk up to the Evans' camp.

There Robert, comforted by a hot bath and a rubdown, was in bed and sleeping peacefully. Miss Evans, having enjoyed the same treatment, was reclining in a big chair before the open fire, wearing a becoming tea-gown and receiving the adulation of her family. She had refused any of these attentions, he learned from Kawa, until assured of his return to consciousness.

Gerald surveyed her with pleasure through the open door, and then, accompanied by the proudly proprietary Japanese, sought his quarters for a change of garments. When he returned to the living-room Miss Evans was alone. He entered with a hanging head, which rose with a jerk when he made the incredible discovery that she was in his arms. There was a long and deeply satisfying silence.

"Then you don't despise me?" he asked at last. "You really think I deserve another chance?"

"Did you imagine I didn't realize what you were going through?" demanded the girl, "because I—I didn't dare to speak of it? I *knew*—and, oh, Gerald, I thought I should go mad! And you were so splendid!"

"Nevertheless," announced Gerald, firmly, after another interval, "I take my first swimming lesson, from Kawa, at the earliest possible moment after sunrise to-morrow morning!"

THE END

www.ingramcontent.com/pod-product-compliance
Lightning Source LLC
Chambersburg PA
CBHW030956260626
47169CB00002B/569